OF BLOOD AND LIES

Bloodstate
(Book One)

First paperback edition September 2025

Book design by Brady Moller
Cover design by Katarina
Editing by Jenny DePierre

ISBN: 979-8-9905953-1-6 (paperback)

AUTHOR'S NOTE

For my family and everyone who has supported me online through this journey.

"The nine most terrifying words in the English language are: I'm from the government, and I'm here to help."

—Ronald Reagan

CHAPTER

ONE

PRESENT

I dreamt of thirty-one beheaded children.

When my mind slipped from the nightmare's hold, I woke in a cold room. I didn't move upon finding consciousness. I didn't dare make a sound. Where I found myself was not where I was supposed to be.

I stayed still and held my breath. The space around me smelled of metal and blood. Beneath the smell was something familiar, but I didn't focus on it.

I slowly opened my eyes. My surroundings were dark. I waited for a moment to adjust to the nothingness, but nothing revealed itself. I was in a void, no silhouettes appearing before me.

I ran the tip of my tongue against the roof of my mouth. Taste buds grazed against dry meat, tasting copper.

The room was deafeningly silent. The stillness felt heavier knowing I certainly was not supposed to be here. I was supposed to be in a world of nothing, rather than a room fronting as nothing.

I wasn't alone. I knew the feeling of being watched. I had learned it at a very, very young age. I would not have survived this long had I not known how to be hyperattuned to my senses. Like I currently had.

Eyes.

My throat tensed. I could feel them, traveling the length of my spine. After a few seconds, I was able to make out a wall in front of me. It was white, but looked gray in the dim light. It wasn't made of concrete or stone; instead, it was padded, and looked like a place I imagined a psychotic cunt might be locked inside of.

My jaw twitched. I couldn't use the wall as a weapon if need be; I couldn't grab the presence in this room and slam them until the wall was painted with brain and blood.

Moonlight filtered into the room. I was able to see it now, the subtle glow on the bed beneath me. I was lying on a few white blankets, which lazily acted as a fitted sheet. Above my still body was another thin blanket. I considered how easy it would be to strangle someone with it. I could do it.

Without making any movements, I concluded I was in a twin-size bed. I felt a flattened pillow under my head. It was damp and smelled of sweat.

I always woke drenched in sweat when dreaming of my beheaded children.

I shouldn't move. I knew this. I should stay still and pretend to be asleep, seep into the nothingness as I had before waking. If eyes were silently watching me, in a foreign room, no good could come from making myself known.

Nonetheless, I turned over to give my back to the wall. I felt my muscles tense and cramp upon moving. I hadn't felt this sore in years—I needed water to soothe the pain of dehydration.

I looked to the ceiling first. There was a skylight in the center of it, allowing the moonshine to fall in and cast shadows around the room. It was too high up to reach, but so far, it was the only means of escape I could see.

Next, I looked to the door a few feet away. It was in the center of the padded wall, perpendicular to the bed I was in. I winced, seeing it too was made of white cushion. I needed a weapon. Anything.

In the center of the door was a small metal slit. A flap covered the opening, and there was a keyhole in the center of it. I assumed if I were to push on it, the flap would not bulge.

There was another door tucked in the corner beside my bed. It was ajar, with darkness slipping out of the smaller room beyond it. It contained a shower, toilet, and sink, but I did not focus on that. Everything inside was made of metal, but nothing seemed flimsy enough to grab and use as a weapon.

My fingers itched and my throat grew tighter. I could feel my heart beating hard against my ribcage. My head was throbbing from how fast blood was pumping through my body.

Trapped. Trapped. Trapped.

The words echoed in my head like some twisted chant. I'd been trapped for an eternity just to be saved and placed into another prison.

I looked at the bed across from mine. It was standing against the opposite wall, mirroring my own circumstances. For a moment, I believed I was looking at my own reflection. But the blankets looked messier. Worn. And there was a man sitting on the bed.

I stopped breathing.

His eyes were as cold as the bodies of my thirty-one beheaded children. His leer was sharp—it felt like he was throwing daggers into a suspended piece of meat. Me. Beneath all of this, I felt fire. Red. Blood. Pure fucking rage replaced the blood running through my veins.

Him.

CHAPTER

TWO

PRESENT

I'd thought about what I wanted to do to Karro if I ever saw him again. Every day in that place, I'd imagined the ways in which I would torture him. I wanted it to be long and painful. I wanted to physically bring him to his breaking point, all while killing his soul word by word. Some of my fantasies had become so vile I believed I'd gone mad.

I wanted him to suffer. Whatever I needed to do, he had to suffer.

But now that he was sitting across from me, I couldn't think. I couldn't move.

Rage was an old friend. Through the lonely nights, Rage had filled me. Through everything, Rage was with me, comforting me. But now, my old friend consumed me; it consumed every cell in my head and every muscle in my body. I couldn't move or breathe.

I wanted to see Karro convulsing, begging for his life. I wanted to see him covered in red. So much fucking red.

I reached for my head, rubbing my temples. I didn't look away from him, despite the migraine racking through me. I didn't remember anything. I didn't remember how I'd gotten free of that timeless place and into a hell where Karro still lived. But even if I'd lost my memory, I would forever remember him.

It'd be impossible to forget Karro.

He sat as still as I did, unbreathing and unmoving. It was just as we'd been trained. Karro had learned the ways of The Blood at a young age, as I had. He and I were one of a kind—we were tools. We *had* been tools.

I looked at the flimsy pillow atop my bed. It was the only thing around that I could use as a weapon. There was no mirror to shatter in case I wished to slit Karro's throat. Any metal in the room appeared to be intact and unmovable. The window did not have any visible screws. If I'd been able to find one, I would have pried it out and punctured small holes in his face until he died of blood loss. Perhaps I would even have stuck one in his cock.

"Naga," Karro warned, once my eyes locked with the pillow. His body tensed. He was much larger than me, yes, but I was angrier. An angry woman was a powerful woman. No muscle could stop an angry woman. And I was an incredibly angry woman.

Karro looked at the pillow, and then back at my face. I watched him from the corner of my eye as I reached for it.

An eternity's worth of memories and feelings had flooded through me at the sound of his voice. I flinched, reaching for the pillow, my hands shaking. I wanted to rip the skin from his face.

I snatched the cushion into my hands, digging my nails into the flimsy cotton.

I wanted it to be so much more painful and bloody. A pillow to the face was the work of a child. But, this had to do. This was The Blood giving me one final chance to release the pain Karro had left me with. To heal the emptiness in my core that he had carved from me. To breathe and exist without thinking about him.

I ignored Karro's warning and propelled myself forward. Landing on the edge of his bed, I straddled him, pushing him hard into the mattress. I placed the pillow atop his face, pressing all of my weight into it, trying to suffocate him as painfully as possible.

Scowling, I bore down harder. The cushion was too thin, and I wasn't heavy enough. I wanted to scream. This wasn't going to work.

Karro let out a muffled laugh, letting me pin him down foolishly for a moment. I felt his stupid face through the flimsy cotton. I wanted to beat his skull in until he was gone from my mind.

He grabbed the pillow, throwing it across the room, then grinned, ear to fucking ear.

Karro began to sit up, but I did not stop. I reached for his neck, aiming for his jugular. Maybe my nails could dig deep enough for me to kill him.

I clawed at his throat until I drew blood. I wanted to rip it out with my bare hands. So many years ago, I would have been able to do it effortlessly. I'd lost count of the number of necks I'd dismembered—most men, but not all. I fucking hated men and their incessant need to lead.

Karro winced, then slipped back into a cold smile. He reached for my fingers, prying them from his neck. Wrapping a large, icy hand around my wrist, he restrained me from scratching or hitting him anymore.

Restraint. That was not going to happen.

"Naga," Karro repeated. He squeezed my fingers, too tight. "Stop." His head tilted downward, his eyes cold and stern against my hard gaze.

I ground my teeth together, looking back at his neck. I'd only ripped a jugular out with my teeth once. His "name" was J993. He'd tried to touch my ass, so I'd responded in the only way I knew how.

I supposed two was a better number.

I ducked down, but Karro pushed me away before I could reach his throat. I fell off him and onto the ground with ease. I'd always hated my weight and size, especially around Karro. He was abnormally tall and strong; no matter how much I ate and trained, I'd always feel like a ragdoll around him.

He was once again sitting on the edge of the bed, looking down at me. Intertwining his fingers, he dipped his head down, and his dark brown strands fell into his tan face. I turned my attention toward the wall behind him.

White.

The ceiling was white. The floor was white. The walls were white. The door was white. The bathroom was white. The bedding was white.

"Am I dead?" I hated that my voice came out as a tremble. A rare feeling rose in my stomach. I shouldn't be here. I couldn't be here.

This had to be hell. Hell was being trapped in this room with him. It was hell for both of us.

I looked back at Karro, my old friend Rage returning. I didn't care if this was hell—I wanted to see him begging for his life. I wouldn't grant him it, no. If I did, it would only be so that I could watch him beg more, and more.

My body tensed. I prepared to lunge at him again.

Karro propped his elbows on his knees, peering down at me through hooded eyes. I loathed him. "No, you are not dead." He almost sounded amused. How was any of this fucking amusing?

"Good." With that, I kicked my foot into his face as hard as I could.

Karro hissed, grabbing hold of his now bloody nose. Narrowing his eyes at me, he cursed under his breath. He looked as if he was planning how to kill me.

I smiled and tilted my head. Oh, what a beautiful sight to see such a heinous man in pain.

"You want to dance, girl?" Karro spat. He pushed himself from the bed, over six feet of muscle now towering above me. I smiled from the floor, batting my lashes. I wanted to kill him. So fucking badly.

I did not need to be asked twice.

I kicked my foot toward his torso. He grabbed hold of my ankle, blocking the impact. Good. That was what I wanted. I took advantage of his distracted state and used the other foot to drive it hard between his legs.

Karro did not wince. He smiled.

My sinister lover.

"You know they trained us better than that." His voice slid against my skin and seeped into me. I hated it.

The Blood had trained us better than something as silly as being brought down from a kick to the balls. I wasn't planning on Karro being in pain, but I did plan on damaging his pretty cock so he could never use it again.

I looked at the hand wrapped tightly around my left ankle, taking the opportunity to use my core to pull myself up toward him. Karro might be larger, and stronger, but I was faster. I always had been.

The second his grasp loosened, I twisted my body—and his. I pushed him to the floor until he lay flat on his back, staring up at me through slits. I placed my foot on his windpipe, pressing down hard. He wasn't even trying to fight me. *Fucker.* I'd rather him hurt me than not try.

"I hate you," I spat. "I hate you so fucking much. I'm going to kill you. Fuck you, Karro. I'm going to fucking kill you." My voice cracked, my soul seeping up my throat. I hated having emotions. No matter how hard I tried, or what I did, I'd never be able to silence them. Pain, hate, and passion alike.

I stomped down harder, but not hard enough to kill. Karro's fingers wrapped around my calf. "You are still so predictable, darling," he whispered.

My jaw flexed as his lips slid upward. I wasn't predictable. I had been so unpredictable at The Blood. It was what I loved most about myself. But with Karro, it was different. Emotion would forever cloud skill with him; he was like a depressant, suppressing who I was. What I was made to be.

Karro pulled my leg, sending me to the ground. I didn't stop him. He wrapped his elbow around my throat, squeezing hard enough to make me gasp. His large thighs encased my hips, preventing me from kicking at him.

My back was against his chest. I bucked, clawed, and thrashed against him, but the floor I was lying on offered no help. I hated him. I hated him so fucking much.

The Blood had trained me, us, early on to suppress emotions in times like this. Emotions were an assassin's nemesis. I'd once been very good at my job, the best The Blood had ever seen. But it would forever be different with Karro.

"Fuck you." My voice came out as a sob, and I hated myself more than him for that.

His arm tightened, restricting my airflow. I relaxed against the floor and stopped bucking into his chest. I'd rather him asphyxiate me than let me go. It was the first time in so many years that someone had touched me, even in such a harsh way. I was not exhausted. I was livid. But I remained still nonetheless.

"You care more about killing me than our—" Karro stopped, gesturing around the room. His breath was heavy in my ear. My pride would survive knowing I'd at least tired him out. "Circumstances."

"Yes," I replied.

I felt his head tilt behind me, brushing against my hair. "Good girl."

He squeezed his arm tighter around my throat, and the room went black.

CHAPTER

THREE

PAST

I sat at the bar, ignoring the weight of Karro's curious gaze. He must have thought I was oblivious to him. In his eyes, I was an insensible girl, unaware of her surroundings. I was a damsel, ignorant of the cold-blooded murderer sitting beside me.

I wrapped my bloodred lips around the straw of my margarita. I made sure that they puckered just enough to catch his attention, to make him wonder about how they would feel around his cock instead of a straw. Slowly licking a drop of tequila from my plump mouth, I looked up at him through my lashes. I met his sage eyes.

Karro tensed. "A margarita in a sports bar? Bizarre." He sipped whiskey from his crystal glass, his eyes still on my lips. I bit my tongue and forced back the smile I wanted to wear. Men were so fucking easy.

There was an empty seat between us. I'd debated sitting down directly next to him when I entered the bar, but I concluded it would be too obvious. He did not know me. But I knew him.

Karro was smart. He'd figure it out.

I sucked in a breath, feeling the mask made of deceit and The Blood cover my face. I had practiced how to smile in the mirror for hours before this. Weeks even. For months, I'd been studying Karro's file. What he liked; what girls made him hard; how those girls smiled. Now, I turned to him and showed him what he wanted to see.

He was gorgeous. I couldn't deny that. His hair was a dark brown, contrasting with his golden tan. I could see tattoos across his arm, and I knew about the ones he was hiding beneath his clothes. I knew everything about him.

He was six foot something, with muscles bulging around his thighs, abs, and arms. He'd been larger earlier in life. I'd seen it in his case file. I wondered if fleeing from The Blood was causing unwanted stress. Was that the reason for his weight loss?

It should be. No one leaves us.

"I don't know," I purred, looking down at the green of my drink. "I just can't handle the rough stuff."

Even if I was living a carefully crafted lie, this may have been the biggest one to leave my mouth. I needed roughness; it was who I was.

I stirred the margarita with my straw, allowing my cheeks to rise. I focused on something that made me angry, like General 32 slapping the top of my wrist like I was some dog. My face heated. To Karro, I must appear flustered.

But it was all a lie. Everything about me had become a lie. I was deceit incarnate, born with a sole mission. *Him.*

Nevertheless, I looked back up at him and took a small sip of the drink. Pride couldn't exist in someone like me, or I'd never make it through this mission.

I looked at his left eye, then his mouth, and then his right eye. I sucked in my own lip when I got to the scar on his bottom lip.

"Hm." Karro grunted and downed the rest of his whiskey.

I looked at my thighs, shifting them together. I was wearing a tight black shirt paired with a black-and-red pleated skirt, topped off with fishnets. Karro had noticed them immediately. In fact, when I took my seat at the bar earlier, it was the first thing he'd looked at.

As I had expected.

Karro liked to fuck. And only fuck. So, he liked girls who dressed like they only wanted to fuck.

In the file, we'd gathered information on every woman he'd been with since he'd left The Blood. They were mostly one-night stands—occasionally less. I'd scowled after seeing he'd fucked someone in an alley, then left her in the rain.

But I didn't know this. I was "oblivious." *Poor little Naga, alone in a bar, ignorant of the murderer beside her.*

I recalled the manila folders sitting on my bed back at The Blood. Everything about Karro was compiled in those folders. What he liked to eat. Do. Watch. When he slept, and when he didn't. The places he went. The things that made his breath heavy. The Blood was prepared to retrieve their runaway, and I was prepared both in deceit and soul.

I sighed, looking up toward the television above us. There were various screens playing sports, game shows, and news. The man next to me didn't care about sports. Case file 3876 on Karro

Sanchez stated that he only watched the news, cursing himself and The Blood for letting humanity come to this.

I looked at the television that broadcasted news of the war in the Middle East.

Our war.

"Terrible, isn't it?" I asked. I pouted my lips and gestured toward it.

It wasn't. The Blood consisted of three sectors: War, Order, and Intelligence. Mine, War, was the reason for what was happening in the Middle East.

Man did not start wars. We did. We played with Man until war was their only solution. They'd rather kill each other than accept something existed that they didn't know about. Us. That they didn't have control—we did.

I'd forever be grateful that I'd been born in The Blood rather than with Man.

"Yeah," Karro started. He gestured his glass toward the bartender, who refilled it. "There is always more to it, though. Can't believe everything you see."

My face twitched. He was right. I hated that he was wise.

To keep up my persona, I shook my head. I downed the rest of my margarita before I spoke. "I don't think so. They wouldn't lie to us." *Oh yes, they would.*

Karro's brow perked. He twisted in his seat to face me. I'd gotten his attention. "You think the government has our best intentions at heart? To protect the world, as they say?"

I'd worn heels as sturdy as the government. Man's government was pavement for The Blood. And they knew it, too.

Karro's eyes had grown cold and harsh, so harsh goosebumps rose on my skin. I liked it. I liked him. If the circumstances had been different—if Karro had not fled from The Blood and I had not been told to hunt him—I might have given him a second glance.

He was intense. His energy was suffocating, even with a seat separating us. I pressed my legs together again. The cold metal of my gun dug into the meat of my thigh.

I looked up at him through my coated lashes. Naive, innocent girl. That's what he wanted, someone opposite from himself. He wanted someone to lose himself in, and forget the man we'd made him to be. He wanted to break someone.

I shrugged. "I don't know. It doesn't really matter, I guess. Whatever they want to do, they'll do."

I bit my tongue, looking back at the television. The Murthaa had been wise in starting this war. Chaos and blood filled the screen. We could contort the world in any way we wished. The Blood had mastered fear and discipline among humanity; we'd mastered Man. If we wanted to, we could kill them all.

But there was no fun in that.

Karro's focus left my face. I felt his eyes touch the cleavage hidden beneath my tight shirt. Then, my clenched thighs, rubbing them together again, running my hand across the netting that covered them. Then tension between my legs was not a lie, though it was not as intense as I played it to be.

Sex was power. Nothing more. Nothing less. Making love was something of Man. It wasn't real. I assumed Karro believed as I did. I supposed I would find out later, once I splayed myself for him.

"What's your name?"

"Naga," I hummed.

I'd debated for many weeks whether I should fabricate a name. Once thrown into the field, I decided against it. In a life full of deceit, my name was the only truth I could hold on to. If

I didn't have it, I feared I'd lose myself to this persona. Whatever was to happen, I would hold my name tight.

"Naga," Karro repeated.

My lower belly tightened hearing it slip off his tongue. It was like silk. *Karro*, I wanted to reply. He had pronounced it perfectly, too. Usually, people could not correctly articulate *Nah*-gah.

"My name is Karro, Naga."

I raised my brow, surprised he hadn't lied to me. Karro, the notorious name that floated around The Blood. It was a name for gossip. He was the commander who'd betrayed our organization.

I would take his place. It was ironic, given my first mission was to retrieve him. Alive, unfortunately.

"Karro," I said, uttering it slowly, as if trying to figure out how to pronounce it. *Cahr-do.* I mimicked how seductive he had sounded when saying my own. "Interesting name."

I wrapped my lips around the straw, looking up at him again. I'd pronounced it too well. My stomach fluttered, afraid he was going to notice how easily it had rolled off my tongue.

The day my dolls were jerked from me and guns placed in my hands, it was the only name I'd heard. The only name I'd said. Karro and I were one, though he didn't know that. He was branded on me. I was his karma, born to replace him. The Blood had made sure of it.

I leaned toward him, close enough that I could feel his soft hair brushing against my cheek. I kept my innocent composure when lesser words formed on my tongue. "I want to scream your name, Karro."

CHAPTER

FOUR

PRESENT

I couldn't move.

I woke up restrained, my wrists and ankles bound tightly together. I was kneeling atop my bed, but my arms were pinned behind my back. Due to the position, I could not move anything besides my head. But I was already looking where I needed to.

I narrowed my eyes in Karro's direction, my teeth grinding together. I'd rather he hurt me than restrain me. He knew this.

His back was to me, far across the room in his bed. I watched his muscles expand and then contract with every breath. If I hadn't been restrained, I would have gone to him and mashed his head into the bed with my foot. Stupid, stupid boy. He should never give me his back. He was smart to keep me tied up, though.

I grunted, pulling at the blankets, which had been skillfully twisted together, acting as a rope. My body ached from having been in this position for however long. I looked toward the window above me. The sky was turning pink. Had I been unconscious the whole night?

I pulled at the blankets again, but the restraints only became tighter. Karro was smart. This was a form of rigging The Blood had taught me. Us. Though I hadn't learned how to escape it. They'd trusted I was skilled enough to not get myself into this position.

I looked back to the skylight. Birds flew past, cawing as the sun rose. I couldn't help but smile. I hadn't seen daylight in so long. It was always night in my timeless prison. Because of him.

When I looked back at Karro, my blood went hot, and my eyes became ice. On the wall above him were many tally marks. I couldn't see much in the dim light, but from what I could tell, there were *a lot* of lines there. They couldn't be marking the time he had spent here. He hadn't aged a day since I last saw him.

My stomach dropped.

He hadn't aged.

Just as I hadn't aged, despite living in that horrid place for what felt like an eternity. The purgatory between Man and something greater, where the sun never rose, and the only animals I could find were barely a meal. A world without Man. My hell.

I looked toward the bathroom door, which was ajar. The ribbed black tank top Karro had been wearing was now hanging from the sink, dripping onto the floor. It was covered in suds from his attempt to wash it.

I was wearing the same thing as him. My breasts spilled from the tight top, and the sweatpants hung low on my hips.

My breath quickened. I was too enraged with him to acknowledge the giant elephant in the room. We were trapped in here with absolutely no apparent way out. This felt too reminiscent of my hell, the hell Karro had found solely for me.

I intertwined my shaky hands behind my back. *You will get out,* I reminded myself. *You have already been to hell and back.*

I focused on my heavy breath as I looked back to Karro. I hated to panic. I could feel it rising up my spine and tightening in my chest. Small room. Alone. Karro. The Blood. It was too much.

Why hadn't we aged? How long had I been there? I'd stopped counting after the third year.

Karro's bare back continued to expand and contract at a steady pace, whereas behind him I was trying to suppress a panic attack. He looked so peaceful. He shouldn't be able to find peace. He deserved everything that was coming to him.

I closed my eyes, attempting to block out the room, and went to the place I had been before this. My hell. It was a place of forest and river. The only sign of life was the plants and animals that were running around. Other than that, it was just my grieving being.

Perhaps I had gone mad.

I swallowed my pride and opened my eyes. "Karro?"

He didn't respond, though his breathing quickened. I cursed and looked up toward the ceiling. Even his name on my tongue made my blood run cold. I fucking hated every part of his essence.

I turned to examine the knots constraining me. My nappy brown hair obscured my view. I wanted to rip the obnoxious waves from my head. They were matted and blocked my only chance of figuring out an escape.

I tossed my strands to the side and returned to my restraints. "Fucker," I hissed. He'd used one of the most difficult knots to escape. As expected.

I shot a glance in his direction and held my breath. He was sitting on the edge of his bed, palms flat on the bed on either side of his thighs. It was impressive how quiet he'd been. I hadn't heard him shift once.

He remained silent, staring into a part of me that I couldn't see. I returned the glare, my tongue bleeding.

He broke the silence. "Familiar?" he asked, scrunching his nose and nodding toward me.

I did not let my expression change. My stomach twisted. I had been in this exact position before, secured with rope rather than a blanket. The circumstances had been far from these. His cock had been balls-deep in my throat back then. The time when I had wanted him.

"Unfortunately," I replied. It'd been very fortunate at the time.

The corner of his mouth quirked before returning to its firm line.

Silence and stares filled the space between us, like ice on ice. Sage colliding with sage. Even our eyes were the same. I hated how it truly felt like we were made for each other.

If I spoke first this time, I wouldn't be able to bite my tongue. And if I didn't, I'd stay restrained for another lifetime.

"Do you want me to untie you?" Karro asked.

I clenched my jaw. I wondered how full the toilet was in the bathroom. Could I drown him in it? Or use my shirt to waterboard him?

"Okay. Suit yourself," he added. He lay back on the bed, pulling the covers up to his shoulders.

Fucker. I swallowed and forced my mouth to open. "Obviously," I spat.

Karro tilted his head to face me. He waited a few seconds before standing and approaching. I tensed, refusing to look away. Was this another form of torture? He'd proven once what would happen if I crossed him: my hell. I had no doubt he would continue to teach and teach until I was nothing but a weeping soul.

"If you try anything, you will end up—"

"Got the point," I bit out.

Karro leaned down in front of me. I focused on the crook of his neck as he reached behind my back, working at the intricate knot. I fanned my breath against his jugular, imagining how easy it would be right now. One bite and he would be dead. It would not taste good, but vengeance rarely tasted good. It was bitter and bloody.

If I killed him, I could be alone, soaking in the bitter and blood. However, I might never know what he knew about this room.

My eyes slid from his neck to his collarbone. I'd never seen so much bone poking through his skin. The muscle usually concealed it.

My body relaxed into his warmth. I hated how his aura felt when it invaded mine. It was comforting. His scent was overwhelming as it drifted into my space. He smelled as I remembered—leather with a mix of spearmint. His pheromones were a reminder of what once was. What could have been. I hated him more than anything for that.

I tensed, looking away from him. He stepped back, putting a few feet between us. Thick air circulated the room, even with the distance. I shook the blankets from my wrists and ankles.

Karro stood still, his arms crossed over his chest. He stared down at me, waiting. I assumed he was waiting for words. I found them fast.

"You smell like shit."

He rolled his eyes and turned his back on me. I did not pounce on him like I wanted to, but watched him take a seat on his bed. I cracked my neck and rubbed at where the blankets had dug into my skin. Not once did I look away from him.

"I've been here for fifty years," Karro started. "Sorry if I don't smell too nice, sweetheart."

CHAPTER

FIVE

PAST

I crossed my arms over my stomach and tapped my foot against the floor, making sure it was loud enough for General Mills to hear. I had a date with Karro in a few hours, and the fat-ass in front of me had decided a meeting was necessary despite the late hour.

"It's been over a week, and you've made no progress."

I pulled my chin upward, looking at him. I'd never learned his first name. His position only granted him a last name. I wasn't supposed to know his last name, either, but Mills could not hold his tongue. We'd been taught to refer to the generals by their numbers. Mills, for example, was General 84.

But I would continue to call him Mills. It made him squirm knowing I had caught his loose tongue.

"Do you know what kind of man Karro is?" I spoke slowly, making sure the general's small brain caught my words. "It's going to take a little more than spreading my legs to lure him back here. Alive, especially."

"Careful with the way you speak to me," General Mills warned. He sat forward, propping his elbows on his desk.

I sunk further into my chair, staring up at the ceiling. I regretted murdering my previous general. Mills was an absolute bore.

I wanted to laugh. I hated superiors. I despised every last one of them with every ounce of my soul. Even if General Mills was higher than me in rank, he was nothing to The Blood. There were hundreds of generals. Me, on the other hand, I'd been born for this—for Karro. If anything, Mills should be careful with how he spoke to me.

I grabbed the bridge of my nose, groaning. Between us, many files had been laid neatly across the table. It wasn't just of Karro anymore. It was both of us. I'd known they would be tracking us together to ensure the mission was on track, but I hadn't expected this many of them. Every moment we were alone was being watched. There were photos of us midfuck, too.

My lips twitched. We looked good together.

I looked away from the images and focused on Mills. "Do not doubt me. I know what I'm doing. I was raised to do this, *General*." I gritted my teeth. Karro was the same way, raised to be a commander. But he'd betrayed The Blood. I'd been raised to replace him and kill him.

I planned on stoning him alive in front of all three sectors. That would prove a point. Maybe after that, I could kill the Murthaa and rise to that level. I could *be* all three sectors. I could be powerful. She oversaw it all. She should have been my superior, rather than some lousy cocksucker like Mills.

"You're drawing this out. Get to it." General Mills threw a photo in my direction. It was of me, my face contorted, holding on to Karro. We were in the bathroom. It was from last night, when we'd drunk a few too many and nearly fucked in the restaurant.

I shrugged, tossing it back at him. "I like to play with my food." This was the largest mission The Blood had seen in centuries. I wasn't going to let this stupid fuck ruin it.

"Well, we don't have time for this. Just get on with it. Do whatever you need to do. Fuck him in whichever way will bring him back here—I don't fucking care. Just hurry up." General Mills leaned backward in his chair, crossing his ankles on top of his desk. "I'm so ready for this bastard to be dead."

He scanned my figure. I was wearing a tight black jacket paired with leggings and tennis shoes. I'd come to The Blood this late to train and blow off steam before meeting with Karro. If I had to estimate, I had twenty weapons hidden within my clothing.

General Mills had no reason to be speaking so bitterly.

"You shouldn't be ready for him to be dead. This is an opportunity. You want him dead because you're a lazy piece of shit. You're rushing me because you're a lazy piece of shit. We can prove a point with this. We will prove a point with this. And I am not going to ruin it because of your insolence." I stood up and spat on his desk.

General Mills laughed, shaking his head. "Remember your place, girl. You know nothing." He waved his hand toward the door. "Go. You're giving me a headache."

I remained still, staring down at him. A few heavy breaths passed before I spoke. "*You* don't know anything. You're a man who grew to this position, and you would have forever stayed

27

in this position. You have hundreds more in line ahead of you, trying to be something they never will be. I may be below you in rank, but I promise you, there will come a day when I am worth more than all of you fuckers combined."

General Mills rolled his eyes, another bitter laugh escaping his lips. The gun behind my back grew hot. "Yeah? If you're so sure I'm going to stay in this position forever, why say that I *would* have? Obviously you must think there is some possibility in my growth."

I shook my head slowly, my brown strands slipping into my face. "Because I'm going to kill you. A dead man would have had so much, but a dead man will have nothing."

I approached General Mills, rounding the desk. He tensed, but I was behind him before he could move. I grabbed a fistful of his hair. This was the War sector of The Blood. We didn't need lazy pussies like him turning the cogs.

I jerked his head backward, letting it hit against my flat stomach. "General Mills, do you want to know something about me?" I asked.

He was frozen, looking up at me with rounded eyes. I looked deranged to him. I could see it in his eyes. His breath quickened and his face paled. "Naga, don't do—"

I bit my lip. I could feel the fear radiating from him. If I could've lapped the taste of it up with my tongue, I would have. I'd find a way to survive off the fear of others. I fucking loved it. Especially when it came to men like this.

I hoped to feel Karro this afraid one day.

"Answer me," I snapped. "Do you want to know something about me?"

Mills closed his eyes, and his lip trembled. At least he knew he was going to die. "Naga. I do not know."

"Tsk." I tilted my head, looking around the office. Red was going to suit his little nook so well. "One thing about you, Mills, is that you're easily replaceable. Me, though? Not so much. Do you know why I keep getting assigned new superiors?"

Mills trembled but did not respond.

"Because I've killed them all. Yet here I am, walking freely. I was raised to kill. You were raised to work and die a lonely man." I reached for the knife hidden in my cleavage. The blade was thick and jagged; it would do what I wanted it to do.

"Naga, please."

I groaned, pulling his hair tighter. "Naga this. Naga that. God, you're all the fucking same." I pressed the edge of my weapon against his throat. He wasn't old, or young. He'd lived enough life.

I pushed the knife harder into his wrinkly flesh. A few blood drops slid down his neck. I leaned down, licking it up with my tongue. He tasted rotten.

"Please don't do this," Mills begged.

"I take that as a challenge, you know." I smiled. I didn't plan on making this easy for him. He needed a fun death after his boring, pathetic life.

I could have stabbed him in the jugular. It would've been less painful, and faster. But in the end, I wanted it to hurt. Bad.

I dug the blade into his throat until the skin began to tear. I waited until I saw fat and veins before I started sawing. Back and forth. He thrashed, kicked, and screamed, spreading blood across the room. I ignored him and smiled. I'd always loved the sight of flesh splitting. There was something oddly beautiful about it.

Mills reached for my face. The stupid fucker got blood on me in the process. I had a date with Karro soon. That wouldn't do.

"I'm having fun, Mills," I exclaimed.

He made a few gurgling attempts to plead with me to stop. Even after he fell limp on the floor, his noises and pleas were still slipping out.

I held his head in my hands, staring into his eyes. Craning my neck, I looked down at the veins and muscles spilling out of him. The bloody tissue grazed my arm; I was going to need to change before seeing Karro.

I smiled harder, looking back and forth between Mills's bulging eyes. They were still moving. He was still opening and closing his mouth. I pouted my lips and spoke. "So strange. We all think we're so much more because we are The Blood. But we're just meat, aren't we?"

I moved his severed head to show him the seizing body on the floor. By that point, his soul had already left him and found oblivion.

I propped his head against my hip and slipped out of the room, looking down the cold hallways of The Blood's Home Office. The War sector was a few halls down, and past that, Order and Intelligence.

I noticed a young girl a few feet away. She was sitting against a wall, her knees pulled up to her chest. She wasn't supposed to be in the Home Office unless she had been summoned by a general; this was where they resided, along with the Murthaa. I didn't recognize her. She was not of the War sector.

She was wearing the same thing as me: a black jacket paired with black leggings. A white "A" was sewn on the sleeve, indicating she was an Anaka—the children under the age of thirteen, trained for careers.

"You," I snapped. She jerked her head in my direction. Her face paled, and she shrieked when she saw what I was holding. "What's your number?"

The girl shrieked again, clamping her hand over her mouth.

I rolled my eyes, impatiently waiting for her response. I looked down at her badge, where 7437 was written in sloppy lettering. 7437 was never going to make it past janitor with a stomach like that.

"Who is your general?" I asked.

She continued to tremble, looking from me to the head. "G-General 47," she replied.

"General 47," I echoed, then nodded, remembering the fire-haired general from the Order sector. I clapped my hands, pushing the head in the young girl's direction. I was late to meet Karro—I had no time to waste on Mills. "Great! Give her this and tell her to report to the Murthaa. Immediately. Say, 'Naga wishes for no more generals.' Got it?"

The girl looked as if she was going to faint. I placed the head in her hands. She shrieked once more, but held on to it as instructed.

"Thank you, 7437." I smiled leaving her alone in the hallway. She would never receive a name. They rarely did. A general was granted a last name, and those above them got both. I'd been lucky to get one despite my position.

Naga. The Great Snake.

I pulled a handkerchief from my pocket, wiping my hands and face clean of what Mills had so selfishly spewed all over me.

After today, I'd decided I would never have another general again. I would become one.

31

CHAPTER

Six

PRESENT

"I've been here for the past fifty years."

I blinked. "What did you just say?" I asked, my lips parting. I looked behind Karro toward the array of tally marks. They were scratched on the white-cushioned wall, though there were not 18,250 worth of days marked behind him.

"You heard me." He lay back on the bed.

I looked down the length of his bare abdomen as his muscles stretched from the movement. Looking away, a muscle jumped in my jaw. He did not deserve a body like the one he'd been granted.

This was all impossible: his age, the room, the place before this. I scanned the space for any sign of wear—specifically, fifty years' worth. The bed was worn, and shredded straps held the flimsy mattress in place, but it certainly wasn't five decades old.

He had to be lying.

"No," I snapped. My eyes narrowed, and I ran a hand through my hair. I was going to rip the knots out. "You're lying to me. That's impossible. I mean, you still look the exact same as when you—" I stopped.

When you left me in that place. I didn't need to say it. He tilted his head, his eyes touching my own. His lips twitched.

When Karro had betrayed The Blood, he had done so by killing almost every officer in the War sector. The Blood still mourned the loss of all those officers; the slaughter was taught in schools, referred to as the Day of Death. The day Karro had escaped and left nothing but corpses.

I'd watched the footage as my way of training for the mission. He'd smiled the entire time. If Karro was smiling at any point, I believed it would end in death.

Something under my skin turned scalding hot.

He reached for his temples, a bitter laugh slipping out. "You're accusing me of lying?"

If I'd had something to throw, I would have thrown it. My chest was tight. I needed to scream, cry, and lash out. Anything. I needed to relieve the tension building inside me before I burst.

It was all too much. This room. Him. Me. The Blood. That place. Why did he look the same age as I did? Why hadn't we aged? We appeared how we had when we first met.

I thought about the place he'd sent me to. Originally, I'd believed it was hell, and that Karro had found a way to bring me to it. It was the same night, repeating over and over. The moon didn't move, and the sun never showed itself. It had felt like death.

"Why haven't you aged?" I asked, my voice coming out soft. Whatever his answer, it would explain why I hadn't. This was abnormal. Everything about it was wrong.

Karro did not respond. His eyes left my face, traveling down to my feet and then back. He wiped the blood from his nose, twisting his head to face the ceiling. My blood grew hotter watching his eyes flutter shut, as if I hadn't even asked him a question.

I pushed myself from the bed, taking two short strides toward him. "You sadistic fucker, answer me."

Karro mirrored my movements, standing from his bed and stepping directly in front of me. He rolled his shoulders back, his posture as straight as mine. I shook, rage racking my body. The sight of his face made my muscles tight, and defensive. Blood was now smeared beneath his nose, where I had kicked him. Even with him covered in blood, I wanted to hurt him more. He deserved worse than death. I wanted to banish him to a land of time, as he had me.

He took a step forward. "You're one of them. You are a conniving little snake." I did not cower. Rather, I held my chin higher. People usually cowered around Karro. "If you think I will *ever* answer to you, you are mistaken. Stupid fucking girl."

My throat went dry, but I showed no sign of it. It was strange hearing him speak so spitefully. I remembered the days when he'd held me as I trembled over things I refused to talk about. As I sobbed, uttering words he did not understand. It had been the guilt of it all. The mission. Him.

My spine straightened. I reminded myself of why I was so angry. He fucking knew. He'd tricked the untrickable. Me. If I were the Murthaa, in charge of everything to do with the sectors, I would have called for his head. Specifically, his head with his cock shoved deep down his throat. I'd find a way to make it a lamp.

Taking another step toward him, I pressed my shaky index finger hard into his chest. I sucked in a breath to steady myself. "You left me there. At that place. Alone for so long. You killed them."

I felt a sharp pain rise inside me. Generals could die. Children, though? I wanted to rip off his head.

Something flashed in Karro's eyes. Surprise, if I wasn't mistaken. I balled my fists, restraining myself. He had no right to act as if he hadn't killed them. They haunted me; he haunted me. I'd been alone for too long, with nothing but the memory of The Blood, lifeless bodies, and him.

Something inside me had broken that day, when I'd discovered what Karro could be. I'd thought I would be able to change him. He had changed me.

Hot anger brewed deep in my belly. My knuckles turned white. Karro blinked, staring down at me with a face that held no emotion.

"Our child. You didn't even give her a chance. Just because you had your poor little heart broken. *Fuck. You.*" I spat at his feet. My fists came to his chest, pounding hard, again, and again. "Fuck you. Fuck you. Fuck you."

Karro, surprisingly, did not stop me. But no matter how hard I hit him, it didn't heal the ache in my chest. Not just for our child, but for Karro.

He smiled, grabbing a fistful of my hair. He used it to jerk my head and force my eyes to his. "You don't know anything, Naga."

Pushing me away, he returned to his bed. I looked down at him, trembling and tight with too many emotions. He lay down and turned over, his back now to me.

I couldn't focus on hurting him. I was too focused on everything crumbling inside of my head.

"You think I'm behind this?" I moved my finger around, gesturing at the room. "Is that why you refuse to answer my questions?"

Karro pulled his pillow over his head, blocking out any chance of conversation.

I turned away when my jaw began to tremble. I wished I could break his heart again. Harder.

CHAPTER

SEVEN

PRESENT

I sat quietly on the edge of my bed, watching Karro sleep. He looked peaceful. Way too peaceful. His lips were parted, and his face was pointed in my direction. The bed beneath him was beginning to sag in the middle. It resembled a cot with a flimsy twin mattress, and the pillows reminded me of the thin ones they would hand out on airplanes. Same with the blanket.

Shortly after Karro had fallen asleep, I fell into my head, recalling what we had been. He had every right to be angry. I'd lied to him. I'd presented myself as a lie, and stuck with the lie like it was my dying wish. My face tensed. He was as much my karma as I was his.

Squeak.

I jerked my head toward the door at the sound of metal scraping against metal. The slit in it opened for a moment, and a small tray of something slid through it, collapsing onto the floor with a soft thud.

I stood up, rushing toward the door. By the time I got there, the flap was already sealed shut. I looked down at my feet, where the small tray lay.

In my hell, I'd survived off the wildlife. However, hunting had been harder than it seemed in such scarce terrain. What had just been pushed through the door was something I would kill for.

Food. Real fucking food. Not roaches, or plants. Food.

I lunged to the floor, kneeling beside the tray. First, I pushed at the flap to see if it would open, but it was stuck in place. I noticed the small keyhole in the center and squinted through it, trying to see out, but all I saw was metal.

I looked back at Karro. He was unmoving, sleeping quietly a few feet from me. If he didn't kill me in this room, the silence and boredom might. I'd been alone with my thoughts for too long. I would go insane if it was the same here.

The tray in front of me was filled with plastic pouches. My stomach turned. This was how The Blood had given out food and drinks in the cafeteria of our sector. Was this why Karro believed I was behind this? He must think it was The Blood. But it couldn't be—this was unlike them.

There were three plastic pouches filled with water, a pouch of what appeared to be chips, one full of dried berries, one containing a bar of soap, and three pouches of dark liquid. I scrunched my brows, reaching for the last one. It was filled with white, chalky balls, smeared against the plastic.

Toothpaste balls. I hadn't seen them in ages. I'd always used a brush and tube like Man did, but I knew The Blood were accustomed to them.

It couldn't be The Blood. Confinement and imprisonment were for Man; The Blood tortured those who needed to be punished and made a spectacle of it.

I opened the bag of chips, pouring half of them into my mouth. My eyes fluttered shut and I began to salivate. My stomach began to ache as soon as I swallowed, but it was worth it. I hadn't eaten this type of food in years. I never believed I'd be given the option again. Even if I was stuck in this room, with *him*, I was grateful.

I reached for the dried fruit next, then looked up at Karro. It was the last bit of food available. I didn't know when the next tray would arrive, or if it even would. Was he hungry?

He could starve.

I opened the bag and started in on the fruit. I chewed it in slow, savoring bites. I shut my eyes, suppressing the groan I was about to let out. Fuck, I'd forgotten how good real food could taste after foraging for so long.

I reached for one of the water pouches, gulping it down between chews. It tasted so pure and cold. It was almost as good as the food.

Keeping my attention on the door, I alternated between eating the fruit and chugging the water. I pushed at the metal flap again, but it still wouldn't budge. There was no door handle, nor any indication on the floor that the door had ever been swung open.

Did it not open? I wanted to know, though I wasn't able to bring myself to speak to Karro, let alone ask him anything. I also wanted to know about the window in the ceiling, and maybe even the metal in the bathroom. Had he checked for loose pieces, and tried to stab the person sending the tray?

"Very generous of you to save me food."

41

I scrunched my nose and continued to eat said food. Karro had pulled his knees to his chest, and his head tilted downward as he stared at me.

I noticed more pouches beneath his cot. There was a surplus of them, though most contained the dark liquid I had yet to touch. My mouth watered at the sight of more chips, fruit, sandwiches, and goldfish. Was he saving the food in case he starved?

There were empty metal trays stacked neatly in the corner beside his bed. There weren't nearly enough for fifty years. He had to be lying.

"Starve," I replied, eating the last berry with a smile.

Karro reached for a pouch of dark liquid. I did not stop him. He tore the bag with his teeth, the smell of alcohol circulating through the room.

"I think this is all amusing," he began. I watched him work at the alcohol, drinking it all without a flinch. "You're a real personality. I mean, if I were a downright bitch, I would also adopt a new identity."

I looked toward the door, grinding my teeth together. The words shot through my skin, piercing an area only he could.

"You know what else I think?" Karro tossed the trash in my direction. "I think they've sent you here to torture me. I believe they got you out of that place, and you conspired with them. To get one last *fuck you* in."

I laughed, and Karro shifted, bracing his elbows on his thighs. I stared at him with a gaze so cold any sane man would cower beneath it. He, however, did not.

I ran a hand down my face. "Use your brain for two fucking seconds, Karro. I don't want to see you. I don't want to be here. I want nothing to do with The Blood. Besides, this isn't them. Not their style."

"Right, because you apparently know them so well," he snapped.

I stared up at him, running my tongue across my teeth.

We'd never been able to talk about it. Karro never gave me a chance. I supposed this was my opportunity to explain myself, and that I did not want to be that person. That I hadn't wanted to lie to him, toward the end. That I'd been trying to leave, for him.

But he wasn't worth my breath. I stayed silent.

I wondered if he still saw his lover when he looked at me. I didn't see one in him. I felt the pain of love, but I didn't see something I'd had. We were strangers now.

CHAPTER

EIGHT

PAST

I was around six years old the first time I killed someone. It was during training, with a few other Anaka. We were all young, learning to fight through The Blood, to survive, and I "accidentally" stabbed a fellow Anaka who kept giving me the side-eye. On that day, we'd been learning how to fight with daggers. That was when I learned I really liked daggers. It was passionate.

After that, whenever I killed with daggers, I felt like I was passionate about what I was doing. Blades, too.

I'd also lost the privilege to train with my fellow Anaka after that. I was put through a more private training for the rest of my childhood. Trained for a specific mission. Often, I wondered if I had been chosen because of what occurred at six.

I'd been given a name. I'd been able to walk away with a slap on the wrist for everything I did. Things that others would be executed for.

They'd chosen me. It became my passion and my power.

Today was no different. Now, holding a dagger tight in my hand, twirling it between my fingers, I stared down at the woman thrashing beneath me. She was crying and screaming something into the pillow. I assumed she was begging for her life. They all did.

I wondered if she had recognized me. Karro must have shown her photos of us. We'd been dating for over six months. Fuck, we lived together now.

"Please." I caught her muffled voice through the pillow.

I groaned and rolled my eyes. Looking toward the ceiling, I cursed The Blood for sending me to do this. I hadn't asked the Murthaa how it related to the mission. She'd simply ordered me to kill this woman and ask no questions.

She had to be testing me—my stomach, the lining reflex I contained, and if I'd squirm or puke.

I wasn't complaining. This was far better than listening to my previous general speaking nonsense. I considered myself a good general; I wasn't lazy like the fucks who had supervised me. The Murthaa knew this. Why was she testing me?

I slid the dagger down the elderly woman's torso nonetheless. The tip ripped her nightgown open, bare wrinkled flesh now exposed to my eyes. I scrunched my nose and tilted my head, hoping this was worth whatever the Murthaa had planned. I trusted her.

The woman cried out again, struggling beneath me. Pleas were slipping out of her mouth and into the pillow. I pressed it harder against her face, trying to muffle out the nagging.

"Say another word and I will cut out your tongue." My voice came out as a hum.

She whimpered in response and nodded beneath the cushion, then let out a muffled cry when I dug the blade into her stomach. After that, she didn't speak anymore. She only screamed. I didn't care about silencing her to hide the crime I was committing. No, this cunt was just fucking annoying.

The only other person who'd been in the home was a teenage boy, and he was long gone. He hadn't even tried to fight.

The woman continued to wail as I trailed the blade deeper into her flesh. I sucked in a breath and tilted my head as I concentrated on the design I was drawing, then gazed at the ceiling. I huffed and rolled my eyes. This was a field agent's job. I wasn't a field agent anymore. I was a general. Killing and carving was the work of an amateur.

I wondered if the Murthaa had given me this test to see if I'd gone soft for Karro. The thought made me want to laugh.

By the time I'd finished the outline of a triangle with a "B" in the center, the woman had gone still.

"Finally," I huffed, throwing the pillow across the room.

Blood was pooling beneath her body, seeping out of the design I'd carved. It was a representation of us, The Blood. A warning to Karro, possibly.

The old lady's face was now pale. Her green eyes had lost their spark, and she stared out at nothing. Even with the life gone, she still looked scared.

I frowned. She had Karro's eyes—another reason for the pillow. It felt like he was watching me.

"For Blood," I muttered. I gave her cheek a light slap before crawling off her. Karro would be arriving shortly. It was Thanksgiving, and soon he would step through the door, the smell of rot overcoming him.

He had invited me here for Thanksgiving, but I'd declined, saying I needed to be with my own family. I did not have a family. All of the Anaka were families. Most of The Blood were born through The Blood, lacking any source but them.

Karro had been born from Man. Rarely did people like him join The Blood. I supposed it was his military background and intelligence that had drawn him to us. That was also what made him weak. He'd been around humanity too much; it did sick things to the mind.

I pulled a handkerchief from my pocket, wiping my bloody gloves clean, then left Karro's mother and brother for the flies to eat.

KARRO ARRIVED HOME A DAY LATER, HIS HANDS TREM-bling.

I was lying on our apartment bed, startled by his sudden entrance. I shot up, then watched as he reached for his suitcase and threw a few outfits in it.

"Karro, what's wrong? Talk to me." I reached over and turned on the light.

He wouldn't look at me. "Nothing," he snapped. For a moment, I wondered if he knew I was the reason he was so upset, but that was impossible. "Just stressed about work. That's all."

I frowned. He hadn't told me about his work. I'd asked, but he'd assured me it was boring and not worth talking about. But his one-time employer—and my current one—was far from boring.

Karro once had *everything*. He'd been the commander of
war, the position I dreamed of. The position I was hopefully
one step away from filling. He could have been the Murthaa if
he'd really wanted to. But he'd left it all. He'd fucked everything
up because of Man fogging his vision. Humanity was weak.

"Where are we going?" I asked, slipping my legs out from
under the comforter. Was he scared? The people he had betrayed had just made themselves known? I understood why the
Murthaa had given me this command. Fear was going to eat him
from the inside out.

I respected her intelligence, but I'd rather be her than work
for her.

Karro's face softened, and he looked down at me. There was
no glint of hate or anger in his eyes. I wanted to smile—he had
no idea what I'd done.

"*I* need to go be with my family for a few days." He leaned
down, planting a soft kiss on my forehead. My stomach fluttered. It wasn't a feeling I could fake. I could feign everything
else, but not that. "I'll be back soon."

With family. I bit the inside of my cheek. Where was he
going to go? What family he'd had was still beneath my fingernails, drying and flaking no matter how many times I tried to
wash them away.

"Please just be safe." I pouted and tilted my head. "Promise
me."

Karro planted a kiss on my cheek. My body heated, and a fire
lit in my belly. "Promise."

He pulled away, staring down at me. My face softened as I
looked up at him. He really was gorgeous—there was no denying it.

"I love you, Naga."

My throat tightened. I looked from his left eye to his right, looking for any sign of a lie or joke. It was the first time those three damned words had come from either of our mouths. And, by Blood, he was telling the truth.

"I love you, Karro," I lied.

CHAPTER

NINE

PRESENT

I woke up panting.

Every inch of my body, as well as the cot under me, was covered in sweat. I pushed myself into a seated position, hoping to leave the nightmare on the pillow.

My throat ached with every breath I took, and my fingers dug into the edge of the mattress. Shame rolled down the length of me. A night terror—I'd been having them since Karro left me in my hell. There was something about being alone with my thoughts. It did something to me.

His mother.

Slipping my trembling hands beneath the blanket, I slowly looked up toward Karro. I prayed to The Blood that maybe, just maybe, he had slept through the noises I'd made in my sleep. I'd worked so hard to build strong barriers with my mind and body, to prevent showing anyone the parts of me that made me tremble. When sleeping, though, I had no control over what came out.

Karro was staring at me, very much awake. His face was lacking any emotion, as always. His back was to the wall and his knees to his chest. He watched me, and I watched him, unspoken words floating between us.

Everything about this room now felt so much heavier.

Letting out a breath, I lay back on my side, facing him. I did not break our stare through my readjustment. He didn't look as cruel as he once had. When I'd last seen him, before he pushed me into that timeless place, he'd been angry. Very angry. But now? He almost looked like the boy who had held me. Loved me.

Days had passed. Silence was all that entertained us, as we both refused to speak. I spent my time searching for escape, but I found none. The metal was not loose. The window was tightly sealed. And the door offered no sign of opening anytime soon.

I was beginning to believe there was no hope. If Karro had any information that would help, he did not offer it. He had bit his tongue as I bit mine. I supposed we were both too stubborn to be together, anyway.

It'd been four days, if I had to guess. Karro slept through the nights, while I chose to sleep through the day so I didn't have to confront him. It was the easiest way for us to avoid each other. Otherwise, we would end up staring silently at each other, like we were currently doing.

I wiped my sweat-covered face on the blankets. It was going to be difficult to wash them with the ragged soap and low water pressure available.

"Tell me something truthful."

I flinched at the sound of Karro's cold voice ripping through the silence. My tongue began to ache from how hard I'd bit it, but I answered nonetheless. "My name is Naga. That was not a lie. Before I was given my career, I was 6657." I stopped. I had taken a vow of blood many, many years ago. I'd promised my life to The Blood, and my tongue as well. I'd sworn I would never speak of it or my life there.

Weak fucking Naga, I told myself. Pride, shame, and guilt squeezed at me. They squeezed so hard, so ruthlessly, that I began to tremble. A scream was on the tip of my tongue, threatening to echo through the room.

"I did not lie about"—I had to spit the last two words out—"loving you."

I looked at Karro's feet. I couldn't do this. "Toward the beginning it was fake. Obviously. But, toward the end—" I turned my focus back to his face. I couldn't bring myself to finish. Not when he was looking at me like everything I was saying was untruthful.

He pushed himself off the bed and took two strides toward me. I could sense the anger and heat radiating from him, even before he got close. I knew the feeling he was basking in, could see it in his eyes. He had a mix of too many emotions brewing behind the sage pierce.

Karro reached for me, digging his nails deep into my neck, tight enough to force out a whimper. We'd fucked many, *many* times. During those, his fingers would usually find their way around my throat. He had always been able to find the right grip to make my thighs slick.

Now, he wasn't looking for that spot. He was holding on like he was ready to kill me.

Despite this, I did not move. I let him squeeze harder, my vision blurring for a moment. I met his dark gaze, lying limp beneath him. Karro crawled on top of me, positioning a knee flush against my stomach. He pushed hard enough that I winced.

It was a rare noise. He was the only one who could make it come from me. He was the only one I'd let touch me, hurt me.

"Here's my truth," he spat. I flinched, but I allowed his mouth to drop beside my ear. "I'd never love someone as pathetic as you."

I clenched my eyes shut. I felt like I was melting into the mattress, seeping into the core of the earth. Even though the words he whispered into my ear were cruel, it was his voice that did it. It was pure venom.

My face twitched, but I let him continue.

"If I could do it all over again, I would. I would kill anyone I needed to if it meant you hurting." His lips curved upward, sliding against my ear. "I'd do vile, vile things if I could do it again."

He was lying. He had loved me. I knew he had loved me. This was not an angry man speaking. He was not angry about the lies and mission. I'd done something to him, something that no one had ever done before. And he had done it to me, just as hard.

I'd broken his pathetic heart.

CHAPTER

TEN

PAST

I didn't need to fake anything with Karro's cock inside me. I couldn't speak, let alone lie when he thrust deep into my cunt.

Maybe that was why I liked sleeping with him so much. I mean, we'd been having sex nearly three times a day since we'd met. When I was on my period, we wouldn't. But occasionally, we would.

"Oh," I groaned. I couldn't finish what I was going to say. His hips hit against my own, the moves hard and snappy against my back side. My palms were flat against the bed, my knees digging deep into the mess we had made of the comforter. His fingers dug into my waist, pulling me backward onto his cock. I could barely hold myself up at this point.

His other arm wrapped around my lower belly, holding my trembling body up. He applied just enough pressure to make my eyes roll backward. I grabbed a handful of the comforter, attempting to ease the tension building in my stomach.

I'd lost count of how many times Karro made me come. Four, if I had to guess. The fifth was approaching fast. The fronts of his thighs were still slick from when he had made me squirt earlier.

My dress had pooled around my waist, giving Karro a full view of my round ass. I could feel his handprints stinging my skin.

Tonight, I'd been extra bratty with him during dinner. I'd learned he liked bratty girls. I was beginning to like playing the bratty girl, too. He'd promised that he would bend me over the edge of our bed, ass up, handprints littering my skin.

He had not lied.

"Please, Karro." My voice came through gritted teeth. The pillow under my head was streaked with black and dark red. I could only imagine how the makeup on my face must look, given I'd cried it all off.

I loved to fuck. I'd been raised to see sex as nothing but an opportunity, a weakness among men. I'd grown to hate it. However, with Karro, it was different. By Blood's name, these past six months he had changed my view of sex. He made me feel like I was being pounded into mush—in the best way possible.

I would let him do anything to me. Some nights, Karro held a gun to my head as he fucked me hard. Other nights, he went slow, whispering a few "I love you's" as his cum filled my belly.

I didn't care. As long as he was fucking me.

My eyes rolled backward again, and I threw my head into the crook of his neck. The bed beneath us was soaking wet with a mix of tears, cum, saliva, and my squirting arousal.

"Oh, fuck Karro," I groaned. I pressed the back of my head firmly against him.

"Yeah?" he asked, pounding harder into me. He grabbed a piece of my neck with his teeth, roughly clamping down on it. He liked to mark me. I'd need to cover that up before meeting with the Murthaa; she would complain about how much I was enjoying this case.

"Uh, huh," I moaned. I let out a loud cry as his cock hit harder inside me, slamming against the spongy part deep inside my cunt. The curve in it made it feel like it had been crafted specifically to hit my G-spot. Some nights, I felt like he was God, and he had created himself just for me. We melded together perfectly.

Karro was going to make it impossible for me to ever look at a man the same way again. Even after the case was closed.

"Karro, it's too much," I gasped, clamping my eyes shut. He was going to fuck me to death one night. I just knew it.

He slid a hand down my bare chest, pinching my tight nipple between his thumb and index finger. He rolled the bud slowly, causing me to cry out yet again. It only fueled what was beginning to drip down my thighs.

"Tell me it's too much again, and I promise I will make it so much more," he growled against my ear.

Slap!

I buried my tear-slicked face into the pillow.

His balls were swollen and throbbing; they slapped against my clit due to our position. He slid his hand between my belly and the mattress, pinching my clit between his fingers. Everything was oversensitive because of how long we had been fucking. We'd barely made it out of the elevator before his hot, heavy cock had been pulsating inside me.

"Fuck Naga," he groaned. It was primal, slipping out of his chest and through his gritted teeth.

He squeezed my clit again, playing with it in circles between his fingers. He acted as if he wasn't about to cause me to black out beneath him. Noises came out of me with every thrust of him, noises I hadn't even believed possible.

"God, you are so fucking good, Naga," Karro groaned. "Such a good fucking girl."

Soon after, it became too much. My voice disappeared as the fifth orgasm racked my body. I gasped for air, forgetting how to breathe. I did not believe in God. God was The Blood. But moments like this made me believe there must be something else out there.

Karro brought me to my own nirvana. A nirvana crafted for just the two of us.

He pressed harder into my lower belly, letting out another low groan as liquids and cum squirted from my cunt. He had filled me with two loads already; some of my cum was mixed with his, which expelled onto his cock.

"Fuck," he grunted, fucking me harder.

I let out a choked noise as the final aftershock rolled across me. He continued to thrust me through the waves. I was shaking, trembling with every pulsation he made inside of me. My pussy was convulsing around his twitching cock.

I wouldn't ever stop throbbing. It was like I always needed to straddle his cock, and take him.

Karro pushed himself inside me once more before he filled me for a third time. I groaned, looking back at him with a toothy smile. His cum was hot, dripping out of me and down my sensitive clit.

I wanted more. I wanted him to rip my body open and crawl inside me. To make a permanent home there, our bodies attached.

Karro breathed heavily, his eyes still locked with mine. He smiled back, slapping my ass once more.

Fuck, he was beautiful.

I didn't fear how dangerous he was anymore. When I'd first been presented with the mission, I'd been slightly afraid of what he would do to me if he found out. I'd heard about how violent he'd been with some of his past lovers. Never physical, but all too manipulative.

Now, it was love I feared.

His love was contagious. It suffocated me, taking me down into the pits of Blood. I wondered if this was what Man called romance.

Karro pulled himself out of me. He stayed out of me, for a minute or two.

"Again?" he asked, after catching his breath. My clit hardened at hearing his raspy, sex-induced voice.

I nodded.

CHAPTER

ELEVEN

PRESENT

The days were becoming routine. Fast.

I wasn't sure how long it'd been. I hadn't kept track. The hours stretched too long due to the painful silence between us.

Occasionally, a mumble would come out of Karro. It was usually a snide remark about my appearance or an insult regarding how fast I ate. Oddly, it was comforting, a reminder that I was not alone in this room. I didn't tell him that.

Twice a day, a tray would slide through the door and plop onto the floor. It fell in the same spot every time. I would sit and wait, trying to catch a glimpse of who was delivering the food.

It was all useless. The metal. The door. The window. Karro. Hope did not exist in this room.

I'd adjusted to sleeping while Karro was awake. A pouch would come in the morning, while I slept, and one at night, while he slept. During the short period that we were awake at the same time, I would confine myself to the bathroom and wash my clothes. I assumed he must be doing the same thing, as every time I woke it smelled of cheap soap.

I stared down at the tray in front of me. My tray. Karro's had been lazily thrown in the corner, empty pouches atop it.

I memorized what we were given, trying to find some pattern to it as the days passed. But it was all random. Some days it was food, water, and alcohol. On other days, it was nothing but random items. A few days prior to today, seven pouches full of soap and rags had been delivered. Each day that passed was becoming a blended mess, even if it had only been a few.

This wasn't The Blood—I was sure of that. The Blood loved order and patterns. They'd taught me to memorize and learn based on patterns, too. Nothing they did was random or chaotic like this. The Blood would frown upon wherever we were. This had to be the work of Man.

I looked down at the tray in front of me. It held a pouch containing some kind of burnt meat and three filled with alcohol. I frowned at the last item: more toothpaste balls. They reminded me of The Blood. They reminded me of the times I'd used them, chewed them, and rinsed my mouth after.

My head began to throb. I hated not knowing.

I held up the bag of meat, examining it in the light first, ensuring there was no mold or maggots on it. Then, I sniffed it. It smelled like steak, but it didn't look like steak. I was too hungry to protest.

I bit into the food and looked up toward Karro. His back was to me, expanding and contracting to the beat of his deep breaths. His hair was a mess, as were the sheets under him. It appeared as though he had been rolling around all night.

The room was too quiet. I felt like I was breathing too heavily, and thinking too loudly. The silence reminded me of that place. I wanted to ask him about that place. I wanted to ask him about this place. I wanted to ask him if he'd been lying, or if he'd truly never loved me.

I bit my tongue.

Creak.

The door swung open beside me. My jaw dropped, and I jerked my head toward it. I stopped midchew, staring out into a white hallway. I blinked a few times to ensure I was not dreaming, or hallucinating. Had I been drugged? Was the door actually open?

I didn't move, but I looked. I could see a corridor just outside. The walls and floors were made of white cushions, identical to the ones in the room we were currently in. There was no sign of anyone. It felt like only Karro's and my souls existed in this place.

"Karro," I whispered. I kept my eyes on the door, afraid it was going to shut.

Silence.

Fucker.

This felt too easy. Too sudden. If it was The Blood, which I still doubted, it had to be a trap.

I stood up, backing away from the door, keeping my shoulders squared toward the foreign land outside our little room. Once I reached Karro, I slapped his bare back. Hard.

I couldn't even blink. I would be making myself vulnerable to whatever was out there.

A breeze brushed against my waist. It was the only sign of Karro shifting. He was deathly swift. Standing from the bed, he took a spot behind me. I hadn't seen or heard him move, but I could feel the intensity of him.

"Go," he said, pushing past me. He bumped my shoulder in the process, walking toward the door as if it were normal. Was it?

I kept my feet planted firmly on the floor, staring at the back of his head as he approached the door. My eyes slipped down to his back. He did not look tense, or worried. I felt stiff as the beds we slept on.

Karro stopped at the doorframe, looking at me sideways. I breathed heavily. This had to be a trap. I wondered if he was a part of it and if he was trying to trick me. Was I about to be brought back to that place? Or back to The Blood?

"It's fine," he exhaled.

"How do you know?"

Karro reached for me, wrapping his hand around my bicep. He jerked my tense body forward, pulling me out of the room. I debated breaking his fingers for touching me.

"How do you know?" I repeated, lowering my voice. I shouldn't trust him. He shouldn't trust me.

He ignored me, pulling me into the hallway. It was identical to our room. White walls. White ceilings. My bare feet sunk into the cushion of the white floor.

Karro stepped in front of me, his body blocking my curious gaze. When I looked at him, his eyes felt so cold I shuddered.

Leaning down, he whispered so softly I nearly missed it, "Do not speak. I'll explain when we return."

I didn't respond.

He pulled away from my ear. His face lingered in front of mine, eyes moving down to my lips. I swore I saw his perk up for the slightest second.

He turned from me, his fingertips sliding from my bicep, slowly drifting down the length of my arm. The touch was so light and soft. It was torturous how gentle he felt. He was far from it.

Then he wrapped his fingers around my wrist. There he was. White knuckles and all.

Hesitantly, I followed behind Karro as we walked down the hall.

My stomach sank at what lined the walls of the hallway. We were not alone.

CHAPTER

TWELVE

PAST

"That's enough for today. You are free to go back to your rooms." I tucked two guns into the back of my leather pants, thirty Anaka staring up at me.

The children before me all looked the same. Their pure eyes were wide, fear swimming through them. All of them were panting. They had spent most of the last hour running from my bullets.

I felt like a mother. They looked up to me—so afraid, yet so needing. My Anaka would not receive a superior until they turned thirteen and stopped training with me. They would leave for a career and have someone else to look up to. But for now, I was theirs.

My Anaka didn't look at me like I was the commander of the War sector. The older people of The Blood had a glint in their eyes when they looked at me. Fear, thankfully. Generals reported to me, and everyone beneath them to the generals. I reported to the Murthaa, and only the Murthaa. I planned to find a way to fix that, too.

The Anaka were different, though. They were young and vulnerable. They didn't understand how good it felt to rise up the ranks of such a powerful organization. The children had not tasted that sin.

I did not view the Anaka as being steps to power. They were my children, in a way, and I refused to ruin that. They loved me, no matter how angry I got. No matter how many bullets I sprayed in their direction, they would forever trust me. I wasn't the commander to them. I wasn't 6657 or the woman I'd constructed to deceive Karro.

I was Naga. I was all they had, besides themselves.

It was terribly dangerous for them to love me in the way that they did. It made them weak. It made me weak. I hated that I loved them, too.

"Naga! Naga!" A young girl ran toward me. I crouched low, preparing for her aggressive hug. She did this after every class. She loved physical touch.

She was one of my favorites—9637. "Naga, look at this," she exclaimed, shoving a little box toward me. There rest of the Anaka surrounded us, anticipation dripping from their eyes as I reached for it.

I smiled and looked around. They looked so happy. Because of me. It felt surreal, especially given I'd been shooting at them a few minutes prior.

I opened the box. A thin silver necklace glinted in the bright light of our training room, a small snake hanging from a chain. I looked up at the children with a narrowed gaze. I looked at all of them.

"Where did you get this, 9637?" I held the necklace up into the lighting. I wondered if I could use it as a bookmark. The Murthaa rarely came into my corridors.

The girl collapsed in front of me, folding her legs beneath her. She was eight, maybe—one of my older children. I did not know my own age, let alone theirs. When promoted to commander, I'd been assigned all of the children under the age of thirteen. There were more in the other sectors, but for War, I had thirty.

The youngest in my class was three, the eldest twelve. I would lose 8374 soon. Once she turned thirteen, she would be off with a general, training for a career.

"We found it on the playground," 9377 explained. She was sitting beside 9637, gesturing toward the necklace. I scanned the group in front of me. They were fidgeting, eagerly awaiting what I would say about it.

I sat down on the floor, in the center of the Anaka. One of my younger children, 3743, climbed into my lap. I wrapped my arms around her, holding on to her trembling body. I looked back up at 9673; she was old enough to know that jewelry was forbidden in The Blood. It was too personal.

"We wanted you to have it. It's a snake. They're smart, just like you."

I moved my attention to the child who'd said it—4738. He was usually quiet, only speaking when forced to. I never forced him, though. I had been the same way.

"Thank you," I said. I smiled, clasping the chain around my neck. The children all gasped and clapped their little hands together. I would need to take it off before leaving the room, but they didn't need to know that.

"You are so pretty, Naga. I want to look like you when I get older," 9848 said, fiddling with a few loose hairs at her hairline. I frowned, looking at her. She was the eldest.

She was the age I'd been when I was sent to the doctors to learn how to make a man feel good, though my Anaka would not go there. Unfortunately, that had just been for me.

9848 collapsed in front of me. Her eyes widened, remembrance flashing in her eyes. "You will never believe what I saw." She stretched her short limbs out on the floor. She had no intention of leaving; none of them did. They would stay here until I kicked them out.

"What did you see?" I asked, tilting my head.

"General 22 and 98 *kissing*!" She mimicked the sound, and the Anaka burst out laughing.

"Oh, stop it," I said, swatting my hand in her direction. The generals were beneath me. If I wanted to, I could have the two of them executed for showing affection in The Blood. But, like the necklace, it would stay hidden in this room—a secret.

"They would never," I continued. "Have you seen 98's teeth?"

The group broke into laughter. I smiled, caressing the back of the small child who lay in my lap. Every Sunday was the same. I would train them from sunrise to sunset, and they would find new ways to stall and keep themselves in the room.

I felt brutal with them. None of it felt right. They would run through a course, and I would shoot at them. Occasionally blades, but mainly bullets. I didn't want to hurt them, but I wanted them to survive; a few nicks was nothing if it meant them coming out of The Blood alive and intact.

The Murthaa had told me stories about Karro when he was in my position. He'd never been good with the Anaka. She'd had to train them when he was commander. It did inflate my ego knowing I was better than him in that area.

Now, 3663 climbed into the small open space of my lap. Four children had climbed into my hold, seeking the warmth of a mother's embrace. They would never receive it as long as they were here. Anaka were born from The Blood; we rarely had a child come from Man and be invited in.

Karro had been in his twenties when he joined. He had been born from a mother and raised among Man.

We were born from mothers, yes. We were not machines. But we didn't know what womb we'd come from. That involved too much connection and emotion. For all I knew, my mother could have been one of the generals I'd killed for speaking with me too tightly.

"Is it true, Naga?" 3663 asked, nuzzling into my neck. "You're hunting Karro? Like, *the* Karro?"

I twirled the necklace between my fingers, staring around my circle of Anaka. My face heated. Karro was more than I'd imagined. So much more. I never wanted the mission to end. I wanted to know of his violence and grace. Being loved by him was addicting, even if I did not feel the same way.

I leaned in, altering my voice to sound as dramatic as possible. "Do you guys want to hear a little secret?"

All thirty children nodded, inching closer and closer.

I pulled my lip between my teeth. I'd been forbidden to speak of Karro to anyone except the Murthaa. I trusted my Anaka with my life, though. They were so loyal and naive. I was their world; it was terrifying. They trusted me more than I trusted myself. I shot at them, with no intention of missing. But they still loved me.

"He and I are boyfriend and girlfriend," I whispered.

A chorus of gasps and giggles echoed around the circle. A few exclamations—"no way" and "he's famous!"—slipped from their lips.

I smiled, looking at them. My heart hurt. One day, they would know "boyfriend and girlfriend" was not as exciting as they thought. It was just seduction and loneliness. On both of our parts.

"Can I please, please, *please* meet him?" 8362 said. She twined her fingers together, kneeling in front of me.

"One day," I promised.

CHAPTER

THIRTEEN

PRESENT

K arro's grip around my wrist loosened. My nails dug
deeper into the top of his hand.

He continued to pull me down the hall, my tongue
bleeding between my teeth. I did as he said, remaining quiet as
we walked further and deeper through a valley of masked soldiers. My body trusted Karro. I did not, but my body willingly
followed behind him.

I kept my eyes on the guards lining the walls on either side
of us. They were wearing white suits with thick white bulletproof vests over them. I noted how fresh and crisp their clothing looked—like they had never been in the face of opposition.
Their clothes were similar to fencing outfits, black shields covering their faces.

The uniform was not of The Blood, but it was the closest thing to it that I'd seen so far. They looked identical. Orderly. Unmoving.

The weapons caught my attention next. Each soldier had a large machine gun propped on their shoulder. The barrels were pointed in our direction, straight ahead, but none of them pulled the triggers. I was grateful we weren't being pumped full of lead.

We continued to walk through the alley of guards. Hundreds of the beings stared ahead as we walked through the hall. They didn't move their heads to follow us with their eyes. No, they didn't even breathe.

They didn't look real. None of this felt real.

I calculated how long it would take to kill them all. I could do it. I might take a few bullets in the side before I got a vest on, but once I got hold of a gun, I could do anything. I felt like a god with a machine gun in my hands. Even amongst a hundred false gods.

I fixed my focus ahead. Karro did the same, his jaw set. This seemed too casual for him.

Once we reached the end of the hall, a single door awaited. It was tucked to our left, two guards on either side of it. I looked around, searching for any other exit. I found none.

Karro shot a warning glare toward me. He removed his hand from mine and entered the room. I hesitated, looking at the soldier to the left and then the one on the right. As I followed Karro through the door, I realized there were fewer soldiers inside, and more opportunity to find an escape.

Goosebumps rose on my skin. I crossed my arms over my stomach, clamping my warm palms over my now-freezing arms. In the center of the room was a metal table with a flickering light swinging directly above it. Beside it was a tray filled with multiple medical tools. The scalpel was what I focused on.

Soldiers lined the walls, as they had the hall. There were twenty, maybe thirty, packed into the small room. It would be difficult to take them all, but not impossible.

I'd need Karro.

I mimicked him, following his every step. When he looked up, I did. When he stared at the floor, I did. I stopped when he sat on the edge of the metal table.

A woman who had been hidden behind the soldiers approached. I looked up at her, watching her every movement. She was tense, but I noticed a slight tint in her cheeks when she emerged. When she looked at Karro.

She grabbed a syringe from the table before coming to stand between Karro's legs.

"Good to see you again," he hummed, looking up at her through his lashes.

My face twitched.

She wore a collared white dress, the fabric loose against her body. I scanned the entirety of her body, though not much was exposed. Her hair was pulled into a tight bun and a white cap covered any exposed strands. The symbol of Caduceus was stitched into the center of her headwear. *A nurse.*

She flicked the needle with her fingers and aligned it with the prominent vein prodding from his neck. He didn't wince when she pushed it in slowly and pressed the plunger.

I stared at the syringe; something black was coming from it. A few dark drops slid down Karro's neck. He didn't seem to mind.

"It's good to see you again," he continued. He hadn't looked away from the woman.

I looked at her belly, where his hand gently fiddled with her dress before he pulled it away. Her fingers were on his neck, tracing gentle circles far from where she was working.

I moved my attention to the closest gun. At this point, I was ready to call it a day and shove a needle into both of their eyes.

"Your hair looks good. You changed it." Karro reached for it, fiddling with a strand that had fallen from the woman's tight bun. I wanted to throw up. On them.

I noted how far the style she was wearing was from the norm at The Blood. *They* had only worn braids; buns were forbidden.

"Thank you," she replied. She bit her lip, a light flush spreading across her pale face.

Karro leaned forward, whispering something into the nurse's ear. Her eyelids fluttered shut, and she suppressed a smile.

I examined the scalpel. It was just out of reach, sitting on the tray beside the door.

The nurse removed the needle and placed it far from us. Grabbing another one, she gestured for me to come sit closer to her. Karro looked up at me, tilting his head toward the space beside him.

I crossed my arms tighter, looking down at him. *Fuck you,* I wanted to say. *Fuck you if you think I'm sitting on that table.*

"Come." The nurse smiled, gesturing toward the open seat.

I laughed and gritted my teeth together. "No."

"Naga," Karro warned. For the first time since entering the room, he looked away from the nurse and toward me. Something about it all made me sick. Angry. His eyes shifted, communicating through his gaze.

Trust me, they told me. Pleaded with me.

Fuck you, mine told him.

I sat down beside him, my muscles tense. The woman approached me, new needle in hand. My stare burned a hole into the side of her face as she prepared the syringe. She slipped it into my neck, as she had done Karro. She did not caress me, though. No, that was just for him.

I did not wince. I wouldn't give her the satisfaction.

I stared at her curls in their tight bun. I wondered if Karro saw something in her, a sort of light, that I lacked. She looked happy. She looked like she would make him happy. I hated that she was beautiful, too.

"All done." She patted my arm, returning to where she'd disposed of Karro's needle.

I'd been too angry to consider what was happening. She'd just pumped something black inside of me.

Karro stood. Was that all? I stayed seated on the edge of the table, my nails digging into the metal. I scanned my surroundings one last time, memorizing the room, the stances, and the tools.

The guards held their guns comfortably, despite the weight. They must have been well trained. Even if I somehow reached a gun and equipment, it would be too risky to take out this many of them.

Karro wrapped his fingers around mine. I looked down at it, letting my stomach flip once before I jerked my hand away. "Don't fucking touch me."

Seething, I pushed him hard into the table beside the door. Tools and instruments went flying across the room, some sliding under the large metal cabinet in the corner. But not all.

I crouched down between his legs. He was breathing heavily, looking at me from the floor. For a moment, I thought he was the one who would rip my jugular out with his teeth.

I smiled close to his face and pushed myself back to my feet. Stepping over the spread-out medical tools, I left him in the room.

I didn't care that Karro had touched me. It had been the sight of chaos, the distraction of it all, that mattered. It had felt good to push that fucker down, though.

I made my way down the hall, Karro close on my heels. Hidden beneath my tank top, the scalpel grazed against my stomach.

CHAPTER

FOURTEEN

PRESENT

I entered the room, Karro's hot energy closing in behind me. I ignored his curses and made my way to the window.

When he stepped inside, the door slammed shut behind him. There must have been a soldier on the other side, waiting for us to enter. It happened too fast.

I squinted and stared up at the window. There had to be a screw there that I couldn't see, a loose bolt or a melting seal.

"You don't ever fucking shove me like that," Karro hissed.

I tilted my head and continued to search for a weakness in the window. "Get over yourself, Karro. You aren't worth my time."

He reached around my neck and clasped his palm around my throat, pulling me backward against his chest. His other arm wrapped around my hips, preparing for my legs to come flying toward him. *Smart.* After a single fight, he'd already memorized how I played.

I pressed the back of my head into his collarbone, attempting to push him away. He felt like a wall of muscle; it only hurt me.

This was such a fucking waste of time. I stared up at the window and went still against him.

"You and I are going to be in this room for a very long time. Stop acting like a fucking brat and get over yourself. Moping is not going to get us out of here any faster, Naga." He spat out my name.

We were not going to be in here for a "very long time." I'd kill myself before I allowed that to happen.

I laughed. Karro dug his fingers into my throat. I was so close to the window, so close to trying. It was out of his reach, even when standing. But together? I could try. I could do *something*.

"You have to be joking. You're such a hypocrite. You've spent the entire time with your back to me, moping, Karro." I spat out his name as he had mine.

He went quiet.

I didn't look away from the window. I debated whether I could pry it open with the small scalpel. "We are both moping," I continued. "Boo fucking hoo. Let go of me and lift me up."

I nodded to the skylight above us. After a silent minute, he released my throat and shook his head. His chin brushed against the back of my hair. "It's no use. I've already tried."

I stepped forward and turned to face him, crossing my arms over my chest. "You are also stupid."

"Shut the fuck up," Karro said.

His eyes slithered away from my face and down to my chest. I crossed my arms tighter. The tank top did no good in covering my breasts. Everything spilled out of the neckline.

When he looked into my eyes again, his expression was tense.

I sucked in a breath and looked back at the window. "Please," I spat. I had to force the word out of my mouth. It made me shudder.

His lips quirked. I would have missed it if I hadn't been staring at them. "Okay," he said, on the verge of grinning. I wanted to slap him. He was amused by me uttering a single word.

I avoided his eyes when I grabbed his shoulders. I attempted to hoist myself up with my upper body strength, but it was no use. His large and calloused hands grabbed hold of my waist, pulling me onto his shoulders in one fluid movement.

My cheeks were on fire. I kept my chin toward the window and my face away from him. He didn't get to see me like this.

I settled my thighs on either side of his head. My stomach too felt like fire. I'd forgotten what it felt like to have someone there, let alone Karro.

I reached for the scalpel and held it tight, then made the mistake of locking eyes with him. It felt all too intimate. His hands holding me in place, my fingers in his hair to keep myself steady, the heat of it all.

I was going to claw at this window until it submitted, if that was what it took. I needed to get out of here.

"You little thief," Karro hummed.

I slid the scalpel through the crease in the frame and attempted to cut the seal. Then, I pried at the pane. There were no screws in sight, but something was keeping it in place. The glass was thick. If I tried to stab at the it and shatter it, I would risk breaking the only weapon we had.

I gnawed at my lip and continued to pry at the frame. "If you had stopped bitching about me shoving you, I would have explained why I did. The tools went everywhere." I hit the window with my fist. Nothing was working. "They'll be searching for those tools for months. They won't even know it's missing."

"Smart girl." Karro's thumb traced a light circle above my sweatpants. I tensed and looked down at his hand.

It had been how he'd once reassured me. Touch. It was how we both expressed our love; how we'd once expressed our love.

I sucked in a breath and continued to work on the window.

As much as I hated Karro, and he did me, there was no denying how ungodly the sex had been between us. I could have sworn he'd fucked me so hard that my brain had rewired itself. My view of sex had once been so distorted, yet Karro had cleared it after the first time. I now understood touch. Love.

"Fuck," I groaned, hitting the glass with my fists. It was too thick. Even if Karro's strength were to be put against it, it would be of no use. The window was offering no hope.

I threw my hands down in defeat. My fists landed a few inches from Karro's. "I thought there would be a nail, or some way to pry it open."

Karro slid me off his shoulders. He practically threw me to the ground, like I was hurting him, despite my low weight.

He looked at my white knuckles. I was holding on to the scalpel like it was my lifeline.

"No," he started, still staring. "I've tried everything. Even with your little scalpel, it's pointless."

I could have killed him.

He was looking at the blade like he knew it.

I was looking at him like I wanted to.

When I looked at him now, I saw The Blood. I saw my Anaka. I saw the doctors and generals. I saw pain. I saw love. I saw sex and lust. I didn't see Karro anymore.

I backed up and sat on the edge of my bed. I focused on the floor and my breathing. My legs felt weak. I hated it. I hated him. Every time I looked at him, it felt like he crawled down my throat and into my head—he found a cowardly girl that I despised and pulled her out. He found the love-sick girl who'd given up everything over some cock and silly love-soaked words.

He didn't move, just stared down at me. I hated that he knew I was going to speak. He knew me too well, without knowing anything at all.

"Did you mean it?" I started. My tongue became heavy. I should be quiet. "That you never loved me?"

A muscle jumped in his jaw. I didn't look away from his darkened eyes. This was the Karro I remembered. The angry Karro who had sent me to my hell.

I blinked and nearly missed the subtle shake of his head. My stomach flipped, and I looked at his feet. I'd rather have the cruel words. I'd rather him whisper in my ear how pathetic I was. I'd rather hear how much he hated me.

I frowned and wrapped my arms around my stomach. I supposed I needed to explain myself more than he did. It hurt terribly to understand, but I did. His rage had a reason, but my lies had none to him.

"They saw something in you. When you were young, they knew you were going to betray them. You weren't even there yet, and they knew. They let you do it, too."

I'd never understood it. The Blood had somehow known that Karro was going to grow up to join them, to rise to commander and betray them. They said it was "The Sight" that allowed them this knowledge, though I'd never quite believed that.

They would not intervene. They wanted it to play as it was meant to. Karro was meant to happen. It was meant to happen. Innocent lives were shed because the events needed to unfold as they were meant to. The Sight was a pathetic excuse for their laziness. They could have stopped it earlier, if they had truly known.

The Murthaa had disagreed. Everyone who died the day of his betrayal died because of some silly belief The Blood held.

I traced my fingers along my biceps and continued. "That's when they decided it was going to be me that surpassed you. They'd trained me since I was born. To be the perfect replacement. I was born to be nothing but you. They used the time, waiting for your betrayal, to get me ready."

They trained me the day The Sight had told them of what he was going to do. Years had passed, waiting for his betrayal.

I didn't understand how they knew. I'd convinced myself I was a safety net in case he did betray The Blood. That there was no way they'd genuinely predicted his betrayal.

But, they had. Everything I had once believed began to crumble, though I never accepted it.

I flexed my fingers around the scalpel, but I did not attack.

My throat felt too tight. I wanted to stop speaking, but I needed someone to hear. Even if it was Karro, who wanted nothing more than for me to suffer.

"I was to be a weapon, not a girl. I was perfect. They wanted me to be you. Karro's karma." I smiled, glancing up at him. He looked like he'd seen a ghost. "And you know I was okay with it. After the lessons with the doctors, I could do anything."

"Stop talking," Karro said. His lips parted, and he stared down at me, his face paling.

He wanted the truth. I knew he did. I would too. It infuriated me that he was looking at me like I was a fucking stranger every second in this room. That everything had been deceitful. We both knew there'd been something there, beyond The Blood, and beyond us.

"You and my Anaka were the only people who made me feel more than what they made me to be. And for that, I was planning on leaving. I wasn't lying about that. There is a truth. So stop fucking looking at me like that."

Karro tilted his head. "Is that an attempted apology?"

I muttered a curse and lay down on the bed. Holding the scalpel, I pulled the dainty covers over me.

I let my confession float around the room for the rest of the night.

Karro didn't sleep. I felt his eyes on me the entire time.

CHAPTER

FIFTEEN

PAST

I knelt on the floor, cleaning up some remaining blood from the Anaka. One of my bullets had grazed a child, but it was nothing they hadn't endured before.

My body tensed, reacting to quiet footsteps approaching.

I tucked the snake necklace into my shirt and turned to face whoever was in my training room. If my gun had not been out of reach, I would have blown their brains out for trying to sneak up on me.

In front of me, the Murthaa stood high, and a child cowered behind her. I was beyond grateful that I had forced the Anaka to leave early. If the Murthaa had seen them so comfortable with me, she might have demoted me or assigned them to herself.

"Good to see you, Naga. I see you're adjusting well to your new training room." The Murthaa gestured to the space I had been assigned. I'd requested something a little bigger, given that I wanted to shoot, not throw knives.

The Murthaa's fingers weaved together in front of her. She had blue dreadlocks that ended at the base of her spine. She usually wore them tied back in a thick ponytail, but today she'd left the strands hanging against her bare arms.

She was wearing a uniform similar to mine. The letter "M" was stitched on her uniform. "A" was on my Anakas'. "C" was marked on mine.

She wasn't wearing a bulletproof vest, though. She had no reason to. She rarely left her corridors at the Home Office. The Murthaa was merely a face for The Blood; I represented our sector.

The child behind her trembled. My mind flashed to General Mills, and how I'd given his head to this girl, 7437. She seemed to be recalling the same memory. Now, she whimpered and hid behind the Murthaa.

The Murthaa would behead her faster than I would if she was given reason to. It was odd seeing someone trust her like this child did.

I dipped my head down, welcoming her presence. It was a sign of honor and respect. I bowed my head to the Murthaa and only the Murthaa.

Her position was mine next, if I wanted it. Commander was the highest ranking until Home Office was involved—the Murthaa being the highest of the Home Office. If anything were to happen to her, a committee chosen by her would takeover.

"Yes. The girls can train easily here. Fewer places to defend themselves," I replied. The snake necklace burned against my skin. It would all be over if she saw it.

I did not fear much, or many, but the Murthaa was one of them. She was something else entirely. She was the daughter of The Blood, the creator herself. She was an ancient woman in the skin of a thirty-year-old. She could die, be killed. But as of yet, no one had tried.

"I assume you remember 7437." The Murthaa pushed the shaking girl in front of her. The child kept her eyes locked on a small speck on the floor.

"Yes," I started. "7437 helped me resolve my issue with my previous superior."

The corners of my mouth twitched remembering Mills. It hadn't been him, mostly. I'd never liked reporting to superiors. When I was promoted, the Murthaa had told me that was the reason she'd known I was going to be commander: I'd rather burn everyone alive than follow them.

"Unfortunately, Theim believes it is best that she is transferred to War. Order was doing her no good. She needs something a little more . . ."

We both looked down to 7437. She continued to shake.

". . . forceful."

Theim, the commander of order. It was uncommon for Anaka to transfer between sectors, especially from Order to War. Theim usually sorted the Anaka out; her brutality was inching toward mine.

"Intelligence?" I asked, looking back to 7437.

The Murthaa shook her head. "That's where she is originally from."

My face softened. I was the last sector. In very rare cases, like 7437's, the Anaka would be transferred from sector to sector. Intelligence was first. Then Order. And now War. If she did not crack and learn to train, she would be euthanized upon the Committee's approval.

"Of course." I cleared my throat. I'd tie her to a chair and shoot bullets in her hair if it meant her learning not to fear a gun. She was not going to be euthanized. "I always have room for more."

"Great. You make me proud." The Murthaa dipped her head and turned to face the door. It wasn't deep enough to be considered a show of respect, but rather a way of thanking me.

I looked back to 7437. She didn't look like she was going to make it long.

CHAPTER

SIXTEEN

PRESENT

Karro and I stared at each other, unspeaking and tense. He was sitting a far distance from my face with his knees drawn to his chest and his back against the bed. The tray beside him was untouched except for the small water pouch he had emptied.

I shifted my head against my pillow, but didn't look away from him. He was everywhere. In my nightmares, in my dreams, and my waking life. He'd taken control over me, without having said a single word. When I closed my eyes, trying to drown out this room, it was him I saw. My match. The other half of my cruel, wicked soul.

His face looked soft this morning. He had a warm glow about him—despite the cold stares and frozen words he'd spat, he always felt warm. He was comforting in some terrible way.

It'd been like this for days, and it'd been like this for the days before those days. Unspoken words wandered around us, thousands of questions on the tip of my tongue. I knew he had questions too. I wanted to speak before he did. I wanted to ask about this place, him, and how he felt.

I cleared my throat and forced my voice. "I have a question."

Karro's fingers tightened into his pants, his eyes boring a hole through my flesh to my soul. I hated speaking first, but I knew I needed to. Karro, even when he was happy, never spoke. I'd have to do it. He'd stare and wait, as he was currently doing.

"When?" I whispered.

A single word, one I'd dreamt about asking for years when I was alone. Now that it came from my mouth, it felt unnatural. It should have been left in the back of my head.

Part of me didn't want the truth. I didn't want to know what had happened to open Karro's eyes, or why he'd kept entertaining our relationship when he'd known he just wanted to hurt me.

I'd spent too much time turning it over in my mind. I thought maybe it had been the day he'd washed my back and read the tattoos. Maybe one had led him to discover that I was not who I said. Or maybe it had been the day I'd come home sobbing and shaking. I'd wanted to leave so, so badly. But I'd kept my thoughts to myself as he held me.

Karro's lips parted, and he ran his tongue along his teeth. "You'd think with all the years alone, you'd have figured it out by now."

I flinched as his voice broke through the thick air. The thought of that place, the isolation, and everything made my stomach drop. It made me sick that he knew how long I'd been there. How cruel it had been.

I shook my head and pulled my knees to my chest. He watched the motion, and his gaze slipped to my neck and cleavage.

"I told you my truth. I wish to know this," I said. I hadn't told him *all* of my truth, but enough.

His jaw ticked. "I owe you nothing." We stayed silent for many breaths, his eyes lingering on my breasts for most of them. When he pulled his eyes back to mine, he said, "Our first anniversary."

My breath hitched as I recalled the night. I'd arrived at dinner with a black eye, and Karro had been tense all evening. I'd believed it was because of the bruise, but no. It all made sense now.

My blood heated.

Before our date, The Blood had been infiltrated by a group of unknown soldiers.

I propped myself up and narrowed my eyes. He followed me through the movement. "It was you. The—"

I looked away. Karro had knocked me unconscious. He was the one who had given me the black eye. And, after it all, we'd eaten dinner together like two fools. We'd fucked like fools after, too.

I was the fool. Karro had known by that point.

Fuck.

We'd been together for three years. Karro knew and stayed with me for two years. He watched me fall foolishly in love, knowing he was planning to break me. To shatter me.

My mouth hung open.

Karro smiled. Hard. "How does it feel?"

I didn't respond, just gaped and stared down at him. He'd tricked me.

It had to be a joke.

I frowned as Karro tilted his head, his smile widening. The pearls of his teeth made me shudder. "Karma," was all he said.

I rolled over, blocking him out. That night, it was our first anniversary I dreamt of.

CHAPTER
SEVENTEEN

PAST

I stood close beside the Murthaa, blue light reflecting on both of our faces. Each screen in front of us broadcasted a different area of the War sector. Some showed the cafeteria, which was flashing red, and others the halls people were scattering from.

I looked over to the Murthaa. Her hood was pulled high, dreads and face tucked in the shadows of her cloak. Even if we all died, it was the Murthaa who mattered. She was the only person who could keep this place running. I would have sprinted through a storm of bullets to protect that power.

The Blood was pitch-black, dark red flashing as the sirens continued to go off. Behind me, a few generals pulled on their suits and awaited my orders. I wrapped my fingers around the straps of my vest, my eyes staying trained on the screens in front of me.

It'd been ages since someone had been able to infiltrate The Blood.

I couldn't wait to play.

The camera feed showed a group of around seven men walking down the halls of the War sector. We needed to act soon, as they were getting too close to where the Anaka rested. I'd trained them on how to defend themselves during a lockdown, but I still didn't want them to have to use their training.

My finger twitched at the thought. I grazed the trigger of the machine gun I had slung over my shoulder. They were getting too close.

"Any ideas?" I asked, not looking away from the screen.

The Murthaa shook her head. It was rare for a breach to happen, but not unheard of. Usually, it was a group of rebelling members wanting to leave The Blood. It happened a lot in Order, but rarely in Intelligence or War.

I focused on the large masked man at the front of the group. He led the other figures behind him further down the hall. They occasionally peeked through doors, shooting rounds into open rooms. I knew this wasn't a targeted attack. They were wasting too many bullets to be searching for someone.

I looked up impatiently. I had an hour. Otherwise, I'd be late to Karro's and my anniversary dinner.

My lips quirked. Karro. I wondered what he was going to get me for our anniversary. I wanted to get this nonsense over with so I could find out.

I turned and faced the generals and soldiers lined up behind me, pointing to the bulky man leading the group. "This man, in the front? Do not kill him. Kill every last one of them, but not this one. I'll deal with him."

General 88 stared up at me, a light behind her eyes that Man would have deemed insane. She licked her lips and stared at the armed men. She didn't just like the blood—she loved the kill. The murder. The guts.

I scanned my soldiers and generals. Their heads were dipped low, showing respect toward me. When I'd first been promoted to commander, I made sure every last one of them knew what would happen if I was disrespected.

"Generals behind me, then soldiers, youngest in the back." Some were as young as fourteen; I'd keep them covered until everyone in front of them was dead. I hated losing soldiers. "Stay in line with your ranks."

The group before me was only a small fragment of the War sector. They were my inner arms, in a way. During a lockdown or emergency, this was the group I called upon.

We left the small room, sealing the Murthaa inside. I held on to the straps of my uniform as we continued down the hall and toward the gunfire. I was in the front, with no helmet or mask protecting my face.

The rest of my generals wore armor covering every inch of them. The youngest soldiers were suited in so much that they often fell over from the weight.

I adjusted my vest and armor. I hated wearing it; it felt so much larger and heavier than I was. I could have swum in it if I'd wished to.

I held a machine gun firmly to my shoulder, the barrel pointing upward and behind me. Two other pistols were strapped to my back to ensure that, no matter what, I would always have access to a weapon. Not to mention the knives. They were against me like a second skin. There was a strap of bullets hanging around my waist, acting as a belt of sorts over my black cargo pants. On my back, the word "NAGA" was written in white paint.

I pulled my hood over my head, hiding my French braids under it. I adjusted the black cotton mask that pooled around my neck, moving it up to cover my nose and mouth. I'd never liked inhaling gunpowder.

The group of opponents rounded a corner, coming into view down the hall. They charged the moment they noticed us. Bullets began to spray around us and toward us. I noted that they weren't shooting at anyone in particular—they wanted us all dead.

I cracked my leather-covered knuckles and pulled the gun to my shoulder. The moment I opened fire, so did my generals and soldiers. Every last person behind me followed my lead, shooting at our attackers as mercilessly as they did us.

All hell broke loose.

Hell was beautiful. Bloody. I smiled through it all, unafraid of being shot. I wanted to bathe in the blood spreading through this hall. The flashing red lights added to it all as well, and the alarm sounded like a song beneath the gunshots. If I could have chosen somewhere to be forever, it would have been here. Not The Blood, but rather, the chaos in the moment. The blood-shed. It felt like peace.

Within seconds, they were all dead. We picked off every last man, all bodies now decaying on the ground. They'd been strong, much stronger than I'd expected. But I'd had more behind me than they did.

Of the men and women I'd brought with me, Generals 88, 9382, 1384, and 1837 had been blown to pieces. It was the most soldiers I'd lost in months.

I looked down at the corpses of our attackers. They did not twitch or groan. We had shot them over and over, continuing even after they'd passed.

The large man who had led the group lay dead at my feet. I kicked his groin to make sure, then scowled and looked behind me. "Who killed him?"

I'd been thinking about the ways I would torture him. I'd planned to pluck off every last one of his eyelashes to prove that I meant to hurt them. Then the fingernails. I'd force answers out of him with the fingernails.

But, he was dead.

6942 ducked her head low. She didn't need to confess. Her bow and tremble were enough.

"Everyone is dismissed." I looked over at the general standing closest to me. His face was covered in blood. I'd have found him beautiful if my heart had not belonged to another. "General 70, return to the Murthaa and tell her it was a success. I'll be there soon for a debriefing."

The group ducked their heads and turned around.

"Except you," I snapped, pointing in 6942's direction.

The young girl tensed, but she remained frozen in her step, keeping her eyes on my shoes. "I'm sorry, Commander."

She was far from a strong soldier, only a part of my arms because I wished for her to learn. She had no talent and no ambition for a career, so her only option was to be a soldier. If she had trained under me when she was an Anaka, I could have shaped her. But she didn't. Now, she trembled at the sight of guns. I needed to force more into her face to help her get over it.

She always stood in the back. I was impressed she'd been able to get a shot in from there. She'd directly disobeyed my orders, though, and that would not go unnoticed.

"Do you know why I wished to keep him alive?"

Her black hair stuck to her sweaty face and her blue eyes welled with tears. She shook her head, trembled, and dropped her gun to the ground. I wanted to roll my eyes. She wrapped her arms around her stomach and ducked her head lower.

"I know you don't," I started. I refrained from sounding harsh. "You are a soldier. You follow orders. Orders I give you."

She nodded aggressively, tears washing away some of the blood that stained her face.

There were some, like 6942, who were too old to be trained. But she was too young to not have a career.

I wiped away a tear that fell down her face.

"I'm sorry, Naga. I will be better."

I shook my head. "No, you won't." She flinched, but I continued. "You are not meant for War. Accompany me to dinner and we'll discuss transferring you to Order." 7437 had been transferred from this sector, meaning they had a position open.

The girl's eyes lit up. In some strange, ironic way, she reminded me of myself. She'd been forced into battle, as I was. I had forced her. I didn't want to force anyone.

"I would love that, Commande—" She stopped, her eyes shifting to something behind me. Her lips parted as if she were about to say something.

Brain matter splattered against my face before she was able to spit it out.

I reached for my gun and did not spare a second glance at the dead girl falling to my feet. I spun around, weapon held high and loaded. It was knocked from my hand before I had even finished moving.

I was met by the barrel of a pistol. It pressed hard into my cheek, pushing me back. I quickly reached for another weapon, but my large attacker had already trapped me against the wall before I was able to move.

There were very, *very* few times I wished I'd been born a man. This was an instance when I envied their composure and mass.

I jerked and attempted to kick at his feet, or even buck my head hard against his. His large hands grabbed mine, restraining them between our torsos. His heavy feet stood on mine, pinning me in place.

No matter how much I trained with a gun, nothing could stop a man of this strength.

I was going to need to punish myself after this. I had let my guard down. Someone with light steps had snuck up on me. I should have cleared the area first. *Stupid, stupid Naga.* I'd burn my thigh or slice my neck for allowing myself to be so incompetent.

Neither of us spoke. I stared up at the void in front of me, a thick black mask concealing every part of the man's identity. He could see me, but I couldn't see him. *Coward.*

It was rare for me to be restrained in this way. Whoever this was knew how to sneak up on someone. Knew how to fight.

"Fuck you, motherfucking fucker," I spat. The gun dug deeper into my cheek, silencing me.

I was going to die here. No one would step foot in the hall until the morning, when the janitor came to clean the blood.

Every inch of my attacker pinned me in place. I wish I had injected myself with some steroid to make me larger. It felt like a weakness; I hated that it felt like a weakness.

I was grateful the dead girl had killed the other man. He had not been their leader. This man was. I could feel the superiority radiating off him, mirrored by my own.

There wasn't much I could do in this position besides squirm and buck against the barrel. I gathered a wad of spit and sent it flying toward him. "Kill me, fucker. Pull the fucking trigger. I will rip out your throat if you don't. Fucking kill me."

It felt like I was begging him. I was.

His body tensed, and the gun pushed further into my cheek. My teeth were on the verge of breaking. I refused to wince and give this soldier the satisfaction of seeing me in pain. No one had that honor, not even me.

I lifted my chin. *Coward*, I wanted to say. However, crueler words always found their way into my mouth. "Stupid cunt. Kill me. I will hunt you down and kill you. I will eat your fucking corpse. Pull. The. Fucking. Trigger."

He pulled the weapon away from my face, and I watched as he twirled the gun around his finger. Once the butt was facing me, he brought it down over my head as hard as he could. Everything instantly went black.

CHAPTER

EIGHTEEN

PAST

"I'm so sorry I'm late," I started. I leaned down in front of Karro, brushing my mouth against his. I bit his lip and sat down across from him.

I winced but replaced it with a smile. My muscles ached from what had occurred earlier, when the group of gunmen stormed into War.

I'd since slipped on a short and tight black dress. The cleavage dipped low, and it was sleeveless, so I'd put on a cardigan to cover the many bruises on my arms.

Five hours. I'd been unconscious for five fucking hours because of the bastard back at The Blood. He'd left shortly after, without attacking the Murthaa.

My head was pounding from the gun that had struck my head and the yelling I'd endured from the Murthaa. I'd failed her. I'd failed The Blood. I'd let one slip past. I could only imagine what would have happened to me if he'd actually attacked her. I'd probably have been stoned by the Committee in front of all the sectors.

My eye was throbbing too. It was a dark hue of purple, and bloodshot. I'd covered it with a bottle's worth of makeup, but it was fairly obvious what I was hiding.

"It was so terrible, Karro." I downed the water in front of me. I was exhausted. "My sister went absolutely insane with Mom. She ended up punching me in the face! I mean, look at my eye." I gestured toward it. It was better to explain it before he could ask.

I didn't know my mother. And I certainly hadn't received the bruise from my nonexistent sister.

Karro's face twitched, but he smiled nonetheless. Was he angry with me? My stomach sank. I'd understand why—I was nearly four hours late, and he hated to be left waiting.

I frowned. "What's wrong?"

His eyes shifted to the knife beside his plate. "Just don't like the thought of someone hurting you. Did you hit her back, at least?"

I shook my head, staring down at my food. He had ordered me spaghetti; my cheeks heated at the thought of him memorizing my order. "No. I wouldn't hurt someone." I sighed, intertwining my fingers. "Even if she punched me in the face."

A few tears pooled in my eyes when I looked back up at Karro. I'd learned how to cry on command at a very young age. At times like these, it really came in handy. "I'm just so sick of this family drama. I wish they'd stop fighting."

Karro's eyes were still on the knife. His grip around his water had gone so tight I thought he might shatter the glass. Did he really care that much about someone hurting me?

"I know, princess. You wouldn't hurt a fly."

I smiled back and reached for him. I traced my fingertips over his bruised knuckles before slipping my hand into his. I wondered who he had fought with. I'd walked in on him beating up many, many men before, but I always hid in the shadows. It would have led to too many questions if I'd responded to it with such a lack of emotion.

Karro nodded to the TV a few feet away. Again, it was broadcasting news about the war, the same war that we'd spoken about the first night at the bar. "It's getting terrible," he grunted.

When I looked at the screen, he turned toward me. Watching me. I focused on the muscles in my face, ensuring that nothing was too tight or too relaxed. It was difficult being someone else.

My stomach pooled with excitement. I loved it. The chaos and bloodshed were beautiful. I wanted to be back at The Blood, hunting down the man who had given me the black eye. I wanted to hang the men who'd believed they could parade through The Blood untouched. Afterward, I wanted the people of The Blood to stone their bodies and release their rage toward Man. Maybe even release their rage toward The Blood.

Despite my thoughts, I frowned and looked back at Karro. "Violence is never the answer. Shooting each other is not going to lead to the peace they wish for."

Karro stared at me. He truly stared, in a way that I'd never seen him stare before. Not much made me uncomfortable, but right now I wanted to excuse myself from the table and hide from his eyes. I couldn't tell if he wanted to fuck me or argue with me.

"How is your mother doing?" he asked with a tilt of his head.

"You know how it is. They argue and argue. Just putting more trauma on the rest of the family. I wish I could help them," I said. My lip even trembled.

Bullshit. Family meant nothing. All I saw in it was weakness among shared blood. Sadness, too. I saw the loyalty that family created, but I did not understand it. Was I supposed to be loyal to someone just because I'd ripped their cunt open?

When I had killed Karro's mother, he'd cried in my arms for days. "Cancer" was what he told me. I held him, despite it all. When he wept, I thought of her eyes. I felt the guilt over and over.

"We can go to that little bookstore after this," Karro suggested. He cut into his steak, his eyes narrowing as he sawed through the meat. "You know, the one you love so much."

I nodded and smiled. Books were something I loved about Man. We weren't allowed to have them at The Blood. History was verbal, never written.

"That would be great." I smiled. He was too good to me.

CHAPTER

Nineteen

PRESENT

A tray full of empty pouches sat between Karro and me, accompanying the silence. We hadn't spoken during the meal. Unfortunately, our sleep had begun to line up since we'd met the nurse, and we were forced to remain silent rather than escape into rest.

For the past few days, I'd only been able to think about our anniversary. I cursed to myself night after night for being so foolish. I hadn't noticed the whites of his knuckles during that dinner, but when I visited the restaurant in my memory, I could see them clearly. I could see the build of *my* masked soldier.

It'd been Karro who knocked me unconscious. And, by Blood, I'd deserved it.

I was an idiot. He knew I had been lying for years, yet I'd continued to lie. What confused me was my survival. Why hadn't he killed me? We'd stayed together, in a knowingly deceitful relationship, for two years after that night.

It all confused me. He hadn't shown a speck of emotion. Well, he had, but not the kind I'd assume someone would express after finding out the supposed"love of their life" was a fraud.

Fuck, Karro may have been a better liar than me.

I dug my nails into my calves, holding on to prevent myself from grabbing the scalpel and slitting his throat.

"I was so stupid," I admitted, staring at his feet. His body was positioned in the same way mine was. We were sitting across from each other, knees pulled to our chests. "I can't believe I didn't realize you knew. For that long."

There had to have been signs. I must have just missed them.

"Agreed." Karro's voice was clipped and raspy.

I frowned and pinched at the growing bruise on my forearm. I hated that I worried less of myself and more about how he felt. *Had he loved me?* I knew I shouldn't care as much as I did. I could focus on my ambition, or anything besides Karro. We hadn't talked since I attempted to open the window. I told myself I would only speak to ask why the door had opened and how he'd known what to do.

But I hadn't. I'd done exactly what I promised myself I wouldn't. I'd poked at a bear that needed to be killed, not entertained.

Surprisingly, Karro continued. Unsurprisingly, his eyes narrowed. "You'd think all that isolation would have helped you sort out the holes in our 'relationship.'"

My stomach clenched as I watched him air quote what I'd been ready to give up my entire life for. It was far from a joke, like he pretended it to be. Beyond the anger and sex, something otherworldly had formed between us. Love. Lust. I debated which word was correct.

"I didn't think about all of 'that.'" I air quoted the word, as he had. "I thought about how I was going to kill you." I looked toward my pillow, underneath which the scalpel was hidden. I continued to think about how I was going to kill him.

More damned silence filled the room. Karro looked up at me, his eyes slightly hooded. By this point, one of us would crawl into the bed and sleep to avoid conversation.

We continued to stare at each other as if we weren't sick of it.

"You knew for two years. Why did you take so long to do something about it?" Too many memories were flooding in. Nothing felt real. The first boy I'd ever loved. Had it been real? Had he truly never loved me? I wanted to hit myself, and then him. I felt like an oblivious bitch being strung along.

Karro stood, moving toward me. He reached for my cheek. I flinched but allowed his thumb to trail down the side of my face. His fingertip stopped on my bottom lip. I allowed him to graze the chapped skin. "Are you replaying everything in your mind, wondering if it was true?" The tip of his thumb dipped between my lips, grazing against the top of my teeth. I let him, softening into the heat of his hand.

He continued. "That's how I felt when I saw you that day. So, I decided you were going to feel the same way. Worse, even. How you feel right now? That's karma, Naga." He smiled and jerked his hand away as if I'd burned him.

I wanted to hurt him as much as I wanted to fuck him.

"What was that place?" I asked. If The Blood was heaven, that place was purgatory, and this place was hell.

"All in due time." He smiled harder. He sat on the floor beside my bed, fiddling with the metal tray.

I looked down at the empty pouches between us. We ate together. We were here, together. It all felt too terrible.

"Your turn," Karro began. "Tell me something true."

I looked at his fingers. "The sex was good," I admitted.

He grinned. "I know that. You squirted against my cock every time we fucked. You couldn't lie about that."

I buried my chin in my knees and stared up at him. The angle provided cover for my flustered face. I hated my body. It was such a traitor sometimes.

I debated what to tell him. Something truthful that he didn't already know. "The case was only supposed to take a year," I began, once my cheeks had cooled. "They wanted me to be forceful about it. Simply seduce and capture you. I wanted to take my time, though. It was the biggest case they'd seen since you left. I didn't want to rush it."

"You wanted to play around?"

I shook my head, staring at my feet. "No. Well, to start, yes. But—" I hesitated. Vulnerable. "I wanted to think for a little bit. By that point, I was thinking of leaving, as you had."

Karro's face tightened.

"The generals started to rush me." I laughed and looked up at him, smiling at the thought. "I killed them all. The ones who came at me. Most were beheaded. I slit the others' throats. The Murthaa understood, though. She told me she would take just as long if she were doing something like you. Once I was promoted to commander, she let me work at my own pace."

The Murthaa had been patient. She had all the time in the world. She didn't age like Karro and I did; she'd been alive for eternities. She could die. She just hadn't.

Karro looked at me as if he'd never seen me before. I supposed, in a way, he hadn't. "I feel like I'm meeting a different person."

"Which do you prefer?" I asked, tilting my head. It felt like there were two people inside me. One was dead.

"Neither."

CHAPTER

TWENTY

PAST

Karro was angry. He'd been angry through our entire dinner. Even as we walked through the bookstore beside our apartment, I could feel the fumes radiating from him.

I wondered what had upset him so. I assumed it was the thought of my sister hitting me.

When we got home, I stumbled backward into our bedroom. His hands were already down my panties, and my tight black dress was pulled up to my waist.

I jumped up, wrapping my legs around his torso.

He put an arm around my waist to support me and walked forward until my back hit the mirror behind us. We'd had installed it directly across from our bed. I always liked to watch him, even when he was blowing my back into oblivion.

"Karro," I gasped, his mouth covering mine. He moved viciously, heat fuming from his pores. I was going to sweat off my foundation if he didn't calm himself. Then, he would see the severity of my "sister's" punch.

Karro made three movements in the time it took me to suck in a breath. He tore my thong, unzipped his pants, and thrust into me hard. I wasn't prepared for the sudden entrance. I cried out, throwing my head backward toward the mirror.

It always felt like a blink of pain welcoming him. He was so fucking big, and I was always so tight, desperate to hold on to him.

Karro thrust ruthlessly into my cunt, so hard the mirror shattered behind me. Shards cut into my back, and I felt blood dripping down the length of my spine. He didn't stop; I didn't want him to. It felt too fucking good.

"Karro," I groaned. My voice was lost in his rough mouth. "The mirror."

"Good," he growled. He pushed me harder into it. I whimpered as sharp pain sliced through my skin in the form of small little shards. His mouth muffled the noise. I loved the pain. It reminded me that I was made of flesh rather than war.

I clenched my thighs tighter around his waist. "Oh fuck," I moaned, feeling his balls slam against the back of my pussy. He fucked me harder than he ever had before. Nearly every night ended in rough sex with Karro, but this was different. He was so fucking angry.

I wanted to bask in his anger. Bathe in it like I wished to bathe in blood.

Blood dripped down my hips as he continued to fuck me into the shattered mirror. I cried out from the pleasure, flaked with the pain. I tightened and released around his cock. He felt so perfect. *Mine.*

"Fuck, there," I gasped, grabbing a handful of his hair. If The Blood was watching, they were getting a show.

I arched further into him, my legs flailing on either side of his waist. He thrust harder into me, no remorse for the pain spreading through my bloody backside. Every movement, and push, made the cuts deeper.

I loved it.

I loved him.

I wondered if something was wrong in my head for adoring the pain and ruthlessness.

My legs trembled around Karro. I couldn't hold myself up anymore. If I slid down the mirror, the shards would cut my back open. Irreversible damage for a fast fuck. But the idea of him being the reason I was in pain? I nearly came from the thought alone.

He grabbed my jaw hard enough for a whimper to slip out. My eyebrows knitted together tightly. I looked up at him with a contorted face. He was breathing heavily, and his dark strands bounced in front of him with every thrust into me. In Blood's name, he might have been the most beautiful man I'd ever seen in my life. It terrified me.

Gritting my teeth, I smiled up at him. I reached for the side of his face, smearing the blood that was dripping down my hips. He smiled back, just as wicked, fucking me harder.

My vision darkened, cum already lubricating his shaft. He was too fucking good at this. I was going to burst despite how much pain I was in.

I grabbed his hair, jerking his bloody face toward me. "I like it when you're rough," I said through gritted teeth.

I liked it for many reasons. Karro was a dangerous man—even I would admit that. But seeing someone so dangerous be this angry made my clit harden. It was the roughness of it all. It felt natural, like I was exactly where I needed to be.

I didn't need to lie. The pain. Blood. Ache. It was my truth.

"Good," Karro grunted. He leaned into my ear, pulling my earlobe between his teeth. He bit until he drew blood.

His free hand slid down my wounded back. It stung and caused me to wince, but I still loved it. I arched into his grip, urging him to hurt me more. Every bit of pain was a reminder of how delicate my body was. How human I was.

I wanted Karro to break me. Karro, and Karro only.

Lust slid its fingers into my mouth, forcing my lips ajar. Noises slid out of me, noises only his cock could drive from me.

He reached for my face, smearing his fingers down my cheek. He looked down and groaned at the sight of me with blood on my face. I felt him swell inside me, twitching. My lips pursed beneath his hand.

I shouldn't trust him as much as I did. I knew this. But I did.

I reached up and dug my fingers into his throat, leaving a small red handprint around his neck. I smiled, slipping my bloody fingers into his mouth. He licked them clean.

"Fuck, I'm going to come," I warned, slamming my forehead into the crook of his neck. My nails dug into his back and shoulders, desperately holding on as he pushed me toward the edge. I'd never finished this fast in my life. It must have been the sight of him with blood on his face.

"Not yet." Karro pulled out of me, cock convulsing upward with need.

I huffed and stared down at his slick shaft. I was on the verge of sticking three fingers inside myself and getting it over with.

OF BLOOD AND LIES

"Get on the bed," he continued.

I did as he said, throwing my dress somewhere across the apartment. The small slashes on my back dripped of blood, following behind me and staining our comforter red.

Karro reached for the drawer beside the bed and pulled the black pistol from the nightstand. He kept it for "protection," though some nights he fucked me, gun to my head.

I should be afraid of him. I knew I should. He was an angry man with a loaded gun in his hands. The Blood would cower if they saw him. Why didn't I? Why did I trust him so much, as hard as I tried not to?

Karro grabbed hold of my thigh, jerking my legs open. The cold air hit my bare pussy, followed by the warmth of two fingers. He slid them in, curling them once.

He spat on the tip of his gun and stared down at me, heat hotter than ever. I couldn't help but feel like I was the reason he was angry; he looked at me like I'd stepped on his toes one too many times.

"Karro," I started, watching as the barrel grazed against my hips.

The gun pressed between my thighs, brushing against the entrance of my cunt. I bucked toward it.

I considered protesting this. I was fine with it being held to my head or shoved down my throat, but inside me? I shuddered and bucked my hips toward the barrel again. I wanted to be fucked more than I wanted to be protected.

His jaw tightened as he used his free hand to reach for my pussy. He spread me and adjusted the gun to my entrance. I did not object.

"Shit," I hissed, jerking my head to the side. The cold metal slid into me with one deep thrust. Karro was not gentle. He never had been. He didn't give me time to adjust.

It was out of me and back in before I could take a breath. I clamped my eyes shut, focusing on adjusting as the barrel thrust into me. It was a mix of bitter pain, bleeding into a force of hard pleasure.

It felt so good and terrible, all at once.

"Fuck. Fuck. Fuck," I chanted, gritting my teeth together. The driving of the gun matched the pace of my moans.

There had to be blood. There was no way I was taking a barrel to the pussy without something being ripped apart. He was fucking me too hard and too deep with it.

I pulled my lips between my teeth at the thought.

"Do you trust me?" Karro asked.

I nodded, afraid he would stop if I said no.

He leaned toward my ear, continuing to pump the gun deep. "There is one bullet in this gun. A random chamber. Do you know what I am getting to?"

Roulette.

My face and blood went cold. "Yes," I croaked. If this was how I died, I'd be happy. I'd die with my enemy's mouth on mine and my skin covered in a layer of bliss.

"I'm going to pull the trigger in five seconds."

I stared up at him, my brows knitting together in confusion rather than pleasure. My stomach contorted and convulsed, cum threatening to coat the barrel at any given moment.

"Are you okay with that, Naga?"

Something felt wrong. Overwhelmingly wrong. Roulette with a gun was a common practice at The Blood; he would know this. The Blood would only play this game when life was in the hands of fate.

I'd done it once. A soldier, my best, had spoken back to me. She hadn't died, but I'd left a bullet in the chamber because of her tongue.

Why was Karro putting me in the hands of fate?

"Are you okay with that?" he repeated, his thrusts with the gun slowing.

I nodded, rolling my hips against it. I deserved all bullets to be in the chamber, not just one.

He leaned down to my face and planted a soft kiss on my lips. It was far too delicate given what was happening between my legs.

"Five."

Kiss.

"Four."

Kiss.

"Three."

Kiss. My cunt clenched around the gun. The fear of death made me drip more around it.

"Two."

I groaned, my eyes rolling backward into my head. I reached for his bicep, holding myself steady as I came. I saw stars for a second straight.

"One."

He planted a kiss on my open mouth, muffling the cry leaving my lips. I was shaking and my vision went black for a moment. Nothing but pure release squirted from my body.

Simultaneously, I heard the gun click inside me.

I'd never met anyone like Karro. I'd never believed I would meet someone as intense and insane as myself.

I would do anything to keep him satisfied. Even if that meant taking a bullet to my cunt.

As long as he came to hell with me.

"Good girl," he whispered into my ear. My breath was choppy, shuddered pants coming from my lips as I came down from the high. He planted a soft kiss on my ear. "Let's go get you cleaned up."

CHAPTER

TWENTY-ONE

PRESENT

I kneeled beside the door, watching as another tray was quickly deposited through the slit.

It landed by my knees. I squinted and tried to catch a glimpse of whoever was outside. Was it one of the guards? Someone else? The flap closed before I could see anything.

Fuck.

"Have you ever seen one of them? The people delivering the food?" I asked. I pushed at the slit, though I knew it would not budge. How were they able to seal it shut so fast?

Karro burned a hole into the back of my head. I did not need to turn around to acknowledge this.

I ground my teeth together. Silence. Too much fucking silence.

We'd been getting somewhere. Every few days, a conversation would spark between us, usually regarding who would get the fruit or who would use the shower first. It was never a constructive conversation, but at least it was something other than this.

I turned to him. I wasn't going to accept silence anymore. "Well?" I shook my head and rolled my eyes. "Have you?"

Karro narrowed his eyes, but he answered nonetheless. "No. That's why I know this is The Blood. They're too fast. The Blood was quick like this."

I laughed. "It's inconsistent. *They* rely on patterns. Consistencies. The pouches have to be a coincidence." I gestured to the tray in front of us.

Today, we'd received six bags of alcohol. I was grateful for the surplus Karro had beneath his bed.

"You would know."

I looked away from him, and then to the pillow on my own bed. I wondered how fast I could get to the scalpel and cut out his jugular. He was big. Strong. I'd have to fight for it if I wanted him dead.

I shifted on the floor until my back was propped against the door. Pulling my knees to my chest, I held the dark liquid into the light, ensuring no particles were floating in the alcohol. It was an old habit I'd picked up after going to so many bars with Karro.

"Fuck you," I replied. I smiled and tore the pouch open with my teeth.

He looked down and let out a heavy breath. It might have been his attempt at a laugh. My stomach sank, and my lips deepened. I'd never thought I would hear that noise again.

I raised the pouch and took a large swig to that. Whiskey. I shut my eyes and leaned my head against the door, letting my breathing steady as the alcohol polluted my veins. It felt good.

"The door," I started, my eyes still shut. "Does it open a lot? Why did you act like it opens a lot?"

I'd been holding onto the question for days. Maybe a few weeks. I wasn't keeping track of time anymore. But I needed to ask. It could be our way out.

"No." I took another shot as his voice ripped through the air. "The door is inconsistent. Sometimes, it will open after a few days. Other times, it will take a year. It's all inconsistent. Like you said. But I do think it's them."

I rolled my eyes. He couldn't possibly believe it was The Blood. He was a fool if he did. If it were, we would be expected to stand by the door at midnight sharp, waiting for our brains to be fried. Sitting here, taking shots, would not be in the realm of The Blood's punishment. This room was grace in comparison.

Surprisingly, Karro continued. "I've memorized it out there. It is just that room. There are no windows or doors. No escape. It's just our room and that room—"

"It's not The Blood," I blurted before he was able to. I knew it was coming.

"This has The Blood written all over it, Naga."

My breath hitched. *Naga.* It felt strange hearing my name on his tongue, especially when he wasn't trying to spit it out.

"Okay," I started. I adjusted against the door, straightening my spine. I opened my eyes and narrowed them in his direction, my lips curving into a smile. "Why don't you ask your little girlfriend how to get out? You know, that bitch of a nurse." I said the last part as if it were the most interesting thing in this world.

Karro let out a bitter laugh. "That's what I'm working on. You know, the reason I asked you to stop fucking talking for five seconds. So I could work with her some."

I slapped my hand to my chest and let out an exaggerated gasp. "Oh! My manners. Shame on me for interrupting your little date."

Karro tilted his head backward, taking back a few shots of whiskey in one go. His eyes stayed glued to mine; I noticed that he didn't wince as the bitter residue slid down his throat.

My words went unnoticed for a few moments. Then he smiled. Hard. "You're jealous."

"Oh, fuck you," I hissed. His smile curled into a grin. My gaze locked on the dimple on his left cheek. This might indeed be hell.

"You are," he said.

Groaning, I banged the back of my head against the cushioned wall. I looked up at the ceiling, gray filling the window. Lightning occasionally struck, illuminating the passing clouds. In the place Karro had put me, there'd been no weather, no storms or rain. It felt like the same day on repeat.

"I don't get jealous." I focused on keeping my voice steady. "Because I'm not weak. Emotional attachment is the reason half the fuckers at The Blood ended up dead."

"But you are 'emotionally attached' to me."

I rolled my eyes at his fingers curling, placing quotes around the words. There was a much simpler word, but neither of us dared utter it.

My heart pumped faster, and I focused on hardening my face. "Was," I corrected.

Hours of silence passed between us. My mind had been racing as I watched the sky. The air between us felt much heavier than it had before he mentioned jealousy; however, in a way, it had made it more comfortable between us. It was as it had been in the past.

"Tell me something true." It was Karro who broke the silence.

I was still leaning against the door, and he was still in his bed, a few more pouches beside him than before.

I hesitated. I thought through every lie I had told him. It felt as though I were reintroducing myself with every truth I uttered, slowly destroying the being and persona I had created. Where would I even begin?

I reached for another pouch. The ache in my heart was overwhelming. I wanted to rip open my skin and ribs, to tear the silly organ straight from its home in my chest. I wondered if I could replace it with some device The Blood had concocted. They must have created something by now; their technologies had been advancing fast at the time of my leaving.

Truth, I reminded myself.

I could start with my occupation at The Blood. I could tell him of the times I snuck out of bed to brief with the Murthaa about wars she wished to plan. Or I could tell him of how I'd gossiped with my Anaka about how it felt to be in love with a man like Karro.

I decided the sex was easier to talk about.

"You were the first man I ever had sex with," I admitted. I kept my eyes on the clouds. I didn't want to look at him when speaking of such topics. "I'd had sex before, but it wasn't like . . ." I poured more alcohol into my mouth before continuing. "It didn't count."

I preferred my brain over my heart. It had protected me. It wouldn't allow me to remember most of what had happened with my doctors, just as I couldn't remember my own age.

I remembered how badly it hurt and how terrified I'd felt. I also remembered deciding I wouldn't feel anything again, and that they would all die.

My throat tightened, milking up a sharp pain. A pressure began to form behind my eyes, but I downed enough alcohol to suppress it. The stupid organ in my chest continued to fight with my head, pleading for me to crawl into Karro's lap. To be held or cared for.

My face hardened, and I looked in his direction. I wanted to slap the pity from his face. "Your turn," I said.

Karro twiddled his thumbs. He looked down at them, quiet, and then back at me. "I found things at The Blood. That was why I left. I didn't have a change of heart. I know that's what they said. The Murthaa. She lied."

I sat up, my brows knitting together. That was what I had believed—that Man had infested his head with their silly morals.

"There was so much more. There were sectors that'd never been mentioned, fully functioning and running. I don't think anyone knew besides her. They couldn't have known. Commanders didn't know."

I waited for him to look at my feet. He usually did when he was lying. My stomach twisted into the most intricate of knots. He was being completely honest. It horrified me.

"What?"

"Do you remember the three sectors?" Karro asked.

I nodded. "War, Intelligence, and Order."

How could I forget? It had been branded in my head since I was a child. War in particular. I had the Roman numeral three tattooed behind my ear, signifying the sectors. Three. There were only three.

Karro drained another pouch of alcohol and grunted. "There is so much more. At least seven other sectors. Time was the sector I had found. It confirmed what I had been suspecting."

That they were lying. I frowned. They were lying. To him and me.

It couldn't be true.

The Murthaa had told me I was her favorite commander among those in the three sectors; she'd said I was her favorite commander in *history*. If there had been something, she would have told me. She trusted me. Even if it wasn't in great detail, she would have at least given me a warning of what existed in The Blood.

I let out a shaky breath. "Impossible."

"Oh?" Karro tilted his head. "In the Time Sector, I found a hall of prisons. Worlds without time. That sounds impossible, doesn't it?"

Bile rose up my throat. It made sense without making any sense at all.

"This place," Karro started. "I don't know where we are, or how we got here, but I believe it is the same. It has to be a prison of a different sector."

I stared at him. Truly stared. I gaped, even. The Blood easily could have had more control over humanity than the Murthaa let on. They were powerful—they could do anything.

"Why are you telling me this?" He wasn't lying. I didn't need to question the truth.

"You told me the truth, so I told you the truth." His lips twitched. "That's how this works. You know, not all of us need to fabricate a life worth of lies just to avoid what we're feeling."

His words went straight to my chest. I nearly flinched. "That was unnecessary," I said.

Karro leaned back in his bed, his back to me. "Whatever. It is going to be more difficult to leave this place than breaking out of a little window. I think. I don't fucking know anymore. I also thought it was impossible for you to leave that prison."

My brow perked. "You planned on leaving me there forever?"

He turned to me, smiling. "I was able to play God, even if it was just for a second. It didn't matter. Making sure you were going to rot for eternity was all that mattered."

We both took a drink to that.

CHAPTER

TWENTY-TWO

PRESENT

M y tongue was numb. When I moved my head, my
vision lagged and blurred.

I'd forgotten how fast my body responded to
alcohol. I didn't drink enough of it to have built up a tolerance.

Before being sent to my apparent timeless damnation, I'd
been trying to lay off the booze. It always made my tongue too
loose, and the Murthaa and I both agreed it was too dangerous
for me to be drinking around Karro.

I wanted to laugh. I wondered what her reaction would be
to all this. She too, the woman I'd once believed to be all-know-
ing, was unaware that Karro had figured it out. None of it mattered. The late nights, the quiet footsteps, and the extensive file
studying. *He knew.*

If the Murthaa saw me now, she'd have me beheaded. Drunk
with my enemy.

I lay on the cushioned floor, my feet propped up on the edge of Karro's bed. I wasn't sure when I'd taken them off, but my baggy sweatpants had been thrown lazily across the room. I was in a pair of black seamless bikini panties and a tight ribbed tank top. He'd seen it all too many times to care.

A thin layer of sweat covered my skin. Alcohol always made me hot, and Karro's close proximity only catalyzed it. I smiled, thinking of the Murthaa. I wanted her to see me now. I wanted her to feel as stupid as I did.

"You even have a different smile." His voice was a slur. Karro sat close beside me, his back propped against the bed, inches from my feet. He'd been staring at me for a while, but I kept my eyes on the stars peeking through the gray clouds.

"Laugh, too. Impressive, isn't it?" I asked.

I'd perfected every detail regarding my false life. For hours, I'd practiced how feminine my laugh would sound around him. I matched it with an innocent, toothy smile.

Karro leaned his head backward, resting it against the bed. His face was close to where my bare calves rested. So close I could feel his breath on me. "You were very good at what you did," he admitted.

My lips twitched. I gasped, grabbing my chest. "Are you complimenting me? *The* Karro? Impressed by my skills?" I rolled my eyes and returned them to the stars.

"Shut the fuck up."

I pulled my lip between my teeth and gnawed it until I tasted blood. "I think this entire situation is hilarious."

"How so?" he asked.

I fiddled with my fingers, mustering the strength to look at him. A few drops of sweat had formed on his brow, most likely from the five bags of whiskey he'd consumed. His cheeks had a tint of pink beneath his tan skin, and his eyes were nearly hooded shut. They were open. Barely. But I could feel them on me.

"It's karma," I continued. "Like, Macbeth-level karma."

Karro closed his eyes and let out a snip of laughter. I flinched, taken aback by the sudden noise.

"So, you're a literature scholar now as well?" he asked.

I rolled my eyes again. Was he fucking illiterate? "It's a common theme in a common piece."

Our gazes caught for too long. His smirk slipped back into a frown.

I frowned too, trying to look away from him. I couldn't. I could see him. I could see the man from so many years ago. My stomach felt terribly ill. Small creatures were inside my belly, and a fire had been lit in my core. They were frantically trying to scatter.

Karro.

I looked away.

I couldn't breathe.

"I'm going to bed," I mumbled, pushing myself up.

His hands wrapped around my wrists, preventing me from moving. I narrowed my eyes on the fingers restraining me. He felt warm.

"What?" I bit out, looking back up at him.

His stare flickered between my eyes and lips. "Nothing," he said, releasing me.

We stared at each other for a few more seconds, as if we hadn't been staring for the past few weeks. Everything about him, and this, made me sick. If I killed him, this feeling in my belly would settle and I would feel better; I'd be able to think straight.

I crawled into my bed, pulling the covers over my face. I attempted to sleep off the disgusting and vile thoughts running through my head.

CHAPTER

TWENTY-THREE

PAST

I sat in the crimson-colored water. My knees were tight against my chest as Karro gently ran the washcloth over my back. Small shards of glass floated in the water, and I added them to my collection on the edge of the tub when they fell within reach.

He was being so gentle, despite it having been our roughest fuck yet.

I tensed as the soapy rag met another gash. He cleaned it of any blood and shards and moved on to the next one. Occasionally, he would apply a little Neosporin to the tip of his finger and rub it into the slits.

I stared at my confused reflection in the faucet. My hair was a tangled mess, and my cheeks were still flushed from the previous moments. I'd never been touched so angrily. Nor had I been touched so gently. All in one night, too.

Karro confused me. All of it confused me.

"What does it mean?" Karro asked. He trailed his finger along my spine. I straightened under his touch.

I knew what he was referring to. Chinese lettering ran from the top of my spine to the base. I'd prepared for *everything*. I already knew what to say when he asked about the ink. I'd planned to quote a Bible verse, as it matched with the persona. I'd planned to say that "I will fear no evil for my God is with me." Something you would expect to find in the home of a church girl.

The lie was on the tip of my tongue, ready, but the truth slid out. "A dead man is a peaceful soul." I hesitated, his fingers slowing as they reached the base of my spine. "But a soul on fire is nirvana."

I caught his reflection in the faucet. His eyes were trained on the ink, and his jaw was tight. He dipped the rag back into the water and continued to wash my wounds.

"Does it mean anything?" he asked.

I shook my head. "It just sounded cool."

Karro hummed, continuing to search my back. I had many tattoos all across it. Visible tattoos were frowned upon at The Blood.

His finger moved across the rendition of a scythe on my lower back and then to the drawings on my ribcage. "What about this one?"

I let out a shaky breath as his thumb ran across a rib. It was a block of script directly beneath a thin bundle of roses. "Veni, vidi, vici," I recited. I should have lied. "I came, I saw—"

"I conquered," Karro finished. His eyes met mine in the faucet. For a moment, I swore I saw anger again. "I've heard of it."

I'd be disappointed in him if he hadn't. It was the motto for the War sector.

I didn't look away. "My sixteenth birthday," I lied. "They had a flash promotion at my tattoo parlor. It was just some stupid quote they had on sale." I smiled at him, hoping he hadn't noticed it was still healing.

I needed to punish myself for this. I'd cracked, lying as Man would. I'd made it so obvious by telling the truth and following it with a weak lie.

He planted an open-mouthed kiss on my rib. I sucked in a breath as his teeth grazed against my skin. "You're good, Naga," he muttered into my flesh. He smiled against the goosebumps.

Karro dropped the rag and went for my throat. His fingers lingered around my neck, reminding me of how much control he had over me. He could push me beneath the water. He could snap my neck.

I focused on not tensing, as someone who was afraid would.

His fingers tightened around my neck. I coughed, reaching for his hand, and he squeezed harder, my vision blurring.

"I don't believe in God," he began. I clawed at his hand, coughing and gasping for air. "I might, *might*, believe in the Devil. And when the Devil made us, he made us one. Tore us apart and placed us on separate ends of this earth."

I kicked at the edge of the bathtub, his fingernails sinking into my skin. "Karro—" I couldn't make sense of his words. I couldn't breathe. He was going to asphyxiate me; I was sure of it.

He planted a kiss on my lips and released me. I gasped, reaching for my throat. I coughed and gasped until I could breathe again. My head throbbed and everything was beginning to spin.

The bathroom went cold.

Karro pushed himself from the tub, leaving me alone in the water. I stared at the door, wondering why he was so angry. Was it the tattoo? Did he no longer love me?

I buried my face into my knees, steadying my breathing. A new feeling began to creep up my throat, an emotion I'd only felt in passing through the years.

Guilt.

CHAPTER

TWENTY-FOUR

PRESENT

I knelt by the door again. The trays never arrived at the same hour, but it was usually around the time the sun began to rise. Still, it'd become my routine to wait and watch the slit.

According to Karro, it was pointless. I waited despite his judgment. Whoever delivered the food might slip up and leave the slit open for too long. If they did, I would be there.

My fingers flexed around the scalpel.

We'd been here for over a month. The days were seamless. Some nights, I'd wake up after only sleeping an hour, believing it to be the next day. It was going to drive me insane. I wasn't sure how Karro had been here for so long without going mad.

He and I were beginning to hold tense conversations, maybe once or twice a day. It was usually when alcohol was involved. We would argue, talk, and laugh until we saw something in each other. It would lead to us crawling into bed and returning to silence.

Karro coughed, a wet noise bubbling in his chest. I cringed, turning to face him. It was the first time I'd looked away from the door in hours.

When he inhaled, it sounded more like a wheeze than a breath, and when he exhaled, it came out heavy. I noticed that his body was trembling despite the thin layer of sweat forming on his skin. It was freezing in our corner of hell—he shouldn't be sweating. I hadn't even noticed he was ill, as we were back in our time of silence.

My eyes slid to his cheeks. His face had a pink tint, and his lips were chapped as he inhaled through his mouth.

I gulped. I hated his wicked lips.

He let out another cough, wincing when his chest expanded and contracted. The noise came straight from his lungs.

The door, I reminded myself. I turned back toward it, tapping my fingers against my thighs. Rolling my lips together, I looked out the skylight. This was taking too long.

My ears perked as Karro's breathing grew more strained. It was becoming too cold at night, and the room offered no hope of heat. The water went cold fast, so steam rarely helped fill the room. I'd spent nights debating whether I should sleep beneath the sunlight during the day.

Or crawl into bed with Karro.

I ground my teeth together, narrowing my eyes at the slit. If someone did slip up, I'd bite off their finger for locking me in this room with him.

"Are you okay?" I asked, forcing the words out. I didn't look away from the door. I didn't want to see his surprise at the question.

"Peachy." His voice sounded as terrible as his breathing.

Back in the timeless prison, I once could have gotten myself off to the idea of Karro's breathing being so strained. But it wasn't going to get us out of here. If something happened to him, so did all knowledge of what he was hiding from me.

"Have you gotten sick in here before?" He must have if he'd survived this long. The room was too cold to hide from illness.

His breath thickened. "Not this bad."

I looked back to the ceiling and squinted at the sunlight. All the generals I'd killed were probably laughing at me. *Fuck you*, I thought. I held myself back from flicking off the sky, imagining it was The Blood.

I took in a short breath before pushing myself to my feet. I rotated to face Karro. His back was to me, sweat glistening along his bare skin. How was he not freezing to death?

My stomach flipped as I imagined my nails cutting into his flesh. I'd clung to him so many times as he fucked me into paradise.

The sound of metal hitting the ground echoed through the room. I jerked my head toward the flap. It was already secured in place, a tray lying on the floor beside me. "Fucker," I cursed. I never missed the supplies arriving.

Karro let out a strained laugh. He winced, and a coughing fit followed.

I scowled and examined the tray at my feet. There were four pouches of water, five alcohol pouches, three pouches of dried apples, and a few clean rags. I noted what I would shove beneath his cot. We had no need for the amount of alcohol they sent— Karro already had a surplus. Some days, exactly what we needed came through the door. On other days, it was all stored under him.

Karro broke out into another cough. I scrunched my nose as wet noises and phlegm bubbled in the air. He sounded like he was going to throw up or choke on something if he didn't sit up.

I watched him pull the covers up his body, then looked at my own neatly made bed. I'd asked him once how the bedsheets were changed, as they didn't look nearly as worn as they should. He'd explained that when the door opened, the bed would occasionally be changed while he was being injected with Blood knew what.

Hesitantly, I approached him. If he had a fever, which I was certain he did, I knew how to break it. It would involve more touching than I wished.

I lowered myself onto the edge of his cot. He was too sick to notice, thankfully. I reached for his forehead, bringing my thin fingers to his skin. We both flinched.

I jerked my hand away. He was scalding hot.

CHAPTER

TWENTY-FIVE

PRESENT

I looked down at my hand. The tips of my fingers were covered with sweat. Karro continued to sleep and wheeze beside me, uncaring of his condition.

"Okay," I muttered to myself. I stood from the bed and paced in a circle. I could leave him to fight through the illness himself—that was what I would do if it were anyone else.

If I called through the door for antibiotics or medication, it would show whoever was out there that we were weak. That wasn't going to happen, no matter how ill he became.

I moved my attention to the floor, where the new pouches sat. Rags. Water. Food.

"Okay," I muttered, again. "Okay."

I bent down, reaching under Karro's cot for supplies. I grabbed a pouch of dried cranberries and one of dried bananas. I bit into the ones that contained rags and collected them with my forearm. I threw the pouches of water down beside Karro. He was going to be dehydrated from how much he'd sweated.

I ran the rags beneath the lukewarm water. It would help break the fever. Staring up at the ceiling, I waited for each one to become fully saturated. *Fuck you,* I wanted desperately to scream. *Fuck you. Fuck you. Fuck you.*

When I reached the bed, I dropped everything down beside him. I leaned under his cot and grabbed a pouch of whiskey. I hesitated, debating whether I should grab one for myself. Part of me *needed* to be drunk when being this close to him. Lastly, I grabbed the thin blanket and pillow from my bed.

"Okay," I repeated, staring down at him. His breathing was coming out in choppy gasps. "Okay."

I winced and approached him. "Make room for Naga," I said, though it sounded like he was too deep in sleep to hear.

The bed creaked as I crawled into it. I shut my eyes, hoping I wouldn't wake him. It would be helpful if he slept through this unfortunate situation.

I positioned myself behind his head, placing a pillow in my lap for him to rest on. My legs were parted, stretched out on either side of his body. Karro shifted, a shudder racking through him. He readjusted himself so that the back of his head lay against the cushion

Every cell and muscle in my body tensed. His head was so, so close to my thighs. Too close. If I looked long enough, I would deem it too intimate, and leave him to suffer.

I looked at his eyes. His lids were hooded as he slowly opened and closed them. Dark circles were forming under his lashes. I wondered if he had slept last night, or the night before. It didn't look like he'd slept in a while.

Unfortunately, he was conscious, all too aware of who was holding his head. I hoped he would forget this. If he forgot anything, it best be this.

"Lie on your back," I whispered. He didn't move. I pushed his shoulder, forcing him off his side and onto his back.

For a moment, I stared down at him. His eyes were open, barely, and set on me. My fingers rested on the side of his cheek; I pulled them away when I realized. I gulped, averting my eyes. My core felt how he looked.

I grabbed one of the rags and squeezed the excess water over his forehead. The droplets ran down his fever-kissed skin. I slowly ran the cloth along his face, wiping away any sweat. It was difficult to ignore the burn of his stare. I focused on his pores to avoid him.

My mind went to the day I sat in the bathtub as Karro cleaned my bloody back. I'd loathed the feeling of being taken care of—it felt weak. But Karro caring for me was all I had wished for in this world.

I grabbed the remainder of the wet rags, placing one under his neck and the other on top of his forehead. I felt him shudder against my thigh as a few cold drops slid off the cloth.

"It's going to be cold," I warned, my voice stern. *Sorry,* I added, in my head.

I reached for the second blanket, adding another layer of warmth to his trembling body. I knew it was a terrible idea to overdress someone with a fever, but these blankets were unbearably thin, and it wasn't offering much heat. My body was probably warmer than the dainty cotton.

My fingers tightened around the rag, moistening his skin again. I wiped all patches of exposed skin clean. When I made it to his mouth, I stopped. Gnawing at my bottom lip, I threw the cloth to his feet. He could deal with the chapped lips.

I looked back at Karro, his eyes already on mine. I frowned. I was tempted to put the rag over his eyes to prevent him from looking at me like that. Like it was just us, in some little snow globe, sitting on the creator's shelf.

My fingertips grazed against his chin. I wondered if I looked as fucked as he currently did. He had reason, I did not.

I moved my fingers to his jugular. My old self would have been ashamed, sitting here with him so vulnerable, and showing mercy. I could kill him. I could make her proud.

I tore open a pouch of water, spitting the spare plastic somewhere in the room. Cupping the bottom of his chin, I tilted it until he lifted his head some, though it was mostly me doing the work. He winced with every movement.

After positioning the pouch against his lips, I looked away, afraid to watch him do something as mundane as drinking water. It was all too much. My hands sunk into his hair, stroking the strands. He felt as soft as I remembered.

Karro downed the first pouch in a few gulps, oblivious to my curious fingers. I reached for another, pouring the water into his mouth until his gulping slowed. I pulled away when I decided he'd had enough.

His teeth chattered despite the heat from his fever—it was even causing me to sweat. I hadn't considered that I might become sick. I didn't care.

Fingers slid around my knee, pulling me from my thoughts. I narrowed my eyes at his hand, now wrapped around the area above my kneecap, and gulped. He was holding me in place. His grasp wasn't tight, but knowing it was his large hand on me kept me in place. I couldn't move. I couldn't breathe.

My attention set on my chest. I was three seconds away from ripping the aching thing right from my ribcage.

Karro rolled until the side of his left cheek rested against my leg. He had to know the effect he had on me. My thigh was tight as a rock under his cheek. He was lying too close to a place he'd once owned.

After a few minutes, his trembling calmed.

When I was young, I'd been taught how to deal with fevers. I'd known the ways of The Blood, and how they treated such illness. I never knew if it was traditional or similar to what Man did in the situation. I'd learned that you sweat out a fever, or you use lukewarm water and hydration. I never could figure out which was more effective, so I paired them together. It always worked.

"You know—" Karro sucked in a breath, wincing as he spoke. "I've never seen you so flustered."

I pressed my lips into a thin line and looked toward the ceiling. *Fuck you.* He'd never made me feel flustered. I didn't think that level of flirting was in him.

He shifted, leaning harder into my inner thigh. His fingers dug deeper into my sweatpants. "Where'd your tongue go?"

"Fuck you," I snapped, still focused on the ceiling.

His face softened, and his grin deepened against me. I relaxed the muscle he was lying against. It felt like he was seeping inside of me, even with fabric separating us.

I reached for the cranberries. All morning, while waiting for the bastards on the other side of the door to arrive, my stomach had growled. I hadn't seen Karro eat in days, though, but I hadn't thought much of it. I assumed it was his way of pouting in the silence.

Oblivious, Naga. My spine straightened, and an urge to punish myself ran down my being. I'd been negligent—old me would not allow that to go unspoken of.

"Eat," I said, tearing the bag open. I poured the cranberries into my cupped palm. "It's fruit, it will help."

Karro nodded and allowed me to dump the food into his mouth. I tensed as his lips brushed against my palm. Even chapped, they felt as soft as they had been in the years I used to suck on them when I pleased.

I placed the pouch beside his hip in case he wished for more through the next few hours.

I grabbed the whiskey last.

He furrowed his brows, watching as I moved the pouch to his lips. "I'm not getting drunk." He broke into a cough, shaking against my leg. It sounded like it hurt, and I felt like I should be enjoying this more.

"It's for the pain," I explained. I tilted my head, focusing on his mouth as I poured in two shots worth of the dark liquid. "I used to give it to my soldiers when they'd been shot. It's good for pain, but too much will make it worse." I pulled the pouch to my lips after, finishing it in one pained gulp.

Karro nodded, clamping harder onto my knee. He leaned back against the side of my thigh and fell asleep after a few heavy breaths.

Once sure he was unconscious, I reached for his face. I trailed the pad of my thumb against his soft, moist cheek. I moved it along his smooth jawline, too. How had he not grown stubble? I assumed it was for the same reason I'd yet to get my period.

I moved another hand to his neck, tracing that skin too. I'd never believed I'd be able to touch him in the way I used to. Everything was so tense now. I hadn't thought it could ever be this soft and gentle again.

I wished I could do it all over. I wished I'd gone into that bar without The Blood in my ear, whispering about how good I was.

After tracing every pore on Karro's face, I leaned my head against the cushioned wall. I fell asleep with one hand tangled in his hair, the other resting cautiously above his jugular.

It was the first night I hadn't dreamt of horror.

CHAPTER
Twenty-Six

PAST

My face remained tight as I held two pistols, one in either hand. In front of me, thirty-one Anaka ran across the course, ducking from my bullets.

Today, I was angry. My Anaka did not fear me, even when angry. They were gullible for that.

I could kill them right now. If I wanted to, I could pick one and pull the trigger once my aim reached their head. I refrained, continuing to shoot in the area behind them, encouraging them to run faster.

I ground my teeth together and thought of Karro. We'd been bickering all night. For the past few weeks, we hadn't been able to stop fucking arguing. I wanted to tear out my hair.

My eyes moved toward the backs of the children. 7437, the newest, was huddled down, shielding herself behind a rock. Her knees were pulled to her chest, and she covered her head with her arms.

Every lesson was the same. She was a coward.

I hated cowards.

I moved both pistols toward her, shooting at the rock she was hiding behind. She screamed and trembled as bullets rained around her. I wouldn't shoot her directly. Around her, yes, but she was still my Anaka. I wanted her to run.

I thought of 6942 as I pulled the trigger. She hadn't wanted to be a part of War either. She too was a coward. And now, her brains would forever be painted beneath the fresh coat of white paint in the hall where she'd been killed.

I shot more at 7437. The other Anaka had finished the course, no bullets in their sides, but, 7437? She'd barely been able to get a step in. She was going to be euthanized if she didn't get past this cowardice.

I ran out of bullets. Silence filled the room, followed by a few Anaka chatting to themselves. I ignored them and kept my eyes on the crying girl. She couldn't even look up at me.

I scowled and threw my guns to the floor, reaching for my blades next. "7437," I snapped.

She whimpered before jerking her head up. All of the children at the end of the course were huddled together. They knew they were safe once they'd finished. 7437 knew this as well—all she needed to do was run.

"Run or you will die." I was harsh, but if she didn't run, she would die. Maybe not by my hand, but some hand would take her when she grew older. The future would eat her alive and spit her out. I thought about the infiltration that had happened over a month ago. What if they came back? If they reached the

Anaka? Would she cower? I wanted to protect her as much as I wanted to pin her to a wall and shoot bullets around her frame.

She whimpered again but slowly stood from behind her rock.

"Stop being a fucking pussy," I began, pulling my knife upward.

The Anaka continued to whisper, most likely about my behavior. Karro couldn't fuck this mood out of me. It was beginning to feel as if every breath he took was wrong.

"Run," I bit out.

And she did. Terribly, but she made her way across the course. I threw the knives toward her feet, my eyes trained on her face. It all felt like muscle memory by this point.

I hadn't looked at her for too long until today. She had a pale, round face, light freckles spreading across her nose. Her baby-blue eyes were rounded too, matching the lightness of her hair. As with the rest of us, her strands were pulled into two tight braids—hers were poorly knitted.

I looked down at her plump lips. They were trembling, tears and snot dripping down them. A shame. She wasn't going to live.

7437 collapsed to her knees at the end of the course. I made sure to throw a knife that landed directly beside her hand. She shrieked, but I did not draw blood. If I'd wanted to, I would not have missed.

"That's enough for today," I called out, my eyes scanning the rest of my Anaka. I could see 7437 trembling from the corner of my eye. "9482, we need to work on your duck next class. You need to arch more—I nearly got your spine."

"Yes, ma'am," 9482 replied. *Ma'am.* I nearly laughed.

"3928." I looked at a young boy. "You were first. Tell the cooks you can have whatever pouch you wish for."

His eyes lit up, and he ran out of the classroom. I wished I could bring them food from Man. Our food was bland and had been sealed in pouches for years.

I groaned, finally looking to 7437. "7437," I started. "Come here."

She buried her face into the tiled floor. It took many heavy breaths, but eventually, she found the courage to crawl to me.

"What are you afraid of?" I asked, crouching in front of her.

She adjusted herself until she was sitting on her ass, pulling her knees tight to her chest again. I wanted to help her. It might not have seemed like it, but it was for her own good. When I saw her cower, I saw 6942, dead due to lack of training.

"I don't want to get hurt," 7437 admitted. "And the blood. I don't like all the blood. It's going to hurt."

I nodded, looking down at the knife in my hands. It was a common response when I asked my Anaka why they were afraid. Their stomachs were too weak.

"Look at me, 7437."

The Anaka behind her all stared, silently crowding around. Their eyes were wide, and none of the children looked away. I was unpredictable. This was probably the most entertainment they would ever receive until they went into careers.

7437 slowly looked up, tears welling in her eyes. I twirled the blade in my fingers, gaze locked with hers. Pushing up the sleeve of my jacket, I placed the tip of the knife against my inner wrist. I inhaled and pressed down hard. I did not wince as I trailed it all the way to my elbow.

Blood gushed from the wound as my skin began to split and gape. It pumped to the beat of my heart. I held my arm above 7437 so the red flow rained down on her.

A few Anaka gasped. I ignored them. It was just 7437 and me.

7437 stopped crying. She looked as if she'd gone into shock, the blood now covering her leggings and jacket. I smiled, clamping my fingers over my gaping forearm. I needed stitches. My skin was beginning to part too far.

"You see," I started, holding the gash together, "a little cut and some blood don't hurt anyone. Does it?" I smiled harder.

7437 shook her head, fast. "It doesn't, ma'am."

Ma'am. There was that silly word again.

"Now, what do you think is going to happen when you go into a fight, 7437? When you are bleeding out with three knives sticking from your face? You will regret not running, won't you?" I stopped, watching her face pale. "You flop like a fish when you die. Do you want to flop like a fish, or do you want to fucking run?"

She began to sob again. I continued. "You are going to wish you got the fuck over it and fucking ran. Get the fuck up and run. If I see you cower once, I will pin you to that wall and show you how good it feels to bleed."

7437 got up, as I had told her to, and ran. She didn't cower once. She ran as if her life depended on it.

CHAPTER

Twenty-Seven

PRESENT

I woke engulfed in warmth.

I knew something was wrong. For the past few days, weeks even, I'd been forced awake by my trembling body. I should not have been warm.

I shifted against the bed. My body tensed as I rubbed against flesh rather than mattress. Blood rushed to my face and scattered under my cheeks.

At some point during the night, I'd shifted from my sitting position. I must have gotten cold and unconsciously moved toward Karro's warmth. I was lying beneath the covers, my face buried in a warm chest. I could smell the lingering kiss of sweat, but he was no longer as damp as he had been. Had the fever broken?

Karro brushed against me, letting out a heavy breath. I tightened. To my back was the wall, and ahead of me was a barrier of hard muscle. I felt too trapped. My heart picked up, and my throat began to tighten. I would need to crawl over him to escape.

I jerked myself away. This felt too good. Nothing could feel this good, especially with him.

Pushing up from the mattress, I propped myself up with my elbow. I looked down at him with rounded eyes, my breathing picking up. *Please be asleep. Please be asleep.*

His eyes were open. Hooded, but conscious. Worst of all, he had a grin spread so far across his face that I could see the silver molar tucked in the back of his mouth. *Asshole.*

"I see you are feeling better," I spat, kicking the covers to my feet. I sat up and prepared to leave this bed as fast as possible.

Karro was still pale, but from the looks of it, the fever had indeed passed. That was the only aspect concerning me; I wasn't in the mood to figure out how to treat a seizure. If he didn't stop smirking, though, I might just have to force him into a seizure.

"I feel fantastic," he teased, his voice coming out as a rasp.

I scowled and pushed myself off the mattress. I swung one leg over his body, attempting to leave my confinement. It was past sunrise—this was the time I'd usually kneel by the door and wait for the first tray.

Karro grabbed my wrist, stopping me midaction. I looked up at the skylight, my jaw flexing. I refused to look at him. My knees were on either side of his waist, leaving me to straddle his bare abdomen. I tried to pull or push myself away, but his grasp was too tight.

I narrowed my eyes at the ceiling. I wouldn't look at him. I didn't want to see the glint in his eyes or the way I was positioned. It was too much.

"Karro," I warned. I hated how warm he felt.

"You are ashamed?" he asked, tightening his hold.

Of course I was ashamed. I shouldn't be here. He shouldn't be alive. I shouldn't have helped him. He shouldn't feel so good between my legs. I frowned. I should have cut his throat when I had the chance.

"I don't care," I replied, still unable to look down.

I pulled my wrist away from him. His hands landed on my waist, holding me in place on top of him. I was going to murder him, so slowly.

"Thank you," he said.

I ground my teeth together, my heartbeat picking up its pace. I couldn't recall the last time Karro had thanked me. The words had never left his mouth, even when we were in a "relationship" together.

His hand wandered from my waist to my hip. I tensed as his fingers lingered on top of my thigh. As terrible as it felt, I let him. My heart pounded in my head, and I held my breath.

I pushed myself off him after a few seconds. Making my way to the door, I knelt in front of it. I continued to hold my breath. Karro would not have the satisfaction of hearing how heavy it had become.

He'd held me. I hadn't been held like that since, well, him. But the circumstances had been different. It had been an act then. This was no act.

I closed my eyes, my back to him. He'd held me after our anniversary, when he'd decided he would play the same game as me. Was he tricking me now? Was this a joke?

I dug my fingernails into my thighs. I thought about the nurse and how she too was being deceived by him. Was I being played the same way? Why was it working? I shouldn't be allowing myself to feel so weak.

The nurse. Something clicked in my head.

"The liquid they injected us with," I started. It had been black—I'd never seen anything like it at The Blood. I'd been to all three sectors, and never had I seen something like it. "Do you have any idea what it's for? It could have made you sick."

"No. It didn't make me sick before. There are numbers on the bags, but that's it. They're counting how many injections we've had. Your bag was labeled one."

I sucked in a breath. I hadn't noticed the number on the bag because I'd been too distracted by the nurse's pink cheeks. I wondered if the liquid had stopped me from getting my period. If it was stopping him from aging.

"What number was yours?" I asked. I pulled my hair behind my back, covering the bare skin his eyes touched.

"294."

I flinched. "You're mistaken if you think that cunt is going to inject me that much," I said. I had maybe one more injection in me before I stabbed her in the eye with her needle. No good was going to come from being injected with some black substance. I'd only allow it so I could examine the room and soldiers.

The tray of food soon arrived—three bags of rice, a bag of toothpaste balls, and some water. Karro joined me in eating on the floor, too close. We argued about who would use the hot water tonight.

I could not look at him the rest of the day.

CHAPTER
TWENTY-EIGHT

PRESENT

A week had passed since Karro's sickness. In a matter of days, he'd gone back to his pessimistic, smart-mouthed self. We could hold a conversation longer now, but it always ended with me crawling into bed to sleep through the tension. It felt like I was sleeping more than I was awake.

I leaned against the wall beside the bathroom and crossed my arms over my stomach. I looked inside, and then to Karro. Unfortunately, there was no door to the bathroom.

He'd be asleep by this point. I never had to worry about him being awake when I was naked, washing my clothes.

"I need to wash my clothes," I stated, looking at the ceiling. I dreaded this. I'd have to wait hours until they dried. It'd been so much easier in the beginning, when we'd slept opposite schedules to avoid each other.

I grabbed the thin blanket from my bed. I could use it to partially cover myself, but if he wanted to see beneath the sheet, he would see beneath the sheet.

"Okay." Karro stared at the ceiling, hands propped under his head.

"Okay?" I replied, my tone as sarcastic as his. "Can you not look?" Did he think I was just telling him what I was planning to do? Communication had never been our strength.

His lips curled into a cheeky smile, and he turned his head in my direction. I flinched when we made eye contact. I wanted to throw something at him for looking at me like that.

"It's not funny. You're usually asleep by now." My cheeks heated. This was not a conversation I wanted to have.

"I'm not laughing." Karro smiled harder.

I scowled and made my way to the bathroom, the blanket draped over my arm. I'd already prepared the cheap soap and let the shower run with cold water. I just needed to take off my clothes, though the thought horrified me. It once hadn't, but now?

I braided my hair into two sections, tying the bottom of my ends into a knot. I slipped off my pants, working them under the water first. He'd seen me in my panties multiple times so far. That wasn't what I was worried about. I was worried about what would happen once the rest came off.

As taboo as it sounded, sex had been our love language. The vulnerability of it all.

"Do you know what I think?" I asked, wringing out my pants. I applied the soap and continued the action. I'd yet to feel his eyes on me; I was in full view of his bed. If he wanted to look, he could.

"What do you think, Naga?"

I squeezed the pants harder. I hated the way he said my name.

"The next time the door opens, I think we should walk down there and kill them all."

Karro scoffed, and the bed creaked.

I hung the pants on the edge of the metal sink. I slid off my panties next, working them under the water. I decided I couldn't control him. If he was going to look, he was going to look.

"You think we could actually kill all of those *gunned* soldiers? With a scalpel? I know you aren't that stupid."

I looked up at the ceiling, grinding my teeth. He'd said it as if I were stupid and hadn't noticed they were armed. "I'll just have to prove you wrong," I started. "Besides, I'd rather die trying than rot in this room. Plus, I'd be content with dying if it meant being able to skin that cunt alive."

"Who?"

I fiddled with the hem of my tank top. I looked over at Karro again, but he was still focused on the ceiling. It was the last piece of clothing defending me from being completely vulnerable. I wrapped the blanket around me and threw the top into the water.

It had been easier to be naked in front of him when I was someone else. I'd never felt vulnerable then—it wasn't me. But it was now. That terrified me.

"The nurse, I mean." My knuckles went white thinking of her. Them. Karro had a reason, I reminded myself. He was trying to trick her. "I'd be okay with death if it meant cutting her skin clean."

"You are jealous." He let out a breathy laugh. "Naga, the apparent stone-cold bitch, is jealous. Fascinating, isn't it?"

I wanted to stab him. I could hear his smile.

"Shut up," I hissed. "I assure you, if another person sticks me and pumps me full of something black, I will kill them too. This has nothing to do with you, or who you chase to rendezvous with."

I stood from the floor of the small bathroom, draping the rest of my soaked clothes over the sink. It'd take hours for them to dry, while I was stuck in the dainty blanket. The Blood *had* to be laughing at my situation.

I made my way to Karro's bed. He didn't look at me. I sat on the floor, directly behind where his head currently lay. It was the farthest I could get from his eyes. This had to be some joke.

"Don't look at me—"

"Fuck, Naga. I'm not a teenage boy. I'm not going to look at you until you're on your knees begging."

My breath caught. He'd said it as if it were going to happen. The words confused me, and I knew I'd focus on their meaning for the remainder of the day.

"Oh," I replied, leaning my head back on the edge of the bed. I was a few inches from his face, though we were facing in opposite directions.

"It's okay," Karro started. "To care, I mean. I hate you. Loathe you. You attempted to trick me. You killed my family. And you're a fucking cunt."

He shifted, his head now tilted against the pillow. I flinched. I hadn't been expecting his breath to run along my face.

"But I still cared. Even after it all, I'd have murdered anyone who looked at you the wrong way. Brutally. I still would."

Looking away from him, I pulled my knees to my chest and gulped. I wanted to kill that nurse for looking at him the way she had.

Karro wrapped his hand around my chin, pulling my head backward against the bed. I winced from how the position strained my spine. My neck was on full display, vulnerable to him. He kept me pinned to the bed despite this, and I arched my back, trying to relieve the tension building.

"I do miss when your tongue was dull, though."

His fingers slid down my throat. I felt like I should be afraid, like I shouldn't be worrying about him seeing how tight my nipples were becoming through the sheet.

"Karro," I choked out. "You said you weren't—"

"I didn't look at you naked."

I focused on his dimples, which deepened when he said this. My heart pounded in my chest seven times. I focused on each beat, trying to bring my attention away from him. Everything felt heavy—electric, even.

After the seventh beat, we both indulged in the strain. I leaned up as best I could, and he leaned down, swallowing me whole.

CHAPTER

TWENTY-NINE

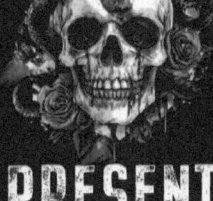

PRESENT

I sunk my nails deep into the meat of my palm. Every muscle in my face tensed, rejecting the feeling of Karro against me. My body's natural response to his lips on mine was to push away.

I didn't, though. I kissed him back as hard as he was kissing me. I pulled his lip between my teeth, gnawing at his chapped flesh. The tip of his tongue caressed my mouth before slipping inside.

My eyes rolled backward when his buds rubbed against mine. The length of his tongue ran up and down, occasionally flicking and twirling around the tip of mine. I explored his mouth, memorizing every inch of it.

I'd forgotten how good he felt.

I arched into him more, his face pressing harder against mine. I reached for his hair and roughly pulled him down on me. His lips, breath, and tongue were going to be my undoing. I wanted to savor the taste of him.

My nipples had become so hard I thought they were going to cut through the blanket. I knew if I were to look down, I'd see brown peaks poking through the thin fabric I was wrapped in. I convinced myself it was the cold air.

Karro's hand moved from my neck and onto my cheek. His fingertips traced gentle circles along my soft skin. I trembled from how lightly he touched me. It felt all too wrong.

He reached for my braids next. He took them into his fist, holding on to them like they were ropes. I winced but allowed him to pull my hair harder. I didn't know if it was the pain of Karro that made me tight with tension.

I whimpered, his mouth muffling the noise. I knew he'd heard it. He'd felt it, too.

He moved his lips harder against me. He bit at me, all while working his tongue deeper into my mouth. I felt the skin around my lips throb, bruises forming from his roughness.

I arched further into him, knowing it'd be easier to take his ruthless mouth than fight it. My fingers tightened into his hair. I latched my nails into his scalp to prevent my curious hands from slipping between my legs. It felt like my core had turned to pure molten lava. And if he kept kissing me, I might just melt into this bed and disappear from existence.

I shuddered, recalling how ungodly it had felt when his cock was inside me.

Karro pulled away, earning a grunt from me. I looked up at him with rounded eyes. No words came from either of our swollen lips. What was there to say?

He grabbed my cheeks with his thumb and two fingers. The gesture forced my mouth open and hollowed my cheeks. Gathering a wad of spit, he projected it into my mouth.

I swallowed, licking my lips clean of every drop. I did not look away from him.

Reality came down heavy, grounding me back in the room. Karro pulled further away, most likely feeling the same thing.

This was a terrible idea.

His lips parted as if he had words for this. I beat him to it. I didn't want to address it. Ever.

"Don't talk about it," I said, jerking my hand upward to block whatever he was going to say. I sat back against the cot, running a hand down my face. My chest heaved from how long I'd held my breath.

This was not a terrible idea. This was a *disastrous* idea.

"Okay," Karro replied. He shifted behind me, lying back in the position he'd been in before deciding to shove his tongue down my throat.

My face tightened and my body went cold. I reached for my swollen lips, wondering how bad I would feel if I were to forget everything for the night. If I were to crawl onto him, without this blanket, and rut out the thick air.

I'd feel fucking terrible, I decided.

I disappeared into the bathroom and sat in the wet shower for the remainder of the night.

CHAPTER

THIRTY

PRESENT

"Naga."

I didn't move. The hairs on the back of my neck stood on end. My limbs were tightly curled in, preserving any body heat I had under the thin blanket. It was getting colder—I couldn't sleep anymore.

"Naga," Karro repeated. Again, I ignored him. His voice was firm, giving no indication that I'd nearly sucked his face off hours before. He was most likely going to curse at me for using what little hot water we had.

"Come on." His hand came down on my bicep. I jumped, feeling a jolt of energy rush through me. "The door is open."

I rubbed at my eyelids and twisted in his direction. Sure enough, behind him, the door had been propped up. I squinted into the dawn-filled hallway. Guards lined the walls, as they had before.

I reached for my pillow. The scalpel was still hidden within the cheap cushion.

Karro grabbed my wrist before I could find the metal. "No," he warned.

I looked up at him, my eyes narrowed. I planned to spew that it was not his decision whether or not I brought the scalpel. His chapped and bruised lips distracted me from the thought. He looked as worn as I felt.

"You said it yourself," I began, looking to the door. "It opens at random. This could be our last chance for a year. Ten years." I sat up, my hand still lingering beside the pillow.

Karro snaked his arm around my waist before I could grab the blade. His hold tightened like he was about to haul me from the bed.

I reacted in the only way I knew how. I tensed, pushing against him, trying to guard myself from whatever violent intention he had.

He didn't choke me to death or bash my skull in, as I'd expected. Instead, his lips brushed against my ear. "When we walk through, watch the soldiers. I don't think they're real." His voice was so low I almost missed what he said.

My lips parted, and I shut my eyes. He felt so warm. It hadn't been his intention to hold me in such a way—he was speaking of soldiers, not love. But it was his embrace that I focused on. I wanted to crawl inside of him.

Karro hauled me from the bed, and I grunted when my chest hit his. If I were to straddle him, it'd put more distance between us.

He placed me on the floor. He did not move. I did not move. The door was open; we could leave the tense room. We needed to.

His eyes slipped down to the nonexistent space between us. His lips twitched for a blink of time, then I pushed past him and toward the door. I was going to die in this tight room. I was going to die because of Karro.

He made his way in front of me. I followed close behind, reminding myself to do as he said.

I stared at the masked soldiers that lined the hallway. As before, there were hundreds of them, standing stall, pinned to the wall, assault rifles propped on their shoulders. They held themselves stiff. Unmoving.

I don't think the soldiers are real. Karro's words rang through my head.

I looked at their chests as we continued down the hall. When I'd been commander, my soldiers had often been more skilled than me. They would breathe. These soldiers did not appear to be breathing. I frowned, continuing to wait for the rise of a single chest. The fall of an exhale.

I scanned them again. They all blended together, statues among statues. But despite it all, I could still feel their eyes. I could feel them watching me, waiting to pump my body full of lead.

I gulped, looking back at Karro's head. I must be overthinking it.

After a few more feet, we arrived at the room again. Soldiers lined every inch of space we walked through. Heat brewed in my lower belly when my eyes locked on the nurse. She didn't look up at me. She didn't spare me a glance. Instead, she stared up at Karro like they were the only two people there.

I too forgot of the soldiers packed in the room and everything outside of it. I could only focus on how she would look without skin.

"Welcome," the nurse said. She dipped her head down, looking at Karro's feet.

My face twitched as her cheeks grew a deep pink. Her ugly, thin lips curled into a smile, and she looked back up at him through her lashes. After her skin, I'd rip those off too.

Karro smiled and sat down in front of her. I joined close beside him. My eyes remained on the nurse's hand, which seemed to never leave his arm. Her fingers lingered after preparing the area for injection. If I hadn't been paying attention, I would have missed the touch.

Karro didn't miss it. He smiled harder, staring at her like I wasn't beside him.

I inhaled, imagining both of them without skin. They'd die like lovers.

I looked around the room, searching for any means of escape. As Karro had said, the injections the nurse was preparing were numbered. I wondered what number would indicate we were done being injected. I had no intention of staying and finding out. We were going to get out of here. Somehow, someway.

I scanned the soldiers next. Like the ones outside, they had guns propped against their stiff, unmoving bodies. There were no windows or hidden crevices within the cushioned walls. How did they get out? In? Did nurse live here? The soldiers? They couldn't be. They must be preparing the pouches somewhere.

I had too many questions and not nearly enough concentration. I was too distracted by the fucking blush on the woman's face.

"You look good," Karro whispered. "As always."

I wanted to scream. I wanted to rip his fake voice from his throat and tear her pink cheeks apart. I closed my eyes and reminded myself why he was flirting with her. We were going to get out of here. He was going to get us out of here. If he didn't, I'd kill them both.

I inhaled and returned to searching around the room. I zoned out the flirting occurring beside me, and my eyes locked with a large metal cabinet behind the nurse. It was filled with bottles and jars of various liquids, though none were labeled or branded with the sign of Blood. In fact, everything was unlabeled.

"Thank you, sweetheart. I look forward to seeing you soon," Karro purred.

I calmed my heavy breath and looked in his direction. His syringe was now empty, and the nurse was preparing my shot. It was labeled with a two.

"Of course, Mr. Karro."

She smiled. Karro smiled. I smiled. We all fucking smiled, and I thought of what I was going to do to her if she didn't remove her hand from his arm.

Karro shifted his attention to me. It was the first time he'd looked at me since we walked in here. He nodded, signaling it was time for my injection. I hesitantly moved closer.

The nurse's demeanor changed. Her light blush paled, and her face went tense. Her gaze stayed glued to the needle and nothing but the needle. She wouldn't even look me in the eyes. With Karro, though, she'd looked at him as though his cock were in her mouth.

Unremorsefully, she stabbed the syringe into my bicep. My lips twitched. Perhaps I could drain her of blood after I skinned her alive. Maybe stab her to death with the same needles she was using to inject us.

I noticed the tremble in her hands. She was trying so terribly to not meet my eyes. Her skin looked soft. She looked like she would be easy to hurt.

"Done," she said, clearing her throat.

I ran my tongue across the roof of my mouth. It tasted of metal. If I discovered that cunt had been poisoning me, only a god could save her. I'd pump her blood full of black until she exploded. That'd be fun.

"Thank you again, sweetheart," Karro hummed.

I hated what he was doing but I understood why. Seduction was the easiest way to get someone to crack. We both knew it all too well.

I stood, ready to leave this forsaken room.

The nurse looked at Karro as he stood. Her face softened, and that ugly pink color returned. "Of course," she started, her voice dipping. It sounded like a heavy breath. "I will see you in a few weeks."

My brows perked. Karro dipped his chin in her direction and left the room, pulling me with him.

A few weeks.

He'd done it. She'd cracked.

CHAPTER

THIRTY-ONE

PAST

I pressed my hand against the cool glass box. Red light scanned the length of my palm once before beeping. The doors to The Blood opened.

The Blood had entrances everywhere. Seeing as it was deep underground, we never had to worry about Man stumbling upon our home. And all entrances led to the Home Office.

The Home Office was larger than all three sectors combined. The area was directly in the center of War, Order, and Intelligence. If anything important were to occur, or if any meetings were called upon by the Committee, it would be in the Home Office.

There was no main entrance to The Blood. Nearly every city had an entrance or some way in which one could be transported to an entrance. The entrance I was currently at was on the outskirts of Chicago. It was tucked in the basement of an abandoned ramen shop.

I stepped into the elevator, which had been disguised as a walk-in freezer. Crossing my arms, I closed my eyes as the door shut. The Blood was *very* deep underground. If we hadn't been, Man would have found us by now.

After a few minutes of descending within the terrain, the car stopped moving. I placed my palm on another glass box, letting the red light scan my palm again. I still did not understand how we'd been infiltrated. The Blood had security for the security. And that security, too, had security.

I walked down the halls of the Home Office. It looked the same as every other sector: cold, bare, and littered with generals rushing to do whatever the Murthaa asked of them. Anaka rarely came to this area. It was too dangerous with the Committee here. If they so much as saw an Anaka question The Blood, they'd send them to be euthanized and have the commander in charge questioned.

When I reached the Murthaa's office, I let myself in and plopped carelessly onto the black leather couch. Karro and I were visiting Chicago for the week, for our second anniversary. I'd asked for the week off, yet she'd still requested a meeting.

The office was large, the largest in the entire Blood. It was painted a dark shade of green with black accents. It'd looked like this for the entirety of her very long life.

"You're late," the Murthaa said. She leaned back in her chair, intertwining her fingers in front of her. A sleek black desk separated us.

"Yeah," I replied, sinking further into the couch. I crossed my arms over my stomach and stared up at her through my lashes. I didn't want to be here. I wanted to be with Karro.

My eyes drifted behind her head, where there were multiple computer screens, each showing a different projection from around the world. One screen illuminated a war in the Middle East. Another showed the president of the United States. Sleeping.

They saw everything.

I reached for a bowl of candies on her desk and grabbed a black one labeled "Adolf." I popped it into my mouth, a tang of bitter blood hidden beneath the sweetness. I winced at the familiar taste; the ones with Hitler's blood were my least favorite.

"Morning," I grunted, spitting the candy out in the trash can beside the couch. I noticed a few fingers at the bottom of the bin, but I refrained from saying anything.

The Murthaa growled, and her body tensed. I knew why. I was being disrespectful. She'd always hated disrespect. When entering any room she was in, it was required that you dip your head before stepping inside. Plus, speaking so casually was beyond disrespectful in her presence. But I didn't care anymore. I was irritated—I wanted to be back in the hotel room with Karro.

The Murthaa's eyes narrowed. I noticed the tint of fume rising behind her dark cheeks, matching the flash in her gray eyes. She reached for a manila folder, throwing it in my lap.

"This is your idea of working on it?" The Murthaa's voice often sounded like a snap of a rubber band. I supposed I needed to flinch.

I reached for the folder. Today's date was labeled in sloppy handwriting on the front. Inside were photos from earlier— of us boarding the plane this morning, us fucking in the small bathroom of that plane, us lounging on the roof of our hotel, us fucking on the roof of said hotel, and us drinking beside the pool.

I bit my lip to prevent a smile. My stomach flipped as I stared at the last photo. I traced my finger along it. I was in Karro's arms as we watched the stars. He'd fallen asleep shortly after, and I'd snuck away to attend this waste of time.

"I told you." I leaned forward, propping my elbows on my knees. Intertwining my fingers, I looked up at her through my lashes. "This is a big case. I want to take my time with it. Have you become forgetful in your old age?"

The Murthaa leaned forward, bringing her hand down hard across my face. I didn't move. I took the hit, slowly looking back at her with a smile. That was not a good idea.

"I know what you told me, girl. Don't you *dare* talk to me that way," she spat. "It's been two years, and you have provided no updates on the case. That is not taking your time. You have failed your assignment."

I leaned back onto the couch and tossed the photos on the cushion beside me. Crossing my arms over my belly, I stared up at her. She was ancient. I wondered how it felt to be in her position. Once she'd been granted it—by someone as ancient as our textbooks—she'd been given the ability to never age. She could die, but she could not age.

"I'm working on it." My voice was stern. I ground my teeth together and reminded myself that Karro was only a few minutes away. I wanted to be with him and kiss him like it was our last night on this stupid fucking planet.

The Murthaa had a choice right now. Life, or death.

She sat back down, running a hand down her face. Her locks were pulled into two space buns, one on either side of her head. Two dark red strands fell from them, framing the outline of her face. I hadn't even noticed the change in her hair; I barely came to The Blood anymore, except to train my Anaka.

I'd once dreamed of being the Murthaa. I used to wish for her beauty and power.

I felt sick knowing I'd spent the past year debating how easy it would be to leave without a trace. Karro had tried, and he'd proved unsuccessful.

"I am beginning to believe your feelings are getting in the way of this case, 6657."

My spine straightened. The Murthaa had chosen death.

6657.

I'd never felt so angry in my life. Despite this, I did not show any trace of rage or fear.

I felt my head slipping into a place I'd worked so hard to burn. I wasn't the commander of War anymore. I was back in that room. I was being beaten to prepare me to be a good little girl for The Blood. I was being tortured to prepare me in case any official ever were to question The Blood. I was back on that cold metal table, being taught how to fuck by my dead doctors. I was on the playground, hiding, wondering why I wasn't allowed to play with the others.

"My name is Naga." My voice broke. I hated myself for it.

I'd been able to numb myself for so long, to scrub my head free of memories and feelings. They were weaknesses, and I had no space for that.

Four numbers made all the work go away.

I went back to the time when I was broken in.

"No. You are 6657." The Murthaa stood from her desk, rounding it and approaching me. I didn't move. I was still in that room, learning every detail of the human body and how to kill it. A chill ran down my spine. It was odd remembering what it felt like to feel.

"You were given a right to a name. Your loyalty. But don't ever doubt that I will take that from you." She grabbed my jaw, squeezing it hard. I hated that it was trembling. I hated everything about myself, and this place. Most of all, I hated her.

Picking up the file, she threw it onto her desk. She turned away from me and made her way back to her seat. "You will be revoked from this case. Your meetings with Karro will end. Immediately. Someone more worthy will be assigned the case. A shame. We really thought it was going to be you."

I watched her finger reach for the intercom button. I assumed she was going to call the Committee in to discuss the case being pulled from me.

I had no intention of leaving Karro.

In one movement, I was up from the couch. In a breath, the blade I had tucked in my pants was in the palm of my hand. I sliced the Murthaa's fingers off in one swift movement.

Now, that was a shame. She'd been *so* close to clicking the button. Now, she had no fingers.

She cried out, stumbling backward until she hit the wall. Her other hand held on to her wrist, staring at her bleeding stumps.

I laughed. She looked terrified.

"I thought you were smarter than that, Murthaa." I crouched down at her feet. She was too distracted by her fingers to realize what I was doing. As swift as before, with one cut, I severed her Achilles. "I thought you would have learned that I don't like to be disrespected."

She fell to the ground, blood from her hands and heels squirting over us both.

The Murthaa was superior. Powerful. But to me, she just looked like a wailing, bloody woman at my feet. That's all anyone was in my eyes.

Except Karro. Karro was different. He always would be different. If someone tried to interfere with that, well, the Murthaa's cries proved what I was going to do.

The Murthaa gasped, crawling toward the intercom. I laughed when she slipped in in her own blood.

"Naga," she warned. Did she still believe she was in any place to be warning me?

I crouched down in front of her. Forcing her onto her back, I placed the tip of the blade inside her belly button. I didn't stab her—that would have been too easy. I merely prevented her from moving.

She started to pant and stared up at me, switching between widening and narrowing her eyes. She looked like she didn't know who I was.

"I know that look," I started, with a smile. "That face you wear. You're wondering what went wrong. What you created. You made me this, Murthaa." My fingers flexed around the blade. I needed to stab something. "I don't even know who I fucking am anymore." I frowned. "Not when I'm here—"

"Only when you're with him," she interrupted. I flexed my jaw. Beneath the point of a knife, people tended to choose their words *very* wisely. The Murthaa did not. "You are in love with him." She started to laugh. Hard.

I pushed the blade further into her stomach. It drew a few drops of blood, as well as a wince. I balled my other hand into a fist and brought it down onto her face. Once. Twice. Thrice.

"You don't fucking know him," I hissed, hitting her again. I wanted to keep hitting her. I couldn't stop—I wanted her to feel how terrible I felt because of her.

When I paused, the Murthaa spoke. "Oh, you stupid, stupid girl. Do you think he loves you? Someone like you? Love is nothing. Fucking nothing. It is for Man. This place is more. You could have done so much more. But poor little 6657 is worried about her heart."

My jaw trembled and my fist tightened. Her words sank into my stomach, my body weighing into the ground. It felt like I was the one who had been stabbed, not her. A feeling that I had not believed possible trembled my body and shook at me, trying to snap me out of this.

I'd be killed for hurting her. The Committee would find out.

"Love is nothing. Power is. When Man falls—and it will—we will be left. You were not born to love. You were born to rule. How could you forget that?" The Murthaa smiled as she spoke. I looked at her bloody teeth.

Inhaling, I focused on everything calming. My trembling ceased, and my breathing steadied. Today was going to be a good day; today this cunt would die.

"You're right," I started, smiling just as she had. "Silly little thing the heart is, isn't it?"

With that, I slid my blade down the Murthaa's chest. She cried out as skin, tissue, and flesh alike split open. I felt like a god, watching a flower of meat bloom for its creator. I bit my lip and watched the blood as it began to pour from her body.

"Power. Love. So many big words for someone who is going to die," I said.

Her eyes began to roll backward.

"Oh, don't die on me yet."

I pushed my fingers through her ribcage, pushing bone and meat aside. I groped around her insides, searching for that pesky little organ that caused it all. When I found it, I ripped it from her.

I was impressed that the Murthaa survived. Barely, but her eyes were still ajar. I held her convulsing heart in front of her face. I wanted it to be the last thing she saw when she finally sank with the worms.

"Look at that," I started, examining the rotten heart in my hand. "Do you feel powerful, Murthaa? Because I sure do."

I sunk my fingers into her jaw. I pulled it down, hard, snapping it in one go, and shoved the heart deep into her broken mouth. It might have been the most glorious sight I'd seen in all my years.

I frowned. I'd never be able to tell Karro how beautiful the Murthaa had looked with her heart down her throat.

My own heart slowed in my chest. I crouched beside her, watching as she seized and began to choke. I wasn't sure what had killed her. She'd either drowned in her own blood, or her body had stopped functioning without that ugly pest.

Whatever it was, I praised it.

This was power, and Karro was love.

CHAPTER

THIRTY-TWO

PRESENT

A few weeks.

I repeated the words in my head during our walk back to the room. Even after the door shut, I continued, afraid I would forget them.

"Did she—" I started, but stopped and sat down on the edge of my cot. Rubbing at my eyes, I forced them to stay open. It was too cold to stay awake.

"Yes." Karro stared at the wall beside his bed, his back to me. The tallies in the cushion resembled claw marks. "That is the first time she's ever said when the door would open."

I hated that it was working as much as I loved him for being so clever.

"It's The Blood," Karro snapped, jerking his head toward me. His eyes narrowed.

For a moment, I believed he was idiot enough to still think I was behind this. If I were, I would not have allowed him to flirt with a woman like he'd been doing.

"She dipped her head. She bowed to me. Properly, too. You were too busy moping to see it," Karro continued, taking a step toward me.

Moping? I would never.

"I was not moping," I replied with a snap. I recalled the nurse standing in front of Karro. Indeed, her head had dipped, as one would do at The Blood.

Could so much have changed over the years that I no longer recognized it? My stomach sank. Karro could be right.

"It can't be." I looked down at my lap. It felt wrong saying it. It *did* make sense. The Blood I'd known had been falling apart before I was sentenced to the timeless place. Something could have changed. It might be different now.

"You were in that place for a very long time," Karro said. It felt like he knew what I was thinking. "As long I've been in this place. Shit probably happened. The Murthaa most likely got promoted to Committee or something, and someone new took over. It makes sense. A new Murthaa, a new order."

The Murthaa was not promoted to the Committee. I burned her corpse.

"Maybe," I began.

A new Murthaa made sense. If one had come into place, things could have changed. But this much? So much that I no longer recognized it? If this was the work of a new Murthaa, her order was pathetic.

"Or this could be a different sector. One we don't know of. The Murthaa could have sent us here—"

"I killed the Murthaa," I blurted. It came out faster than a breath.

Karro blinked, staring down at me. I pressed my lips together, and a weak smile spread across my face. "Shit, it feels good to get that off my chest," I huffed. "The first one would make more sense. There *definitely* is a new Murthaa."

"You killed the Murthaa? Like, the really old one?"

I nodded, pressing my lips into a thin line. I refrained from telling him why I had killed her. I'd never forgive myself if I admitted that to him. It had been the one and only time I'd let myself succumb to my emotions.

Karro smiled. "Good girl."

I looked down at my lap again, and my face grew hot. "So, yes, I do believe you. It could be a new Murthaa. It'd explain why everything is so different. I also agree that the soldiers aren't real. I should have gutted that cunt when I had the chance."

"No. I needed the confirmation first. If I was wrong, and you had, we'd both be dead."

I didn't understand why he couldn't grasp that I was okay with dying. I frowned. Everything I had was gone. My Anaka were gone. Karro was gone. The Blood was gone.

"Well," I started, clapping my hands together. I forced my lips into a deep smile. "Here is your confirmation. Let's kill her now."

Karro shook his head and backed up against his bed. He sat on the edge, his back curved as he leaned over. He did not look away from me. It terrified me that he wouldn't look away from me.

"And what if there is no way out of here? Or a way only she knows. Then what?"

I stayed silent. He had a point. There was a chance she could help us leave.

"There is no consistency to the door opening," Karro continued. "If what she said is true, and it opens in a few weeks, then we can trust her. Find a way out with her. Then, I will help you do whatever you wish to do to her."

Karro might have been as insane as I was. He was acting like we were speaking about something as simple as the weather.

I crawled under the covers, shivering. It hurt to look at him, but I couldn't look away. "I'm going to ask you a question," I said, pulling the thin blanket further up my body. "And I want you to be truthful. You can lie about anything you wish from this question on. But, I swear to Blood, do not lie to me about this."

Karro didn't respond. He leaned back in his bed, his eyes lowering. I knew I had no right to be speaking of truth and lies. But my Anaka were too pure to know deceit; what had happened to them was the work of a monster.

"Did you kill them?"

I watched him very, very closely. I watched his breath and waited for a hitch or any sign of a lie. I memorized his muscles and waited for them to tighten. Anything. I needed closure. I needed to know. And if he hadn't, I did not have the slightest clue who had.

"No," Karro replied. His voice was steady. His eyes stayed with me. His breath had not faltered or been held.

He was telling the truth.

"Okay," I said.

He had not killed my Anaka. I did not know who had, but I knew it was not Karro.

CHAPTER

THIRTY-THREE

PRESENT

"Tell me something truthful," Karro said, breaking the silence.

Neither of us could sleep. It was too cold. Every time I almost dozed off, I was woken up by my own trembling.

I stared at the ceiling, ignoring the weight of his eyes. Something felt lighter, despite only a few hours having passed since we last spoke. I believed something had shifted inside me. I no longer saw my Anaka when I looked at him.

"Hm," I hummed, scanning my memories. My lips quirked as I thought of the Murthaa's burnt corpse. I turned on the bed, lying on my side, my hand propping up my head.

"You know how old the Murthaa is," I started. Karro rolled onto his side, mimicking my position. "You'd think she'd be so hard to kill. She really wasn't. She died like a fucking pussy, too.

I killed her when we were in Chicago. We went to dinner right after."

"You're such a lying cunt," Karro said, though his lips slid into a smile.

It'd felt so fucking good to kill the Murthaa. She was long overdue.

"Yeah," I replied. "I put her ashes in the Committee's tea."

I wouldn't have gotten away with it if I'd left the body. They'd have found her. But after the Committee had ingested her, I knew I'd gotten away with it. Fuck, I'd killed the Murthaa and gotten away with it.

"Why did you do it?" Karro asked, his brow perking.

My throat tightened, and I looked toward the floor. That was a conversation he could not torture out of me.

"For giggles. Your turn. Tell me something truthful."

He bit his lip and laid his head on the pillow. I watched his eyes looking around the space behind me.

"In Chicago, I suppose after you were done killing one of the oldest women alive, we went to that bar. Remember?"

I nodded. It had been the next day. I'd drunk too much trying to repress my fear of the Committee.

"A man looked at you the wrong way. You were too drunk to see it." I winced at his words. I hated being drunk, even in front of him. It made me so vulnerable. "Even when I hated you, I couldn't stand seeing someone look at you like that."

I smiled, and a bitter remark formed on my tongue.

He beat me to it. "So, after you fell asleep, I took him to an alley and cut off his cock."

My mouth hung open. Again, he showed no sign of lying.

"Oh," I gasped. "Even after you . . . knew?"

Karro nodded. "Only I can hurt you."

I furrowed my brows, my gaze flickering between both his eyes. *Only I can hurt you.* Oddly, I felt the same way about him. It was some twisted mix of pain and pleasure.

I burst into a fit of giggles, looking away. I'd forgotten the sound of my own laugh.

"What's so funny about me cutting off a man's cock?"

"I don't know," I said. "I mean, thank you, I think?" I laughed once more before silence returned.

A heavy weight pressed back down on me, and my curled lips deepened into a frown. My hold tightened around the blanket. Karro looked at me for too long. I looked at him for too long. I was about to tear myself apart and show him how ugly I was inside. I needed to make him look away.

"Come here," he hummed.

I shook my head, looking down. "Why?"

"Sleep with me."

I pulled my covers up over my cheeks, attempting to conceal their rosy tint. I looked up to the ceiling, again cursing those who were above, laughing at me. It was too cold to turn down any extra heat.

If we ever escaped, I'd burn every last one of their corpses. Then I'd be warm forever.

Without speaking, I crawled out of bed, bringing my blanket and pillow with me. I kept my head dipped low, afraid the moonlight might expose how his words had affected my face. I blamed the thick air for how flustered I appeared, too.

Karro's body took up three-fourths of the small cot. I slipped into what little space was left, throwing a second layer of blanket atop us. Pulling the pillow to my chest, I hugged it tight, as I usually would to fall asleep. I kept my back to him.

I'd forever hate him for making me a coward, over it all.

"Tell me something else true." His voice ticked against my earlobe. I felt his breath fan down the back of my neck. I assumed it was followed by his eyes, trailing to where his crotch and my ass met. I would have looked too.

"No," I said.

"No?" I felt his stupid smile. "Then tell me lies."

I closed my eyes. His hand landed on my hip, fingertips tracing light circles above the hem of my sweatpants. He needed to shut up.

"No," I repeated. I twisted my head until I was facing him. "Stop talking."

With that, I leaned into his lips, with no intention of pulling away.

CHAPTER

THIRTY-FOUR

PRESENT

My lips intensified against Karro's. I slid my tongue into his mouth and traced every taste inside of him. He mimicked my movements, exploring the roof of my mouth and the back of my tongue. If he kissed me any harder, he would be in the back of my throat.

I shuddered at the feel of his buds dragging along mine. He tasted as he had before, and as he had so long ago. Sweet. Every drop of him was so fucking sweet. I wanted to run my tongue along his entirety and claim him as my own.

He was mine.

Unfortunately, I was his.

I rolled onto my side, my front going flush against him. His hand slid between us, lowering until the tips of his fingers met the small strip of skin above my low-slung pants. Goosebumps engulfed my skin, but it felt like fire was eating at me.

When we first kissed in this room, it had felt different. Fast. Like we were getting it out of our systems, in a way. This, though? This felt like passion. Slow and hard.

Karro continued to rub circles against my lower belly. With every gesture, his fingers moved closer and closer to my waistband. I whimpered against his mouth.

He was close. So, so close. All he needed to do was slip his hand down the hem and latch onto the heat a few inches away.

I moved my thigh to rest on his hip. It parted my legs, giving Karro the consent he wanted. He slid three fingers down the front of my pants. I didn't break the kiss. It was my only way of muffling the noises he was about to pull from me.

My body jolted into him. Soft, clothed breasts hit his hard chest. I clamped my eyes shut tighter and kissed him harder. I didn't want to make a noise; I didn't want him to see me. It felt too real. This was me, not someone I could hide behind, and that terrified me.

Karro's fingers clamped down on the apex of my thigh. He squeezed the flesh hard, fondling it in his calloused hands. My belly began to throb. He was *so* close to where I wanted him to be. I could buck my hip up, and he'd be there. I could take matters into my own hands if I wanted and fuck his fingers with one simple shift.

"Please," I gasped. I pulled away from his face and gritted my teeth. I hated that I'd begged. I wanted to rip out my tongue.

I dipped my face down, blocking his view of me. Resting my cheek against his chest, I looked down between our bodies. It was a beautiful sight. His tan, strong arm disappeared into the depths of my pants. I grabbed a handful of his shirt, keeping myself steady.

His smallest finger left my thigh and moved to my panties. I shuddered as he ran it up and down my covered slit, molding the fabric to my wet folds.

I threw my head back, shutting my eyes. His mouth sunk onto my neck, pulling my skin between his teeth. I reached for his hair, pulling him harder into me. Karro let out a quiet and low growl. The vibrations from the noise shot through me and down my body.

I shuddered, rolling my hips against his pinky. I needed something inside me. Anything.

"So impatient," he hummed into my neck, continuing to mark me. I wanted to do the same. I wanted him to be covered in dark marks the next time we walked into that cunt's office.

I didn't respond. I couldn't speak. I don't nodded, my brows knitting together as my need grew too intense. I could feel pleasure dripping down my legs. I didn't want this anymore, I *needed* it.

"Karro," I said. My teeth stuck together.

I felt him smile against my skin. He took another spot on my neck, bruising it until it went numb. I tightened my fingers in his hair, pulling and tugging hard at him.

Moving his hand away from my thigh, Karro planted three fingers on top of my panties, sliding them down my slit. His tips lingered above the wettest spot of the fabric, directly above my entrance. He applied enough pressure to force another plea from me.

Once his fingers began to sink inside me, he pulled away and returned to my clit.

Karro was a tease.

I did not like being teased.

I arched my back, pushing my front harder into his. I couldn't get any closer without crawling inside of him. If I could, I would have.

"You're wet?" Karro released my neck. My eyes fluttered as his lips brushed against my collarbone. Everything about him felt so fucking divine.

"Shut up," I replied, rolling my hips against his vexatious hand.

He pulled away from my chest and rested his forehead against mine, our heavy breaths mixing. He began to rub large circles against the entirety of my cunt with his three fingers.

I wanted to scream. How could one person feel this fucking good? It felt like he knew the perfect amount of pressure, and the perfect direction to rub me. I despised him. I hated him. But fuck, he felt good.

Karro pushed my panties aside and sank his fingers into my pussy. A guttural noise came out of me as I adjusted to the sudden girth. He curled his fingers inside me and pulled me closer to him.

The sadistic bastard pulled me by the pussy. It hurt so good.

"Shit," I groaned. I clamped my eyes shut, concentrating on how hard he was working inside my cunt. It was the only distraction I had from his voyeuristic eyes. I didn't want to know he was watching me. It made me want to crawl inside my own skin and hide.

My body jolted with every movement he made. My nipples were tight, rubbing against his hard chest. His fingers curled more roughly inside me, finding the spongy spot with ease. It was a spot only he could find. I couldn't even find it when fingering myself. Only him.

I let out a breathy cry, unable to stifle the noises that were coming out of me. "There," I gasped.

He began to roughly fiddle, rub, and curl against the spot, making my vision black and my head spin. "I know," Karro replied, his mouth against my ear.

He curled harder against my G-spot. My legs began to shake around him. I pulled myself tighter around his hip. I wanted him inside of me, but I couldn't handle the idea of him pulling his fingers out. I was tightening around them, trying to keep him in me.

My belly was getting hot. I felt like everything inside of me had liquefied into heat. His cock hardened against my stomach. The feeling of him twitching against me nearly made me come.

I reached for his throbbing length as he continued inside of me. I was able to wrap my fingers around his shaft for a moment. He felt hot and heavy, even with his pants protecting him. I squeezed around him, stroking once. He slapped my hand away.

I grinned, smiling up at him. His eyes had darkened, but he did not stop working inside my tightening pussy. With his free hand, he constrained both of my wrists. My hands were shaking. I hoped he could feel how good he felt. My pussy tightened and dripped on his fingers—he had to feel it.

"You know I don't do hand jobs or blow jobs," Karro began. His eyes flickered down to my lips. I hadn't realized I'd opened my eyes, and grown comfortable with him watching me. It felt too good to crawl inside myself. "You either feel good, or I fuck you until you bleed."

His hand tightened around my wrists. His fingers continued pumping hard inside me, knuckles hitting my lips with every movement. I needed to grab ahold of his hair or latch onto his skin. Anything. I hated being restrained.

My face contorted, and I shut my eyes, taking his ruthless fingers. Something inside me snapped. It didn't feel good anymore. It felt like a need. The world around us faded into the blackening of my vision. As did this room and this place. I'd risk it all if it meant coming. I needed more. More girth. More speed. More Karro.

"Fuck me until I bleed, then." Humiliation ran down my spine. I didn't recognize my own voice. I rolled my hips into his hand, chasing what he was giving me. It was becoming too much—I was going to explode.

"Not yet," he said, his lips against my neck. He toyed with my skin as roughly as he did my pussy. The palm of his hand rubbed against my clit, hard, while three fingers continued to curl inside of me.

I rode them harder, chasing the rut I wished for. I was on the verge of passing out. It was overwhelming; it was so fucking good.

"Fuck, Karro," I moaned, fucking his fingers hard. I never begged. No matter who, or what the circumstance, I never allowed myself to act too weak. But right now, I was begging him to keep doing exactly what he was doing. Curling. Thrusting. Pumping. Existing.

I would kill him if he stopped.

I buried my face into his neck as I came. I clamped my legs together, trying to ease the intense feeling between them, but it did not stop him from fucking my cunt through the orgasm. I shuddered and gasped for air, trying desperately to ground myself. If God was real, Karro was fucking me to him.

"There you go," he praised, pumping harder inside me. My cunt milked his fingers, latching onto him as if he were going to disappear. "Good fucking girl."

I came back to earth after a few more thrusts. I let out a quiet cry, and my body shook harder. I could feel and hear the cream soaking his fingers.

He pulled them from me when I stopped shaking.

"Fuck, Karro," I sighed, collapsing onto my pillow. I closed my eyes, catching my breath as the aftershocks wore off. I thought of how cruel a creator had to be to have made him that skilled with my body.

I looked at him once my breathing had calmed. He'd licked every drop of me clean from his fingers. My head was still spinning as I tried to ground myself after being finger fucked to nirvana and back.

"Sleep now," Karro said. I was grateful he wanted to avoid the aftermath as much as I did.

I fell asleep within a breath.

CHAPTER
THIRTY-FIVE

PAST

7437 sat against my door. Her knees were pulled tight to her chest, and her braids were falling out of their tight stitching.

It was late, around 0200 in the morning—far past the curfew for any Anaka. Once they turned thirteen, they were allowed to stay awake until 2300; 7437 was far from turning thirteen.

She was not supposed to be in the hall designated for commanders and generals, either.

"7437," I started. "You should be in bed. This corridor is restricted for Anaka. Surely you were taught basic rules in your previous sectors."

Even if that wasn't the case, she'd been in War long enough to know that she was not supposed to be near this hall. She was supposed to be in bed, waiting for training and education.

I reached over her and placed my hand flat over the door. With a beep, it registered that my prints matched the room. I didn't open it, but instead looked back down at 7437. She hadn't left.

"I know," she said from her seat on the floor. "I was taught that. I just—" She stopped and took a swig of something.

Her back was flush to my door, blocking me from entering. I noticed that her bloodshot eyes were locked on her bare feet. Her face always looked soft. Tonight, though, it was tight and flushed, and it hardened further as she took another swig of alcohol.

"7437," I sighed, reaching for her pouch. I tossed it a few feet away.

Pulling my hand away from the handle, I slid down the door, taking a seat next to her. It wasn't uncommon for my Anaka to seek me out. But coming to my hall? This was a first.

"Why are you here, 7437?" If the Murthaa had been alive, I would have needed to report this: the alcohol she'd been drinking, the curfew she'd broken, and the restricted area she'd chosen to sit in.

She swallowed and rubbed her palms up and down her pants. She was in her leisure clothing, a pair of black, loose-fitting cotton pants and a matching oversized black shirt. I was still dressed in my war attire. Guns and all.

"I don't know. I just needed someone to talk to. Even if it was you," 7437 admitted. This was a common response from my Anaka. Usually, it was not this bitter, and didn't happen this early in the morning. It happened, though. They needed someone.

7437 did not look up at me. Even after she'd learned that I was not going to shoot her, she still feared me. She wasn't afraid of the guns and bullets anymore. She was scared of me.

My stomach turned, and I leaned my head against the door. I could only imagine how lonely my Anaka felt. If 7437, of all people, felt the need to seek me out, she must feel lonely. She wanted comfort from the person who made her afraid earlier in the day. No sane person had done this.

8274 had once come to me sobbing about how she wished to be a part of Man. She knew I could report her for speaking such blasphemy, but she still came.

"I just needed someone. I need someone," 7437 repeated, rubbing her hands against her thighs harder. Her pants were creased and stained with sweat from the action.

"I know," I replied quietly. I ground my teeth together. I knew what it felt like to be lonely, especially at that age. I'd never been with the Anaka—I had been trained alone.

I knew how it felt to not be able to sleep, as I assumed was the case with 7437. Instead of rest, we'd be consumed by a lonely void of thoughts, which a mother, friend, or father would fill if we'd been among Man. I understood the Anaka, and I understood how dangerous the need could become. A need for a mother. A need for a friend. A need for a lover.

Some Anaka grew into great generals who were granted the right to marriage and pregnancy. It was rare. *Very* rare. But it happened.

"I don't know what's wrong with me," 7437 began. I looked down at her hands. The sound of cotton and calloused palms scratching together filled the quiet hall.

"If you're referring to your training, you're fine," I lied. She wasn't. She was behind in ways I could not figure out how to fix.

But I wouldn't bring it up. She would not be euthanized under my rule.

Shaking her head, she buried her face in her knees. She didn't cry. She knew not to cry in front of me. "Not the training. I don't know. It just feels like I don't feel things the same way as everyone else. I feel too much."

I stayed quiet, watching the side of her face. Her muscles softened the more she spoke about how she felt. It was the opposite of how I was. I always tensed and deflected when speaking of emotions.

"What do you mean by that?" I asked.

She shook her head again. "I don't know. I shouldn't be here."

She did not try to leave. We sat in silence, both staring ahead at the wall in front of us. I looked over when her breathing grew heavy.

"I know this sounds silly," 7437 continued, "but I have dreams. Dreams about things happening, but before they happen. Does that make sense?"

I physically prevented myself from rolling my eyes. I blinked, hard. The Sight bullshit was something I'd never believed in. It was superstition for Man, and those who came from Man. Karro would probably believe in something as idiotic as The Sight.

It was a gift given to those who could see into a realm away from ours. I thought it was beyond bullshit. There was no other realm, and there was no ability to see.

"And I have dreams about things I need to do. I don't know how I know, but I know. I know that I need to do the things I dream of."

I sucked in a breath. "What medication do the nurses have you on?"

7437 shrugged, twiddling her thumbs together.

The Anaka were put on various medications. I had once been on a variation of X that caused me to believe I was half-alien. I made a note to seek out 7437's nurse in the morning.

"Okay." Everything about this conversation was against what I aligned with, but I kept going. For her sake. She needed someone. "What kind of dreams have you had recently?"

7437 flinched. "Well, a few hours ago, I was resting, and I had a dream that I came here. I sat and waited for you. It was the universe telling me I needed to come talk to you. I don't know why, but I did it. It just felt right."

I ran a hand down my face. *The universe.*

"Have you learned of Project Xi yet? We have technologies to go deep into space. Deeper than Man has. Do you know what we've found?" I asked.

7437 shook her head once more.

"Nothing," I said, pushing myself from the floor. I stood up until I was towering above her.

She kept her eyes on her feet. "Sorry, Naga."

"I'll talk to your nurse in the morning. I was once on a medication that made me have delusions. Sometimes they affect your psychological state." I hated speaking about my childhood, but perhaps if she had someone to relate to, then she'd feel less lonely.

7437 looked up. It was not 7437 looking at me. An expression was painted on her face, an emotion I'd never seen her or any other Anaka possess. She looked terribly angry. For a split moment, I saw myself after I'd beheaded the Murthaa. I'd been shaking, with too many feelings scrambling together.

"I'm not crazy," she snapped.

My fingers flexed. I'd never had an Anaka snap at me. The only people who'd ever spoken to me in such a way were all dead.

"I'm not saying you're crazy," I hissed, lowering my voice. My face twitched. A little girl had just given me a tone. "I'm just saying, some medication—"

She stood up, interrupting me midsentence. That too was a first. "I keep having dreams about you," she said.

I crossed my arms and looked down at her. Despite my height, she kept her chin high. I'd never seen her with anything but fear in her eyes. Now, it was molten. I could feel the anger radiating from her skin.

"Oh yeah? Like what?" I'd once been told by someone who possessed "The Sight" that I was going to die young. I'd spat in her face and killed her. It was all bullshit.

"Well, I dream of that place you go to," 7437 said, crossing her arms over her chest like me.

I laughed, looking up at the ceiling. I did not have the patience for Man superstitions tonight.

"And, I have another where I am in your body. I can feel everything you feel. It's more of a nightmare. I can feel how angry you are. How scared you are. It's overwhelming. It's what you felt when you ripped out the Murthaa's heart."

My blood went cold, and my entire body tightened.

7437 smiled and continued. "I don't ever want to fall in love if that's what it feels like."

I blinked. Every word that had swum in my mouth got lost in my throat. I almost gagged. The Blood would have my head if they knew I had murdered the Murthaa; the Committee would come for me. My face paled. I debated slicing apart my skin to prevent 7437 from seeing it.

The Murthaa had been dead for weeks. I'd been careful disposing of the body and covering my steps. I'd seen one person when entering the office that day—an officer. He was rotting beside the Murthaa's burnt corpse. The Committee was coming soon to investigate, but I was not afraid. I'd been so good at covering my tracks.

Until 7437.

She shrugged. I felt sick. "Who knows? Maybe you're right. It's just the medicine."

She smiled and left me alone in the hallway.

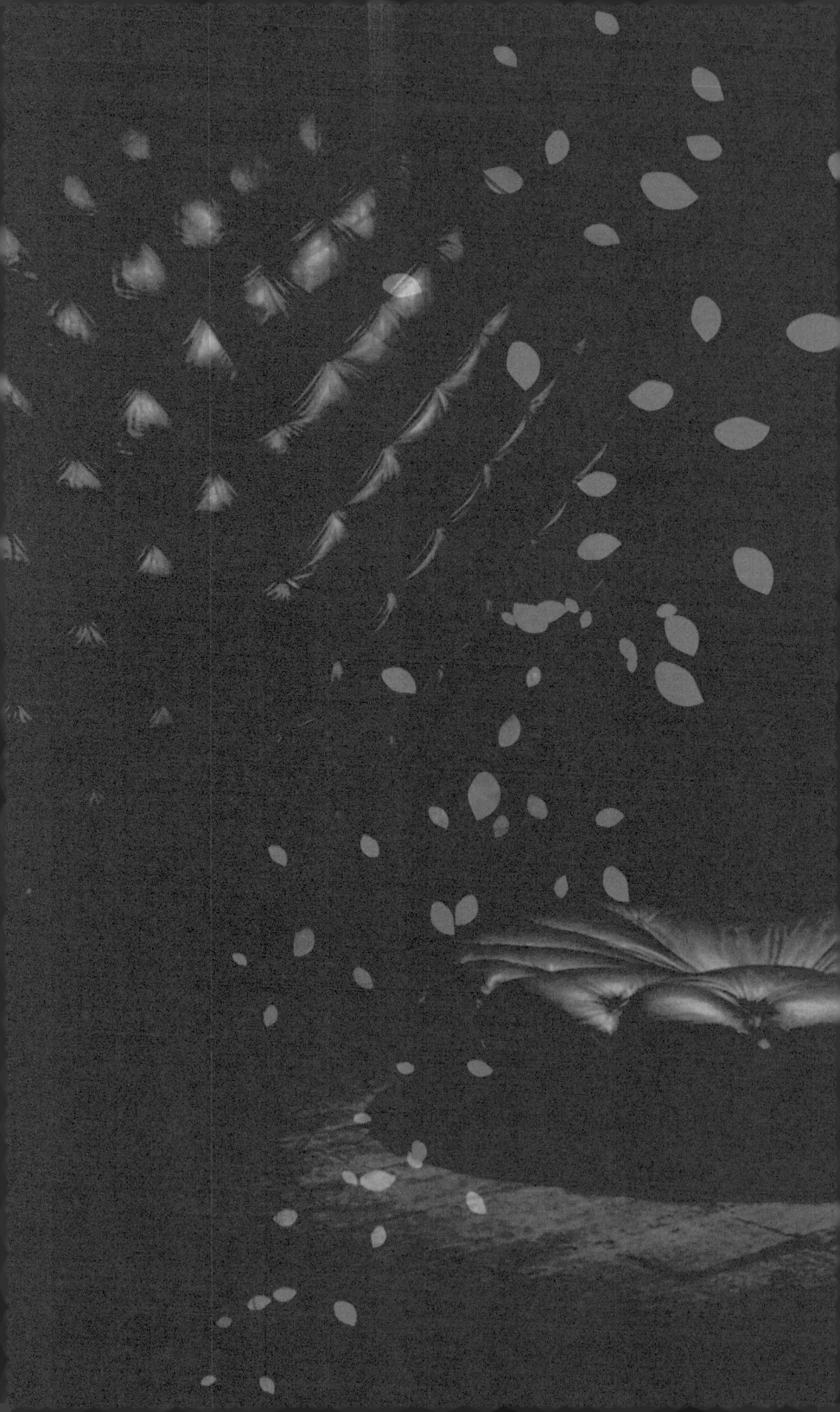

CHAPTER

THIRTY-SIX

PRESENT

A night passed, and I could still feel him.

When I woke, I did not feel a heavy weight on my chest, pinning me to the mattress. My skin tingled and buzzed, the remaining waves of orgasm lingering across my skin.

Karro had never made me feel like this before. So raw. So real.

I knelt beside the door, tracing my fingers lightly across my arms as I stared up at the small slit. I wanted to make myself feel this euphoric. I wanted to find an excuse for how he made me feel this good. If I made myself feel electric, then I would no longer have to credit him for his existence.

My eyes slowly shut. I was turned away from him, trying to ignore the hole being burnt through my backside.

Karro had slept more than I did last night. I'd stayed in his bed, even through my wakeful periods. His fingers traced light circles along my skin through the night.

I continued to rub my arms. I *needed* to make myself feel how I had last night. He couldn't have that power over me.

I hated how easy it was to seep back into him, to forget the harsh words we'd thrown at each other. It terrified me. Everything about Karro terrified me. No man, no gun, no war, and no doctor would ever compare to how horrifying it felt with him.

We'd forever be aligned with each other. I had no control over that.

I cleared my throat, pulling myself from the labyrinth I was spiraling toward. "If I had a hanger and a decade, I could get this door open," I said, unable to turn to him. I looked at the tray beside my knees. Today, we'd been given three sandwiches and five bags of soap. Once again, I felt gratitude for the surplus beneath his bed.

"I could," I reiterated. "If this is The Blood, then it's made of magnets." I assumed it was made of magnets. I didn't hear many clicks when the slit opened each morning. Plus, when the door was open, there was no sign of a lock on the other side.

I braved Karro now, focusing on the tallies behind his face. It was better than having to meet his eyes. "How long have I been here?"

"A little over a month," he said.

I looked back at my thighs, fiddling with the loose fabric. "That's what I thought." I frowned.

"Ready to leave me?"

I looked up at the ceiling, cursing my people again. My cheeks felt like they were going to melt off my face in gooey flesh.

I wanted to rip myself apart. Or kill Karro. Either would solve the issue in my chest and core.

"I haven't gotten my period," I said. I didn't in that place, either. There was a large scar on my belly. A scar from Karro's wrath. I wondered if his blade had damaged me—something inside me.

Karro shifted behind me, lying on his back. I needed a drink, to raise a glass to his apparent surgical skills. My nails dug into my thighs.

I crawled across the floor and reached for a spare pouch of alcohol. Karro alone had made it through an entire pile of whiskey. I wondered if it was because of me that he was so stressed out. I knew he was what pushed me to drink.

I downed a shot of whiskey. And then a few.

My fingers lingered on my stomach. I had once been so ready for life to bloom in my womb. I'd taken it as my life mission, to bring up a child in the opposite way from how I'd been raised. It'd heal me, in a way.

I wasn't ready now. I wasn't as selfish. I would never want to bring something as light and pure as a child into this world. It'd be torture, and I wanted no part in that.

I gulped and looked up at Karro. He stared down at my hands on my belly.

I looked away when his face softened. He had no right to show pity. He'd created life and then taken it from me. Over *love.*

I recalled the night when 7437 had showed up against my door so many years ago. *I never want to be in love if it feels like that.*

I didn't know what it felt like. It felt like too much brewing together; I couldn't figure it out. Some nights, love felt like an enemy. Other nights, it felt like a friend.

I decided it was both.

No matter what happened, it would be there, haunting me. If Karro were to hold me as I spoke about the horrid things that had occurred in the dark, I'd feel love. If he held a gun to my head and pumped it full of lead, I'd feel love.

My jaw trembled. I kept my back to Karro. He would not see me like this—not over something he had done. I swallowed anything trying to rise up my throat. I could hear my generals. I could hear the Murthaa. *Weak fucking girl.*

I did feel weak. I was weak. But I was growing accustomed to the feeling.

CHAPTER
THIRTY-SEVEN

PRESENT

"That place I sent you," Karro began. I jerked my head up toward him. I feared he'd heard the thoughts I'd just disappeared into. "What was it like?"

I threw an empty pouch at my feet. My head was beginning to spin. "It was just like earth, but without humanity. Before life. There were animals, sometimes, and plants. But it just felt . . ." I paused. "Empty."

"If it makes you feel any better, I was not given a day of freedom before I woke up here."

Freedom. I narrowed my eyes. It didn't make me feel better.

"Do you remember how you got here? Anything?" I'd been afraid to ask. I praised the whiskey for making my tongue loose.

Karro shook his head. "Not really. Nothing past that night. I was in the Time Sector, where I stored you." I scoffed at his choice of words, but he continued. "I left after making sure you couldn't escape. I went back home, drank a few margaritas in your honor, and woke up here."

I scowled and reached for another bag of whiskey. "Great to know that you were getting drunk after"—I winced—"that."

Karro's eyes skimmed the front of my body. I looked down to where his attention fixed. My sweatpants hung low on my hips, exposing the patch of skin below my belly button. It'd always been his favorite spot on my body. Especially when it came to coating it with his seed.

My face heated, and I averted my eyes, hiding from him. "Why must you make everything so sexual?" I asked.

From the corner of my eye, I caught a glimpse of his hips lifting. He readjusted his pants. "Why don't you come over here and find out?"

Our gazes locked. I opened another pouch, tossing a shot down my throat. I kept my eyes hard on his. My thighs felt like they were becoming numb. I hated how weak he made me feel. I hated it. I hated him. I hated myself.

My stomach tensed. It felt like he was already fucking me. "-No," I replied.

Karro's dimples sunk deep. I winced and tried not to look at them for too long.

"You know, now that I know *you*, I don't take you for a margarita girl."

I was grateful that he'd changed the subject. I was two breaths from crawling onto him. "Random," I replied, tilting my head and looking up at him. This was not the type of conversation I'd imagined having with him. Ever.

"Yeah," Karro continued, drawing out his words. "I imagine tequila. No lime. No salt. Just the bottle."

I rolled my eyes. "That's specific, is it not?"

He shrugged. "I don't know. It's just what I imagine a conniving, lying little bitch to drink."

I stood up. My nails dug into the meat of my palm. My face felt like it was on fire. My teeth were going to break if he did not stop talking.

Karro perked up. A grin spread across his face. He was looking at me like I was some form of entertainment. Nothing more.

He swung his long legs off the bed and planted his feet flat on the floor. I watched him run his hands up and down his thighs a few times. I did not speak. I stared, trembling from how tightly I was holding onto the anger.

"Are we going to fuck it out, Naga?" Karro asked, his smile growing.

"Fuck you."

"Gladly."

I scowled but slowly sat back down on the edge of my bed, across from him. When I relaxed, he did as well. It felt like looking into a mirror.

Karro eventually lay back. It'd be easy to attack him. So easy. I refrained, but the thought remained with me.

"Was I good?" I asked once my breathing had calmed.

Lust flickered behind his eyes. "You need to be a little more specific.".

"At my job. You know, the whole 'conniving, lying little bitch' thing."

He ran a hand through his hair. My stomach flipped when I saw his fingers. I wondered if "fucking it out" would help lighten the mood, even if just for a moment. I needed to breathe. I needed to scream. I believed that Karro could help me with that.

"Yes," he said, pulling me from thoughts of vile positions. "You are good at being a conniving, lying little bitch."

"Was," I corrected. I couldn't hide behind her anymore. Unfortunately, I was myself. I wanted to tell him that. I couldn't, though. Then he would know *me*. He would know I'd cut myself open and let every inch of protection part; he'd be able to see me.

"After I found out, I started to watch you more," Karro said. I swallowed. I did not want to be watched. "I analyzed you more. I tried to figure out your 'tells.' On our date, after I knocked you in the face with a gun, you'd lied straight to me about it."

"Well, *did* you figure out any of my tells?" I asked. If he had, I'd need to work on them.

He shook his head. "No. I assumed everything you'd said before was a lie. Because of that, everything you said before that day, and after, was a lie."

I looked down at my lap. No. He did not get to believe I was lying about being in love with him. I wished I could lie about how I felt. The shit I still could feel in my chest. I wanted that to be a lie so badly.

"You did slip a few times. Not with your lies, but—" Karro stopped. He tested a few words on his tongue. "You came through. *You*."

I recalled the day in the bathtub when he'd asked about my tattoos. I hadn't lied then. I should have, but I didn't. And the day that I'd come home, an absolute disaster, pleading with him to leave me. Or to run away from me. I'd broken down in front of him.

I didn't think he remembered.

"Do you want to hear something true?" I didn't recognize myself.

Karro nodded.

"Do you remember that night I came home, so upset? One of my Anaka could see through her Eye. The Sight. All that bullshit. I didn't believe in it—at all. But she knew about something I'd done. Something very, very bad. I was scared. I wasn't lying that night. I wanted to leave with you."

I felt sick. I'd never been that afraid before. Death would have been a gift compared to what the Committee would do to me. They were not above the Murthaa, but with her gone, they'd be in charge. They'd do anything in their power to find what had happened to her.

I'd been told a story about a girl who'd had to deal with the Committee. First, her brain was fried. I'd never been given the details of how. Then, they'd made a spectacle of her body and allowed men to do as they pleased to her, until her body broke. After that, the women and children took out their rage out on the convulsing sack of guts that had once been her.

Or maybe it was one of The Blood's false teachings, implanted to make us afraid.

"What did you do?" Karro asked.

I looked down. I shouldn't give him the details. I'd get tortured if they ever discovered me. Even after all this time.

"I killed the Murthaa. As I said, one of my Anaka knew. She dreamt of it." I wondered if Karro believed in The Sight or Eyes.

"Why did you kill her?" he asked.

I pressed my lips into a thin line and looked up at him. He didn't need to hear the word. *You* floated between us.

"Oh," he breathed. "Impressive. No one had even come close to harming her."

I laughed. I'd killed a nine-thousand-year-old woman because of a boy. I'd liked it, too. I'd do it all over again. Committee be damned, that cunt was bound to die.

I'd only regretted killing two people in my lifetime: Karro's mother and brother.

"How about you? Tell me something true," I said.

I knew everything there was to know about him. I'd memorized it so many years ago. I learned more through what he chose to tell me, though.

He leaned his head against the wall. His eyes were hooded. "I like you more like this. If you had come into that bar that night as yourself—" He pursed his lips and looked away. "I would have fallen in love with you."

My lips parted. Empty words floated around the space—too many words with all too much meaning. I wanted to respond, but I didn't know how.

"I need a drink," Karro groaned.

CHAPTER

THIRTY-EIGHT

PAST

I burst into the apartment. The door handle slammed hard into the wall, so hard Karro jumped from his sleeping position in bed.

It was an hour after 7437 had left me gaping in the hall.

I threw the duffle bag I was holding onto the floor. It was filled with items I had left at The Blood, a few books I had hidden and some outfits I stored there for after training. I wasn't sure if I would go back. If I didn't, the Committee would know I was the one who had murdered the Murthaa. If I did, 7437 would forever have something to hold over my head. I did not like either option.

Karro was seated in bed, watching my every movement. I crawled onto him without speaking a word and buried my slick face in his chest. I tightened my arms around his torso and rested my legs on either side of his. I held on to him tight.

I couldn't kill them all.

The only way to regain control would be to kill everyone— every soul in every sector. I'd have to kill every person in The Blood, and with them, Man as well. Terrifyingly, I was willing to do it.

But, it was not possible.

Karro's arms slid around my waist. He wasn't holding me in the way I was him. It didn't matter, though. I felt like I was falling apart. No matter how hard he held me together, it was inevitable.

My skull began to throb as twenty-something years' worth of tears accumulated. I was so close to snapping. I couldn't break. I needed to stay in control. I needed to figure this out.

I couldn't breathe, let alone concentrate on getting myself out of this. A quiet whimper slid past my lips. The vibrations were muffled by Karro's bare shoulder.

"Naga," he hummed. I was going to cut out his tongue. I didn't want to remember that he was here, witnessing it all.

"Don't," I snapped. The words came out as a sob. Shame crept up my back, heat scattering across my ears and face. "Please, just don't." My body was shaking. I wanted to hold it in. I didn't want him to hear the noises coming out of me.

I couldn't kill them all, I reminded myself. I was completely and utterly out of control.

The moment 7437 squealed and told The Blood about the murder, I would be dead. I was going to die at the hands of The Blood—my mother, my father, my life.

My body stiffened. I could kill her. A child. I wondered whether I had it in me.

Karro squeezed me harder. I softened into him. My fingers dug at his bare chest; I wanted to tear him open and crawl inside of him. Even this close, it would never feel like enough. Nothing would feel safe. I needed to be molded to him, every part of his being branded and fused with my flesh. I wanted his soul, body, and mind to be intertwined with my own.

"I'm sorry, I'm sorry, I'm sorry, I'm sorry," I chanted. I wasn't sure he'd heard it. I didn't want him to hear it.

The beat of his heart against my ear grew louder. I listened to how fast his blood was rushing through his veins.

"If work stresses you out this much, you need to grow the fuck up." His tone was bitter. I heard his heart skip when he uttered the word *work*. To him, I was a teacher.

I jerked my head up and looked down at him. My eyes became slits, forcing out the tears I'd tried to hold back. I snarled and pushed myself off him, stumbling from the bed and into the bathroom. The door cracked from how hard I slammed it shut.

I slid down the wall next to the door. I folded into myself, covering my head with my arms and burying my face in my knees. I needed to scream and tear at my flesh—anything to let out the emotions crawling under my skin.

My jaw trembled and tears filled my eyes. I wanted to throw up. I felt so fucking weak.

I held my breath as sobs began to rise. I would vomit if I heard those. The tears were terrible enough.

I never cried. Ever. But, fuck, when I did, it resembled a hurricane.

"Naga," Karro said, the door bending as he leaned against it. It was locked, thankfully.

I dug my nails into my bicep. I hated the sound of his voice. I hated him. He was giving me somewhere to go. If he hadn't been involved, I would have figured it out. I wouldn't have had a place to crawl to and break down in; I would have killed the little cunt within a breath.

"I'm sorry, Naga. I have no filter. Open the door."

I winced and recalled just how nonexistent that filter had been recently. Every chance he got, Karro had been letting insults loose. His cruel remarks were so witty I had to stop to consider whether or not he meant to insult me.

Our relationship was getting worse. Karro was growing colder by the day, blocking himself from me. I, on the other hand, felt like I was opening my soul up for him to invade. I was becoming so vulnerable. I'd do anything as long as it meant him staying with me.

"Yeah, that's been happening a lot," I spat. I narrowed my eyes at the door.

He laughed. "Open up."

I stared at the lock, my body rushing to it and opening it without another thought. I did not look at him. He wasn't going to see me like this.

Karro entered and slid down the wall beside me, pulling his knees tight to his chest. I looked at him from the corner of my eye, digging my fingers into my thighs. The sobs had settled, thankfully, but the shaking continued.

He reached for me. His fingers wrapped gently around my jaw, and he pulled my eyes toward him. "What happened?"

My breath got lost in my throat. I almost let my tongue free. I'd be dead soon, anyway. I wasn't going to kill a young girl for something she knew nothing about. I'd let the Committee kill me first.

Oh, nothing. Just murdered your former employer. You know, my current employer. And, apparently, a child can see through her Eye.

"Just a bad day," I replied.

Karro's jaw tightened. I'd stared at him for too long. I frowned. I wanted to tell him how much I loved him, and how that terrified me. I wanted to tell him how nothing felt more real than him.

"Okay," he said.

I knitted my brows together. Why did he sound disappointed? "Karro," I began. I lowered my voice, afraid of wires, cameras, and ears. Fuck, I feared that 7437 was off sleeping, imagining this exact scene unfolding in her Eye. "Can we leave? Go away to some cabin? Anywhere but here. *Please.*"

I stared up at him, my lip beginning to tremble. Maybe, just maybe, he could figure out what was upsetting me. I couldn't utter the words. They would know. But he could figure it out. I wanted him to figure it out so we could leave. Together.

Karro laughed—a bitter, cruel laugh.

"I'm serious." I shifted and reached for his hand. He pulled away from me. "I really think we should just leave. Please. It doesn't matter where we go, just as long as I'm with you. *Please.*"

Mentally, I felt like I was my hands and knees, begging him to run away with me. Karro did not see that. Karro saw something . . . funny?

He laughed and leaned forward. I shuddered as his lips brushed against my ear. "You can't leave your job."

CHAPTER

THIRTY-NINE

PRESENT

Drinking had become how we passed the time. Some nights, we were silent as we lay beside each other and drank ourselves to sleep. Other nights, we would laugh until reality crept into the room.

I didn't know what tonight was going to be.

We were sitting against the door, eight empty pouches of whiskey between us. "Do you know what I think is funny?" I said.

"Oh, do tell," Karro slurred. He leaned his head back, looking at me from the corner of his eye. The past few hours had been a mix of bickering and light conversation. I'd told him about my routine, and named every general I'd ever beheaded. He praised me for it.

"Everything," I continued. I slid down until I was lying flat on the floor. Through the window, I could see it was a clear starry night. "I think everything is funny. I mean, everything is a fucking joke. Man. The Blood." I laughed. I didn't understand what I was saying, but it felt like I was making sense. To the whiskey, it was clear.

"Continue," Karro said. His fingers fiddled with the ends of my strands. Goosebumps spread down my neck.

I bit my lip and continued to focus on the sky. The rest of the room spun. I wanted to count every star to keep my mind from going insane. How had Karro not gone insane? Had he?

"Do you think there is a sector for space?" I asked. Order. Intelligence. War. It was branded into me. But I believed him. It all made sense. The timeless place, the power the Murthaa had over aging, and this place—there had to be other sectors.

"Probably. There was so much. I wish you could have seen what I saw. I can't even describe it. You just had to be there."

Karro looked down at me. I looked away from the window to meet his eyes. If I hadn't been so drunk, I would have told him that I *could* have been there, but he'd chosen otherwise.

I grunted and shifted on the floor, twisting my body until it was perpendicular to his. I rested the back of my head on the top of his thighs, keeping my focus on the stars. I was scared they would disappear.

Karro hadn't looked away from me.

"I want to see it," I admitted. I sounded like a slurring mess. "Before we kill them all."

"We?" His brows rose.

"Of course." I grinned hard, then sat up and pointed at my chest. I thought I was going to say something. Well, the alcohol had something to say.

A passing dark cloud distracted me. My hand fell limp and rested on Karro's chest. I stared up at the sky, mouth open. "You will," I stated. "Because you are my bitch."

I laid my head back down on his lap. He shifted and held it in place against him.

"Oh no." He barked out a laugh. I flinched. "That's not how this works. I think it's the opposite, actually."

I dug my nails into his thighs, my drunken attempt at harming him. My tongue was too loose to offer some sharp response.

"I was going to say that it is funny. Man has no idea about anything. We don't know anything, either. Yet we were the ones controlling it all." I frowned. I didn't understand what I was saying anymore. "That's funny."

"Real funny." Karro sounded bored.

"And they just don't care about . . ." I hesitated. "Well, I don't know how to word this without sounding like a conniving, lying little bitch, as you so gracefully put it."

"You've said it more than me at this point."

I'd have slapped him for that remark if I'd been sober.

"They don't care or try to understand it all. They just accept it. Like, look at how they live. So comfortably. They work their shitty little jobs. Live their shitty little lives. They just accept that they're going to die. Poof."

Karro stayed silent, brushing a hair from my brow. I fixed on a star in the sky.

"I'm not sure which is worse, though," I continued. "To walk among Man or to walk among The Blood."

My head shot up, and Karro jumped. "Have they ever delivered spaghetti in those pouches? Fuck, I'd kill someone for some spaghetti right now."

"No," he answered.

"Fuck," I hissed. I returned my head to his thighs. "I will kill the cooks after I kill the nurse."

Karro laughed at this. I shuddered at the noise.

I locked my gaze back on the specific star I'd been fixed on all night. "That star is you," I blurted.

"Which one?"

I pointed toward the window with a wobbly finger. I doubted he could tell which one I was talking about. "The one in that cluster. It's brighter."

Karro didn't look up. He was still looking at me. I sucked in a breath and tried to ignore his hot stare.

"Which one are you?" he asked, brushing another strand from my face.

I frowned at the question. I was too drunk to be thinking this critically. I quietly scanned the sky for any sign of myself, but couldn't find any.

"I don't think I'm there," I admitted. "I'm probably a giant asteroid that once fell from space and wiped out an entire civilization."

Karro laughed and threaded his fingers deeper into my hair, massaging my scalp. My eyes fluttered shut. I opened my mouth to speak again, but his lips slid against mine before I could. I was grateful for it. I would have started something I did not wish to discuss.

Karro kissed me hard through the night, harder than he ever had before. He kissed me until we were an entangled bundle of limbs on his bed. Until we both fell asleep against each other's mouths, forgetting everything prior.

It horrified me how happy I felt.

CHAPTER

FORTY

PAST

"I swear, every time I smell smoke it's because of those damn cigarettes," someone said from behind me.

Twirling the cigarette between my fingers, I stared out at the empty playground ahead of me. I rolled my eyes at the comment and wrapped my lips back around the filter.

I didn't need to turn and see who was there. I knew it was J392. He was a floating janitor. Some of them were confined to specific sectors, but floaters would travel from sector to sector, depending on their needs. J392 was my favorite.

He was around sixteen years old, but I could have sworn he had the heart of a sixty-year-old man. I'd never seen his face. Given that janitors were ranked the lowest among The Blood, his entire identity had been stripped from him—from all of them. They were each forced to wear a mask that covered their entire face and head. I did the same thing to my soldiers, though my intention was to prevent our enemies from knowing whom they were fighting.

"Nasty habit," I admitted. I looked down at the three spent buds.

J392 continued to sweep behind me. "You mind?" The broom fell to the ground with a clink, and he sat down close beside me, holding his hand out.

I lit the end of a spare cigarette and passed it to him. "Nasty habit, J392," I teased. I'd been around his age when I caught it myself.

I couldn't see his mouth, but I felt his smile. I wondered what had happened to him. If he was a janitor at this young of an age, he must have proven himself skill-less. Janitors were usually old, and worn.

J392's fingers curled under the edge of his mask. I looked away, through from the corner of my eye I could see him pulling it over his mouth. It was considered awful manners to even show your lips if you were a janitor. The Blood would decapitate him if they found out how disrespectful he was being.

I didn't care anymore. I just wanted to be with Karro, free.

"Long day?" J392 asked.

"Something like that." I frowned and looked at my shoes. It felt wrong. In common practice, we weren't allowed to ask janitors about themselves. We weren't allowed ask how they were doing, and we couldn't socialize with them, either.

"How was your day?" I continued.

J392 shrugged. I didn't know much about him. There wasn't much to know. All sense of self had been taken from him. He wasn't allowed to wed, impregnate, court, or sleep with another. If he picked up a hobby besides mopping, his hands would be cut off. I'd seen him with a book once; I turned the other way. The Blood would be too cruel to someone like him.

"It's been so tense here. Since, well, you know," J392 began.

I tightened my jaw. He referred to the Murthaa with such ease. I felt like I was going to throw up. A member of the Committee would be arriving soon.

I would die soon.

"Yeah." I reached into the pocket of my sweatshirt and threw an assortment of plastic sticks at his feet. Seven, to be precise. Seven cruel reminders that I was not going to be the only one dying at the hands of the Committee.

I didn't want it to be true. Not now.

J382 gasped softly, and I squinted at the playground, taking another pull of my cigarette. I didn't want to look at the sticks. I didn't want to remind myself of what was brewing in my belly.

I'd been trying all day to imagine my own blood running around the playground. I decided this place was too horrific to bring a child into. If I did, I would be a cruel, cruel mother.

"Holy shit. Congrats. You probably shouldn't be smoking that, though."

"Yeah," I said, bringing it to my lips. "Probably not."

It'd be best if I killed it now, before sentencing it to The Blood. I'd kill my child with my own hands if it meant not having it suffer here. I needed to leave before we both died.

Karro wouldn't come with me. We were fighting too much now. He didn't love me the way I loved him.

My throat pricked. "I don't know how I'm going to tell him."

I wasn't sure if it would make things better or worse. Everything had been so tense between us. Brutal. I was sure that

I would return to our apartment to find all of his belongings packed, no trace left of my love.

"Do what you just did. Throw the piss sticks at him."

I scoffed and shook my head. "He's a little more complicated."

"Forgive me if this is rude," J382 began, clearing his throat, "but is it his? I have to ask."

If anyone else had asked that question, I would have killed them. Everyone knew by this point—they knew that the mission had taken a turn. *Complications.* I was too embarrassed to admit I was in love.

I nodded. "You know, I could have your head for asking something like that."

J382 laughed, leaning backward. "I know you could."

CHAPTER

FORTY-ONE

PAST

I arrived home shortly after talking with J382. My stomach was in knots.

I opened the door slowly, hoping that perhaps Karro was asleep. Unfortunately, he was awake. He was standing on the balcony, his arms stretched out far on either side of him. His shirt was on the bed, and I watched his muscles tighten when he heard me come in.

Fuck. I did not want to do this.

I stepped out onto the balcony and joined him. Cars honked at each other while clubbers cheered at the rage with drinks in their hands. I wanted it to be that easy—to live a boring, simple life.

I sucked in a breath.

I'm pregnant. I'd repeated the words in my head, and aloud, over and over. I had rehearsed them with J382; he'd told me the worst that would happen. Karro could kill me. Uttering those two words felt so much worse than dying by his hand.

"Hi," I squeaked.

"Hello." Karro's hands tightened around the railing. He leaned forward, dipping his chin as he looked down toward the street. We were over twenty-seven stories in the air. I could push him—it would kill two birds with one stone.

I'm pregnant. I'm pregnant. I'm pregnant.

It was so easy in my head. *Spit it out you fucking bitch*, I told myself.

"How was work?" His voice was stern. I couldn't do this.

"Good." Again, it was a squeak.

Karro noticed this time. I squeezed the iron railing. My breathing grew heavy, and my foot tapped fast against the ground.

"Come here," he said.

I braved a look at him. It made it so much worse. His gaze darkened. Lately, it felt like every second of the day he was angry. I didn't understand what had happened. One day, he'd just snapped. He'd stopped loving me.

He lifted his arm and gestured for me to join him. I slid in front of him, my ass pressed against his upper thighs and my breasts against the railing in front of us. I gulped at how little space there was between him and falling to my death.

Karro pushed harder into my backside. I wrapped my fingers tightly around the railing, holding myself in place. Leaning my head backward, I slumped into his chest.

I missed him. I missed him so badly it felt like an ache.

We hadn't had sex in weeks, it felt like. It had gone from three times a day to maybe once a day. Then, three times a week.

Now, the idea seemed like a joke. Sex was how we'd expressed our love. There wasn't any left.

I closed my eyes. It terrified me knowing I wasn't just pregnant, but far along. I had started to lose weight in my legs and arms. My stomach always stayed bloated, though. I felt so fucking stupid for not realizing earlier. The Blood had taught me to kill, not check for pregnancy symptoms. I was lucky to even have been granted sex.

Karro's large hands wrapped around the railing on either side of mine, grazing them. I needed touch. I needed him.

"Why are you nervous?" he asked, his lips moving against my jaw.

I looked down to the street. Twenty-seven stories would be a far drop. He could push me. I could push him.

"Because," I said, my breathing becoming choppy. His hands slid away from my face and down my neck. I shut my eyes, melting into the feeling of his curious fingers.

He spread them across my cleavage. "Because?"

"You are angry with me." My voice shook. *Coward.*

His lips pursed against my jaw. I winced as he grabbed a piece of skin in his teeth. I had a small scar beneath my jaw, and his tongue trailed against it, sucking on the memory.

"Why am I angry with you?"

I remained silent. That, I did not know.

"Naga?"

"Because I'm a piece of shit. A terrible person. I don't deserve you. I'd hate me too. I do hate me. And I'm a bore." The words were spewing out faster than my mind could process them.

His entire body hardened behind me. Every delicious inch. He smiled against me, and I clamped my eyes shut tighter.

Karro's hand slid down the front of my leggings. It was almost inhuman how fast he could find my clit. Any spot that men couldn't find, Karro was able to devour it within seconds.

"Fuck," I cursed, folding over the railing. I dug my nails into the iron to keep myself balanced. I was not in the mood to become a bloody puddle for drunk clubbers to slip in.

Karro snaked his arm around my waist, keeping me pinned to him. "You are not a bore," he corrected. Three fingers rubbed roughly against my clit. I folded over further, coughing, choking, and gasping. He applied enough pressure to form friction deep in my core.

I felt defiled, and he'd only just started.

"Shit, Karro," I hissed through gritted teeth. My eyes widened as I watched the crowd on the busy street below us. If they looked up, they would see me contorted, gasping for air as Karro worked in my leggings.

His free hand grabbed my tank top, holding a fistful of the neckline. "Do you want them to see you?" he asked.

He pushed two fingers past my folds until he reached knuckle depth. He pulled back out, my pussy tightening to keep him in place. He pushed back in. Over and over.

"Yes," I managed. It was a strangled noise.

Karro smiled against me. His fingers continued to pump deep inside my cunt, wet noises smacking with every slide out of me. I wanted him deeper. I wanted more.

He pulled my tank top down until it ripped clean from my chest. My nipples tightened. The wind blew against my bare chest, reminding me of how exposed I was.

"That's not boring," he replied. A third finger slipped inside me, working loose a low moan. My pussy stretched and then tightened around him. I felt so full with his fingers in me.

Karro twisted me around, pumping into me through the movement. I reached for his back to steady myself. I was going to fall from the balcony—the railing was too flimsy, and we were too high in the air. But it felt too good to protest.

Karro slid his fingers out. His arm wrapped around my waist, and he lifted me onto the railing. I gasped, holding his shoulder as I wobbled against the metal bar. I looked behind me and down toward the street. One strong gust of wind or slip from his hold, and I would splatter.

He reached between my legs and tore at the middle of my leggings, exposing my pussy. I looked back down at the street, my nails sinking deep into his skin. I wouldn't break the railing with my weight; it was Karro I feared.

"Karro," I started. "It's a little high—"

He took the words from me. His cock sunk balls deep into me. He slid out, and back inside, hitting deeper and harder than his fingers had. My eyes rolled backward. I held on to him tight, taking him as he fucked me hard against the railing.

"Fuck," he groaned.

My heels hit his lower back with every thrust. I tightened my legs around him, urging him to go deeper. The angle caused the tip of his slick cock to hit a spot deep inside of me. My head flung backward, and my mouth hung open. Senseless noises came out of me.

I smiled, hard. If I died from the fall, Karro's cock would be the last sensation I felt.

I arched myself into him. "There," I croaked. I rolled my hips toward him, meeting him with each thrust. His slick cock continued to ram into the spot, making my vision go black. He drove throaty, primal noises from both of us.

"Fuck, Naga, you feel so fucking good." He let out a low noise and fucked me harder. I was going to be bruised in the morning. My hips were slamming against the iron railing with his hard thrusts.

I opened my eyes, watching the street through blurred vision. My head spun from how hard he was and how I'd held my breath to concentrate on how good it felt.

I reached for his hair, letting go of his shoulders. His arms around my waist were all that kept me from death. Leaning back, I gave into the trust. It made the pleasure overwhelming. My legs trembled, and my face was twisted. My cunt was clamping and releasing around him.

I looked up at him. He looked otherworldly, in a way. I'd never seen anyone even remotely as ethereal as him, especially when he was inside of me. There was a glow about him. His lips were parted, and his eyes remained with the hot, throbbing pussy he was invading.

I ran my fingers through the hair that fell into his face. It wasn't the fullness that felt good. It was him.

I groaned and threw my head backward. He was perfect. Fucking perfect.

"I love you," I whispered. I was quiet, hoping he wouldn't hear it.

He thrust harder into me. My walls dripped around him. Everything inside my core felt electric, inhuman. I trailed my finger along his sweat-stained face, zoning out his thrusts and focusing on him. The beauty and pain of him.

"A lot," I added, with a groan. It terrified me.

His jaw tightened. He looked away from my pussy and to my face. I waited for something. Anything. He remained silent.

Karro hit harder inside me, pushing past my tight walls. I clenched around him, milking us both through the orgasm. He went still, throbbing and swelling inside me. His hips spread as he came, filling me with his pleasure.

I held on to him for dear life as my orgasm slid down my body. It was hot; it was uncontrollable. I frowned, burying my face into the crook of his neck. Soft, feminine-sounding breaths were slipping out of me and into his ear.

Sex was supposed to feel good. It did, but it didn't. It felt like I was avoiding the inevitable. We were falling apart. Fucking would not bring us back together.

Once Karro began to soften and my breathing calmed, he pulled me from the railing. I adjusted my leggings, attempting to cover some of the hot cum seeping from me. We never used condoms. That was our first issue. We liked it raw and rough.

I didn't let go of him, just kept my face buried in his neck. "I'm pregnant," I whispered. I felt ashamed, even though it was he who had put it inside of me. I was bearing it; I didn't want to bear it. "I found out today. I kept getting sick. I don't know how long—"

Karro tensed. He grabbed my chin and pulled my face away from his neck. My jaw started to tremble. I looked down. I couldn't bring a child into this world—I couldn't be a mother. I'd actually debated killing 7437. If The Blood didn't break my child, I would.

He looked between my eyes. "Are you lying?"

I blinked. "Why would I lie about that?" My voice began to tremble.

Karro let go of my jaw. I searched him for any emotion. I looked for anger or excitement. Fear. Worry. He remained blank and unreadable.

"Okay," he breathed. "We will figure it out."

With that, he pushed past me, leaving me alone and used.

CHAPTER
FORTY-TWO

PRESENT

I woke up entangled in Karro. The blankets from his bed were over us, containing our body heat. I couldn't imagine sleeping alone now. It was too cold, lonely.

The side of his face rested flush against the top of my breasts. My fingers were threaded through his hair, holding him close.

He held on to my waist, fondling the extra bit of fat that I had.

"What do you think will happen if we get out of here?" I asked, breaking the silence. I dreaded the question. Would we stay together? If Karro wanted to leave me, then I would leave him just as fast. If he wanted to stay, then so did I.

He hummed into my chest. I arched my back, pressing myself closer to him. The vibrations from his mouth shot straight to my belly.

"I'm going to make you spaghetti." His slurred voice was muffled by my chest.

I bit out a laugh. According to him, it was all I ever talked about when drunk.

"Okay," I replied. I continued to stroke his soft strands. "I'll make you a margarita, then. I am an expert, after all."

His lips slid into a smile against me. I shuddered as he spoke into my skin. "I will kill you if you do."

I zoned out staring at a cushion on the wall. My lips deepened into a frown. Since we had come up with the plan for our escape, using the nurse, a question had lingered on my tongue. Would it go back to hate?

It would be easier if it did. It was easier to hate him.

Did he still hate me? Did I still hate him? I didn't know what I felt. There was too much happening in my head.

"Karro?"

"Hm."

I gulped and shut my eyes. I'd never thought I'd feel nervous speaking to someone. Especially a man. Fuck, how pathetic I had become.

"Are we going to, I don't know . . ." I stopped. I sucked in a sharp breath. "Like stay together? Not like, *together*, but you know. I—" This was fucking stupid. I planned to put a bullet in my face after this.

Karro pulled away from my chest. He looked at me through his damned lashes. I scoffed upon seeing how hard he was grinning. "Are you nervous, Naga?"

"Shut the fuck up." I tugged hard at his hair. He bit his lip and returned his flushed face to between my breasts.

Karro's hand splayed against my belly. He traced light circles against my bare skin, where my shirt had ridden up. "Do you know why I didn't leave you?" he asked.

My body tightened. I felt the ache in my chest return, but I kept my face firm. I wished he had left me. It would have made things so much easier.

Karro made me hurt. Nothing would ever hurt as much as him. Just as nothing would ever feel as good as him.

I stayed silent.

"Truthfully," he started, "I don't think I can be without you. Even if I hate your guts. And I *really* hated you. But I couldn't leave. I don't think we were made to be apart."

I gritted my teeth, biting back the sharp feeling rising in the back of my throat. "Okay." My voice was clipped. How did he expect me to respond? With a thank-you? I tilted my head backward and stared at the ceiling. "It explains why you were so angry. You lived with someone you hated. Your enemy—"

"No," Karro interrupted. "I was angry because I still loved you. The same way you currently hate yourself because you still love me."

My entire body went rigid. He didn't need a response. He could feel it—the confirmation of what I would never admit aloud.

"Doors open, soldiers aren't real, we convince the nurse to help us," I said. I was beyond ready to get out of this stupid fucking room.

"Yes."

"And if that doesn't work?" I couldn't be confined anymore. It had to work.

"It will."

I winced. If we were wrong, and everything tumbled, we were dead. If Karro's assessment of the nurse was wrong, we were dead. If my confirmation of the soldiers being fake was wrong, we were dead.

"If it is The Blood, they will kill us after we escape," I said. It felt like the only way to get away from them was through death. Perhaps it was for the best.

"Okay." Karro sat up, propping himself onto his elbow. I looked down at his lips. His breath fanned down my face. "I will make you spaghetti. You can make *yourself* a margarita. And then we will kill them all."

I liked the sound of his delusion.

CHAPTER

FORTY-THREE

PRESENT

Karro stood tall above me, scalpel in his hand. "Stand up," he ordered.

I hesitated, looking at the edge of the bed and then back to Karro. He spun the tool in his hand, maneuvering it in between his fingers until the handle faced me.

I reached for it and stood. "What are you doing?" I asked, my grip tightening around the scalpel.

"Stab me with it," he replied.

I blinked, unmoving, awaiting a flicker of amusement. Any sign of a joke.

None appeared.

Was he insane?

Karro huffed, his eyes fixed on the blade in my hand. "If worse comes to worse, you stab her with it. The soldiers aren't real. But you haven't fought in years. Stab me with it. Practice."

My face twitched. I was rusty, but he did not get to tell me that.

"You aren't going to hurt me," he continued. "I think we both know who has the upper—"

I cut him off by lunging toward him with the scalpel. He was right—I hadn't fought in years. A child could tell what I was about to do. He effortlessly dodged the blade and twisted my arm around me.

One moment, he was in front of me. The next, he was behind me. His elbow locked around my throat, preventing me from moving.

He held the scalpel to my face. "Dead," he hummed into my ear. I scowled. He waved the blade in front of my vision, but just out of reach.

"Fuck you," I spat.

"Again," Karro instructed. He pushed the blade lazily toward my chest.

I was quicker this time. He hadn't finished handing me the tool before I jerked it from his hand and thrust it toward his ribcage.

I was fast.

Karro was faster.

He was better than me. I hated it.

He grabbed my wrist and twisted my arm until the scalpel pressed against my neck. I winced when the cold metal kissed my skin. It wasn't hard enough to split open my flesh, but it was close.

"Dead," he hummed. His lips slid upward.

"Okay, it's a stupid fucking nurse. You're a trained commander. There's a difference." My face heated. I was going to slit my own throat open if it meant avoiding failure again. I was so fucking weak.

"No. You don't know how their training has advanced. What if she's the one behind this entire thing? She could be the Murthaa for all we know. A commander. Get a grip, sweetheart. Again."

He placed the scalpel in my hand.

Sweetheart. I scoffed at the odious word as I planned my attack.

Distraction always worked. I kept my eyes on him, ensuring he had no idea where I was going to attack. This time, I kicked toward his thigh. Hard. Immediately after, I thrust the tip of the scalpel toward his jugular.

My foot never made an impact. Karro grabbed hold of my ankle before I made contact. He caught both of my wrists with his free hand, twisting and contorting my arm until the blade touched my neck. Again.

"Dead." Karro grinned, too hard. "You were a commander?"

I smiled back. "I've been killing birds, not men, as of recently."

"You do well with eye contact. I never know *where* you are going to hit. But, you are hesitating right before you do." He stopped, a cruel smiling tugging at his lips. "Why are you hesitating, Naga?"

I ground my teeth together. "Because I don't want to kill a good fuck before it happens. Again."

The room grew heavy after the word *fuck* left my mouth.

He passed me the scalpel. I wasn't going to hesitate this time. I couldn't. He would know he was right—that there was a reason.

It was no longer Karro standing in front of me. I imagined it to be someone else. For a moment, the nurse appeared. Then the dead Murthaa. I ended up settling on the doctors, the brutally murdered ones who had trained me to be such a good girl.

I jabbed my fist into the air above Karro's shoulders. As expected, he caught my wrist. I'd wanted him to do this. It didn't matter. I tossed the scalpel behind his head. My free hand caught it and pushed it into his throat.

With my restrained hand, I threaded my fingers through his hair. I jerked at it, forcing his head backward, then pressed the blade harder into his throat. I watched as the skin began to break. He hadn't held it this hard to my throat.

The outer layers of skin separated, revealing red meat. It continued to part as I applied more pressure. Blood began to drip from the wound. If I didn't pull away soon, I'd see fat. That would mean stitches. Infection.

My trembling hands tightened hard around the tool. I wanted to kill them all. Every last person who'd ever stepped foot in The Blood.

I sucked in a breath and jerked my hand away. "Dead," I muttered.

Karro let go of my wrist. The tips of his fingers traced along the cut I'd left him. When he pulled away, they were coated in blood. It flowed freely, but not at a concerning speed.

I huffed and collapsed onto the floor, throwing scalpel across the room.

It had been over fifty years. They were dead. I wanted to kill them again, and again. I wanted to torture the doctors. I wanted to torture the Murthaa. I wanted to hurt everyone.

Karro joined me on the floor. I zoned in on the scalpel a few feet away. It was coated in blood and a shred of skin.

"Who did you pretend I was?" he asked.

It terrified me how well he could read me. He knew me better than I knew myself—even after all of this time.

"No one important."

Karro touched my knee. I gulped and looked down at his large hand. If I were to press my thighs together tight, a single hand would almost conceal both of my thighs. He was so big. Every aspect of him.

His thumb stroked a slow circle around my sweatpants. I turned my head to face him, and his hand slid up my thigh.

I looked at the cut on his neck. I could have sliced his throat open. He'd practically given me the opportunity.

"I'd like to fuck you now."

I flinched, taken aback by his words. I looked away from the cut.

"Are you okay with that?" Karro continued.

If I hadn't had respect for myself, I'd have gotten on my knees and begged him.

I reached for the hem of my shirt. "I suppose."

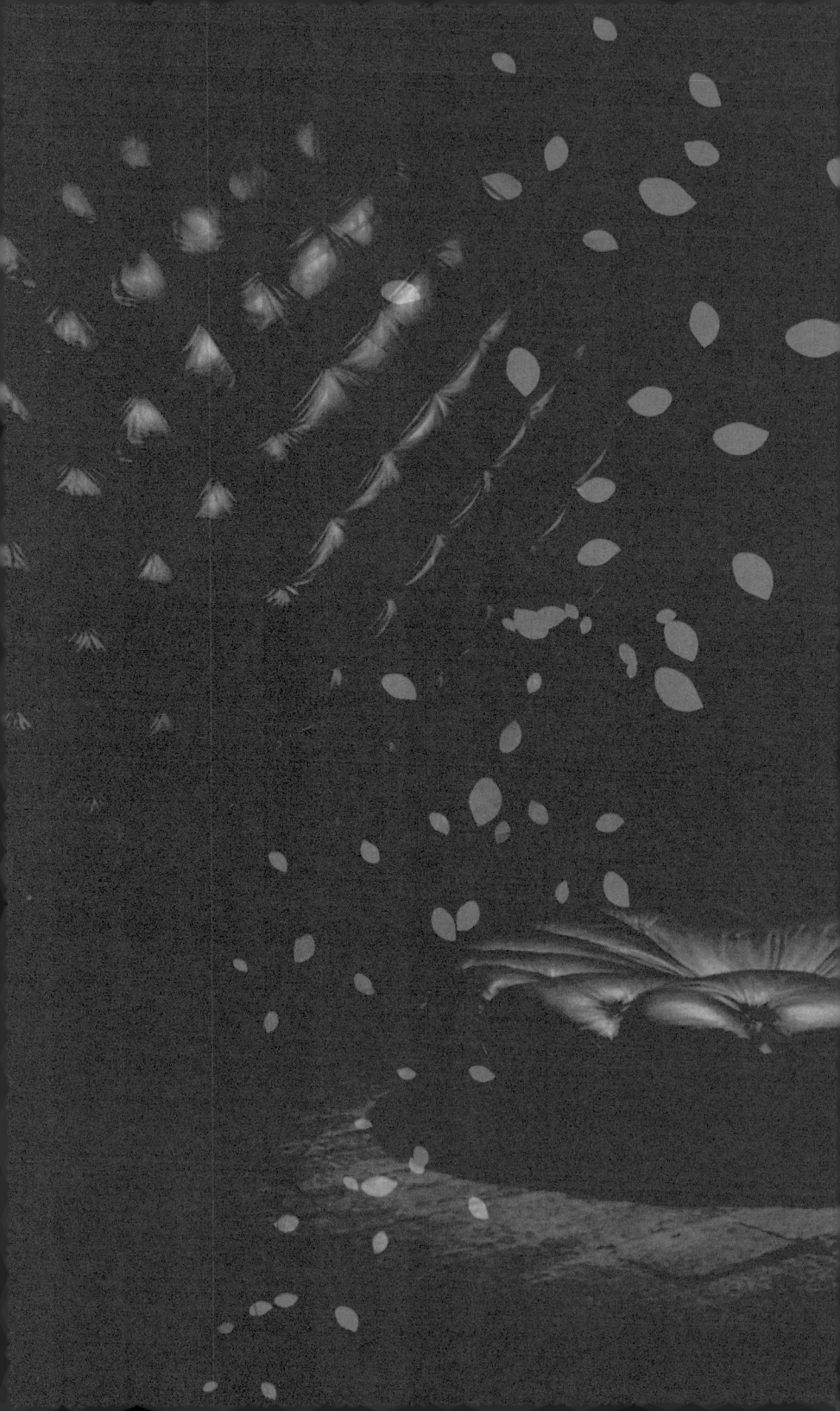

CHAPTER

FORTY-FOUR

PRESENT

I trailed my finger along the ridges of Karro's abdomen. He'd lost weight since I last saw him, but he still felt hard in mass. He shuddered under my touch.

We knelt in front of each other, and he dipped his neck downward, pulling a breast into his mouth. I shuddered as his lips wrapped around my areola, concealing it entirely. His other hand crept up my belly before grabbing a handful of my breasts.

"Shit," I gasped, my head falling forward. I stared down at his lips as he continued to suck, bite, and run his tongue along my nipple.

My breathing staggered. His hand drifted from my breast and back down the length of my fast-rising belly. I pulled away from him. He was going to make me lose myself.

I leaned down, bracing myself on my hands and knees. I curved my back, and my ass rested high in the air. I reached for the hem of his sweatpants.

My lips lifted as I pulled them down. Karro rarely let me suck or stroke his cock. He'd fuck my throat, but I was rarely in control. I liked to play—and tease. Karro liked to rut.

His cock sprung free. His swollen head grazed my cheek during the process of removing his pants. I felt the stickiness of his precum coat the skin he touched.

"Naga," Karro warned, looking down at what I was doing.

I grabbed base of his heavy cock. My fingers lingered around his balls. He looked *godly* from this angle. He knelt, gazing down at me as his hot cock throbbed in my hands. I tightened my fist around his shaft and brought it down to his base.

Karro sighed and looked up at the ceiling. I watched annoyance jump in his jaw.

My dimples deepened. I loved the control. He hated me having it. If it were up to him, I knew my face would be fucked so hard that spit, cum, and blood dripped down my neck.

I jutted my tongue out, then flattened it and pressed it flush against the base of his cock. He sucked in a breath at the contact. I slowly pulled my tongue up his shaft—painfully slowly. I liked to watch how impatient he became, how insufferable it was when I held my mouth on him.

I supposed that was why he rarely let me suck his cock.

I swirled my tongue around the tip of his cock, and Karro grabbed my hair, pulling me away. I grunted when my back hit the cushioned floor. He repositioned himself, now kneeling in between my legs.

Karro leaned into me, pinning me harder against the floor. His cock twitched against my stomach. "You lost that privilege a *long* time ago." His breath ran across the sensitive spot behind my ear. I smiled, despite the threat lacing in his tone.

"Pussy," I replied. The last time my tongue had been against his cock had been in a museum. Every time he was about to come, I'd "accidentally" gotten distracted and had to stop. Or I would pretend someone was approaching and watch as his orgasm retracted.

It was fun.

Karro did not find it fun.

He dug his fingers into my pants and jerked them down to my knees. I kicked them far across the room. I wanted skin on skin as much as he did.

I tilted my head backward, preventing him from seeing my face as it contorted. His cock ran up and down my slit, spreading his precum between my lips.

Karro pushed into me. I sucked in a sharp breath and squeezed my eyes shut. There was a slight discomfort as he seated himself inside me. I steadied my breathing and focused on how full and warm I felt.

He did not give me time to adjust. He was out of my folds and deep inside within a second. Over and over. "Fuck, Naga," he groaned.

I opened my eyes to watch him. His eyes were hooded, looking down at the area where we were joined. My eyebrows knitted together, and my head hit the floor hard. My back arched and flattened with every thrust.

His hand pressed against my lower belly, intensifying the feeling inside of me. The other hand dug into my thigh, holding it against his hip as he continued to pound hard into me. I was about to slide against the floor. He was completely, and utterly, primal.

Karro jerked me upward. The angle caused my ass to rest on his thighs. My hips tilted upward, deepening where he hit. "This should have happened earlier," he groaned.

I nodded and arched further into the ground. I hoped he couldn't see how dissatisfied I looked.

I propped myself up on my elbows and looked down at the area where he was working. It felt like he was in my fucking chest. He pushed inside me fast, but I was able to catch a glimpse of his cock midthrust. His shaft was coated in slickness—my slickness.

I groaned and threw my head backward.

I couldn't tell whose body was whose by this point. We were molded flesh, a tangled mess of sweat, pleasure, and limb. I closed my eyes and focused on the buildup inside of me.

I felt good—I was full and warm. But that was it. Karro felt like another warm body inside of me.

It once hadn't felt like that. It had once made me believe in something greater than us—that something could exist that had crafted our bodies for each other. Now, though, it didn't feel that way. Karro felt like any other fuck.

"God, Naga, you're fucking beautiful," he groaned, his thrusts becoming sloppy.

I nodded in agreement.

Karro's cock twitched and swelled inside of me. I felt him leaking, coating my insides.

I frowned, clamping my eyes shut tighter. I should be enjoying this. I tried hard, so fucking hard, to focus on it. To feel good. He felt good. He was enjoying this.

He was just a warm body.

Karro pulled out of me before he came. He stroked himself, beating hard above me. I watched the ropes of cum splatter on my stomach. He closed his eyes and groaned as he stroked himself through his orgasm.

I wished I felt as good as he did.

I felt dirty. His cum burned against my skin. I wanted to scrub myself until I bled, to wash away the reminder that I had let him back inside of me.

Once Karro finished, I quickly got dressed and crawled into his bed. I frowned, facing the wall. I pulled the cover close to my face.

Karro was wrong. I was not angry at myself for *loving* him.

I did not feel like I loved him at all.

CHAPTER

FORTY-FIVE

PAST

R*ed.*

Everything around me was red.

My lips were stained with a dark color, matching the tight dress I had on. My hair was curled and pinned to the back of my head with a crimson-colored pin. Pulling it all together was a pair of tall red heels.

It was Karro's favorite color. Thus, it was mine.

I reached for my lips, my fingers lingering on my smile. I felt good. I felt so fucking good. We'd been fighting *so* much, but something had been different about tonight. We'd gone to dinner, and drunk wine, just like we had in the early stages of our "relationship."

It was getting better. It had to be.

I continued down the hall at The Blood. On the way toward my corridor, I needed to walk through three hallways: the A1 ka's corridors, the training rooms, and the officers' corridors. Then, I would be in the secluded area. The commanders' corridor.

I stopped midstep and knitted my brows together. The door to my training room was propped open. It was almost 0200— no one should be awake at this time. Especially in *my* training room. The only individuals I'd permitted in there were my Anaka and the Murthaa. And that cunt was dead.

I pulled my fingers away from my lips. Frowning, I looked up at the light, which was flickering. The lights shouldn't be on, nor should the door be open. No training was scheduled, and all of the Anaka should be asleep.

I slipped my hand down and groped for the leather strip I wore around my thigh, holding a blade tight in place against me. It was the only weapon I had on me. I couldn't remember the last time I'd had only one weapon on me.

I stayed silent and slowly pushed the door open.

I'd expected some child to be sitting in the center of the room, crying about how much they needed a mother—it happened all too often. Or perhaps 7437 smiling, telling me of how she had alerted the Committee of my actions.

I could not have been further from the truth.

For a blink of time, all I saw was red. Blood coated every inch of the room. The ceilings and walls were sprayed with thin streaks of it. Even though their bodies were small, the arteries had produced enough blood to coat the walls. Beneath them, blood pooled in a puddle.

It was still expanding. This had been recent.

My knuckles went white around my blade. I stopped breathing. I listened to the quiet drop of blood dripping from the ceiling and into a puddle.

I slowly turned, the room blurring and lagging as I moved my head. Bloody handprints coated the walls. Small. Childlike. My throat tightened and my body began to tremble. I hadn't let out a breath since entering the room.

The handprints accumulated at the door, most concentrated in the area beside the handle.

They'd been trying to escape.

I dropped the knife in my hand. It fell into a puddle, splashing blood onto my clean legs. A quiet sob came from my throat. I gasped for air, stumbling into the wall behind me.

I wasn't going to count them. I could see them all. My Anaka, spread across the floor, covered in their own blood. Their heads were far from their bodies.

I clamped a trembling hand over my mouth, gasping and sobbing into my palm.

Death had had fun in here. Death had fun dancing among the innocent and giving purity something that should be reserved for the wicked. It seemed that was all Death could do in this world.

I looked down at my feet. Part of 8392 lay near me. He was looking up at the ceiling, his mouth stuck ajar in a screaming position. He used to bring me flowers every Sunday.

Next, I looked at 9420. She would always fill me in on which generals she'd seen kissing. Now, her mouth hung low, jaw broken. I could not find the rest of her body. I did not want to find the rest of her body.

I closed my eyes and reached toward my face, wiping away the few tears that had formed there. I steadied my breath and began to assess every last person who worked here—they were all going to die.

LAYLA GRIM

Picking up my blade, I stormed out of the room. It felt like part of me stayed, though—like I was leaving something behind that I would never get back.

Red. It was the only thing I could see. I'd never been angrier in my life.

I made my way to the double doors that separated the generals' corridors and the training hall. A guard stood positioned in front of them. His eyes were shut, and his head rested against the wall.

He was asleep. He was fucking asleep.

"You," I hissed. "You were supposed to guard the halls." Another sob slipped free, and I sliced his throat before he could fully wake up. He fell to the ground, seizing.

I stepped over him and continued down the corridor. I rounded the corner and pounded on the closest chamber to me. "General 94," I yelled, slamming her door with my fist.

A few curses and thuds sounded from inside. I continued to pound on the door until it swung open. A woman in her thirties stepped into the door frame. Her blonde hair was brushed, hanging long by her sides.

For a moment, she appeared angry, but she paled when she saw me. I could feel the burn of blood on my face.

"Someone has beheaded all of the Anaka. I want a list of every fucking guard that was on duty tonight. Have them sent to a holding cell until I can come to kill them," I spat. My fingers were trembling. General 94 looked down at my hands as I hid them behind my back. "Look at every second of footage to see what the fuck happened. I want a list. A janitor on duty? Put him on the fucking list."

General 94 nodded, wrapping her body in a nearby coat.

I left her, my hands still shaking. I looked down at my palms. The tips of my fingers were covered in blood. My palms were covered in blood. Their blood.

My face twitched as the lights began to flash red. An automated voice echoed "Lockdown." I continued toward my room, ignoring the generals that were running down the hall toward the atrocity. The motion and chaos felt like it was passing in a slow blur. Every step I took felt heavy.

I stared at my door, swallowing down a bundle of needles. I recalled 7437 sitting in front of it, proving to me that The Sight actually existed. She was somewhere amid the flesh now. Dismembered.

I pushed inside and walked toward my vanity. I felt like I was floating—my body and spirit had disconnected, and my body was on autopilot. I dug my nails into the wood and stared at myself in the mirror. I had blood smeared across my face, beneath my eyes. I didn't recognize myself. I didn't look sad, or angry. I felt angry, but I looked like nothing.

My teeth cracked from how hard I was grinding them together. The blood on my face resembled the smears around the door handle.

They'd been trying to escape. I was on a date while they were suffering. I wasn't there. I wasn't there to help them.

My fingernails picked up wood from my vanity. I shut my eyes and dipped my head low. I tried to concentrate on my breathing, to hold in the sobs. I couldn't catch my breath. It was all coming out too fast.

I needed to scream.

"Fuck. Fuck. Fuck," I cried. I gasped and let out strangled sobs, throwing my fists into the mirror at the beat of my curses. I shattered my image, continuing to hit the mirror until I felt the glass dig too deep. I deserved to be hurt. I deserved whatever the Committee would do to me. They were dead.

"What's your name?" The voice ripped through the air, stinging as a whip would.

I jerked my body around to face whoever had spoken.

I flinched. My hands braced behind me, pressing into the glass I'd just shattered. I couldn't feel it. I couldn't feel anything.

Karro stared at me from a shadow in my room.

CHAPTER

Forty-Six

PAST

I blinked, staring at Karro.

He was sitting outstretched in the chair. His legs were extended in front of him, and his arms were relaxed behind his head. He was too comfortable.

I gulped, the image of the bloody handprints returning.

My Anaka.

My Karro.

It was him. It had to be.

"You," I spat, narrowing my eyes to slits. I probably looked like a stranger to him. I was covered in blood, trembling from the tension I was holding on to. I couldn't breathe. I wanted to rip my chest apart to be free of the ache.

"Me," Karro replied. A sly smile crept onto his face.

I did not want to cry in front of him. But I did. The mascara and lipstick I'd worn for him were now a streaked mess. I wrapped my arms around myself, trying to hold myself tight.

"You killed them," I said. I sobbed. I couldn't hold it in anymore.

Karro stood from the chair. I should be afraid of him. I was more worried about my composure than him. "What is your name?" he asked.

"You killed them," I gasped. My vision blackened. Rage and grief came together, squeezing at my throat. I reached for my neck, clawing at it. I clawed at myself until I bled—I wanted to breathe.

"I don't know what you're talki—"

"You killed them," I repeated, my head spinning. I grabbed the closest object to me—a lamp. A mix of cry, whimper, and sob came out of me as I threw it in his direction. I'd been aiming for his head, but he easily deflected it.

I didn't want to hurt him. I didn't want to exist. I wanted to crawl into a corner and hide in the warmth of myself, as I had done when I was a child.

"You're a liar," Karro said.

He said something else too, but I didn't listen. My body trembled, and noises slipped out of me. I convulsed, trying to calm myself down.

Karro took a step closer to me. I looked down at the gun in his left hand and then the knife in his other. There was no blood on the blade—no blood on him. I wanted to see it. I wanted to see the proof of what he'd done.

I reached for the gun that was hidden beneath my vanity. Pointing it in his direction, I prepared to shoot him before he could shoot me.

I was met by the barrel of his own gun. It pressed hard into my forehead. No one had ever gotten this close to killing me before.

I pressed my gun into his chin.

Neither of us pulled the trigger. We were fucking pathetic.

I dropped the gun, which landed a few inches from his feet, and walked backward toward the wall. Karro followed me, engulfing my small steps with his large strides.

When my back hit the wall, I slid down it. I wrapped my hands around my head, trying to sink beneath my own skin. I wanted to cower from this world—I was such a fucking coward. I wanted to disappear inside myself and wait until the world fell back into place.

Karro threaded his fingers through my hair, the gun against my scalp. He jerked my head up, forcing my gaze onto him. He looked terrifying. Beneath the flashing red light, his look was something beyond anger. I'd never seen anything like it.

"Don't be a coward now, Commander."

Karro's large hand wrapped around my bloody throat. The self-inflicted scratches stung against his palm. I choked, grabbing onto his hands, and pried at his tight hold with my nails. It was useless. He was too strong.

He tilted his head, looking down at me. "Are you not going to speak?"

I removed my struggling hands from his. If he wanted to kill me, I didn't care anymore. He'd be killing *both* of us. Based on the tight grip he had around my neck, it didn't appear he cared about killing our child, either.

"You killed my Anaka." My voice barely made it past his tight squeeze. I coughed and gasped, trying to catch my breath.

His face twitched and his brow curved. I knew that look. He was confused. How dare he act confused? It had to be him.

I reached for his face, digging into his skin. I was going to rip the smug expression right off of him. "Stupid fucker," I hissed. He jerked his head backward, out of my reach. I balled my fists and hit at his chest, arms, and face—anything I could reach. "I would do it all again."

Words spewed from my mouth. All I could think of was my Anaka. "I would do it over and over. I wish you could have seen me kill your mother. And your brother." I laughed, gathering a wad of spit to send into his face. "She cried. You should have seen it, *fucker.*"

Hot tears were trailing down my face.

Karro was expressionless. He jerked me toward him before slamming my head hard into the wall. My vision blurred, and I felt peace trickle across my skin. He pulled my back toward him, and then into the wall again. My head spun, and I felt a crack in the back of my head.

"I loved you," he admitted, after the third blow.

I could barely stand. "So fucking sad," I growled.

Karro smiled, and my head hit the wall once more. This time, everything went black—I could finally breathe.

CHAPTER

FORTY-SEVEN

PAST

I woke up with an ache in my spine, shifting and groaning against the table beneath me. My vision was blurry, a few stray tears slipping down the sides of my face. My skull felt like it had split open.

I turned my head and looked around the room. Everything was spinning, producing a blur around me. My stomach throbbed, tearing my focus away from my head. As the spinning stopped, the pain intensified inside my core.

I looked down at my belly. The dress was hiked above my waist, my belly and lower body bare to anyone who witnessed the sight. My jaw began to tremble; I'd never been in so much pain in my life. I felt like I'd been stabbed, over and over.

My stomach was covered in blood. I tried to reach for it, to feel for the bump, but tight bindings around my wrist kept me restrained. I was too weak to try and tug on the cloth holding me down on the metal table. I pulled my eyes away and up toward Karro. It took a moment to focus; I recognized him through the haze of whatever damage he had inflicted on my head.

His arms were crossed over his chest as he watched the woman beside him. She was a blurry mess, but I could make out the knit of her face as she worked. Her hands were fiddling above my belly.

She was working on me.

I squinted and saw she had a needle and thread in her hands. Beneath the blood, I saw a few stitches holding my stomach together.

Red filled the room, and then darkness. Over and over. I couldn't have been asleep for that long; we were still under lockdown.

I looked around, catching glimpses of my surroundings through the strobed light. I recognized this room. It was not *the* doctor's office, but perhaps another doctor's office I'd been to. Maybe when I'd been assessed and examined, to make sure my dead doctors hadn't broken anything inside me.

My consciousness slid into darkness. I shut my eyes and let my head fall limp to the side.

When I came to again, there was more blood. It was oozing out of my belly as the nurse beside Karro frantically tried to stitch me up. Karro didn't look at me. He was watching the nurse's movements.

My eyelids grew heavier, and I felt my body threatening to slip back into unconsciousness.

I looked at the tray beside her before I passed out again.

I stiffened. There was something on the tray. It was wrapped in a bloody white towel, which concealed most of it, but I was able to see two tiny, bloody blue feet sticking out at the bottom. Too small. Too bloody. Too blue.

My head fell to the side again, and I moved my gaze up to Karro. He still hadn't looked at me. He ran a hand down his face, and his foot impatiently tapped against the floor.

"It's done, sir." The nurse pulled away from my belly.

My vision had cleared slightly, and I was able to scan her figure. Her black strands fell loose around her shoulders, and two streaks of gray framed her face. She was wearing Blood attire. *A traitor.* It was rare. I couldn't imagine how hard she'd had to act to avoid being caught. How had I not realized?

"Thank you," Karro replied, dismissing her.

He leaned down, unfastening the restraints that held me down. He wouldn't look at me. He looked everywhere but at me. I did not fight him. I stayed limp and weak, allowing him to do as he wished.

His lips pressed into my ear. "You can't have a child where you're going, anyways," he whispered. I could barely hear him through the fuzz and ringing in my ears.

He scooped his arms under my back and legs, hauling me from the table. I closed my eyes, my mind threatening to fall back into unconsciousness. He carried me out into a cold hallway.

"Just kill me," I whispered, limp in his arms. My stomach ached so terribly—I couldn't feel anything anymore.

"No." His voice was stern.

I let my head fall limp against his chest. Everything was gone. If there had been a gun within reach, I would have put a bullet through my head.

Karro.

The Anaka.

The Blood.

It was all gone. I was gone.

"Please kill me," I slurred. I could feel some form of drug swimming through my head. "I just want to die."

Karro shook his head, eyes looking forward. "Rot in hell," he said.

I slipped back into an unconscious state.

CHAPTER

Forty-Eight

PRESENT

I gasped and shot upward in the bed, kicking at the covers until they pooled at my feet. Frantically, I reached down, feeling for the wound I had felt so vividly in my dream.

I squeezed my eyes shut and held my belly tight. *It was a nightmare,* I reminded myself. A memory of something I did not need to worry about. The time for mourning had passed. This was a burden.

"Hey," Karro whispered, sitting up next to me. I looked over at him, my cheeks slightly hot. I must have crawled into bed with him during the night. I didn't remember.

He wrapped an arm around my waist, pulling me into him. I stiffened, but let myself fall into his chest. He felt so warm, despite how cold and bitter his insides were. The nightmare was a burden, but it was also a reminder of him. His cruelty.

My body tightened, trying to reject his touch. I shouldn't be acting like he hadn't ripped a child from my belly. I shouldn't trust him.

Karro squeezed me tighter, forcing me to relax against him. It was strange that the person who had caused me to hurt so terribly was also the one who now comforted me—the only one who could comfort me. Perhaps the wound on my stomach was a play at control. His sadistic way of showing that he could hurt me, and heal me.

I'd promised myself that the day a man hurt me would be the last day a man took a breath. Yet he sat there, untouched. It was me. I was weak—so fucking weak.

Karro's lips came to my ear, brushing against the softness of them. "I'm sorry, Naga. So fucking sorry."

I looked down at my stomach, which I still held, as he spoke. It hurt. It hadn't stopped hurting. Ever since our child had been removed from my womb, I'd felt it. It was a mix of pain and emptiness, biting at my insides every day that Karro walked free.

The pain was a cruel reminder of what cruelty I was forgiving—the boy who held me.

Karro continued to whisper into my ear, holding me closer. I ignored every word. Was this how he had tricked me before? Had I been blinded by love, like a fool?

I pushed off of him and stood from the bed. He shifted, like he was going to follow me, but I held my hand out. "Just give me a second," I whispered, my throat tightening. I stumbled into the bathroom and slid to the floor.

I remained here for hours. Or minutes. It was difficult to know the time when the skylight was all that helped in the matter.

I sat against the bathroom wall, my knees tight to my chest. I felt Karro on the other side of the cushion, sitting with his back to me. I'd heard him shift a few times, but neither of us had spoken.

My arms remained around my stomach. With every passing second, guilt grew heavier and heavier on my chest. I shouldn't have let him in. I should have killed him. I'd disappointed myself. My child.

"The soldiers aren't real." I flinched when Karro broke the silence. "Convince the nurse. Get out of here. Spaghetti and margarita. Then we kill them all."

I leaned forward, resting my chin between my knees. I wished it were that easy. It couldn't be that easy.

I ran the tips of my fingers along my biceps, staring at a speck on the floor. My skin felt raw from scratching—I thought maybe if I clawed myself until I bled, I would forget the guilt of his touch.

There was a wall between our backs, but I could feel my soul trying to sink out of me and into his. I hated being confined with him. There was no way to stop myself from trying to join with his essence.

It always had been like that.

"You know," I began, clearing my throat, "when I was young, I was forbidden from ever leaving the room I lived in. They were afraid we might cross paths. And later on in life, my mission would have been compromised if you had seen me. One night, I snuck out. I wanted to see the rest of The Blood. I wanted to go to the playground to collect flowers for my room."

I stopped, looking down at my feet. I shouldn't be speaking. He could use this all against me. He could hurt me, again.

"On my way back one night, I saw you. I was so fucking scared you were going to see me. You were so young at the time, and I was—" I scoffed, shaking my head. I didn't know my age. They'd taken *everything* from me. "I was really, *really* scared you had seen me watching you. But you were so beautiful. I didn't understand why I couldn't be around you. Around everyone else."

I shifted, fiddling with my sweatpants. "I knew who you were. Knew you were the person they were preparing me to go after. But it felt weird. You looked so normal."

"You put a rose on my gun," Karro stated.

I nodded. I'd dropped the rose atop of the weapon before fleeing to my room. It had been my way of rebelling against The Blood, without doing anything drastic.

"I didn't know what I was doing. If my general had known, they would have locked me in my room."

As a child, I'd been punished a few different times. Before I started my period, they'd used snakes, spiders, and bugs to punish me. They would lock me in my room and release the creatures. After I started my period, I realized it wasn't the bugs I feared anymore.

"I kept it," Karro admitted, pulling me from my thoughts.

I looked down at my stomach. I imagined young Karro, bloodlust and all, keeping a rose from a shadow in the night.

"You were my enemy, not my lover." I swallowed, preparing for the truth to come past my tight throat. "I hated you so much when I woke up here because I forgot that. I don't hate you for tricking me. I admire you for it."

"What do you think now?"

I looked down at my feet. "Ask me when we're out of this room."

CHAPTER

Forty-Nine

PRESENT

I sat on the edge of my bed and ran my hands down the front of my shirt, smoothing it. My face and eyes felt puffy, carrying the emotions from the night before.

I slowly lifted my gaze up toward Karro. His head was flush against his pillow, and his face was positioned in my direction. There was a large empty space in front of him. It was where I had recently been sleeping, beside him, conserving the heat.

"You good?" he asked. His eyes were heavy, on the verge of slipping into slumber. His voice rasped and dripped with the need for sleep.

I looked down at my lap and twined my fingers together. I didn't feel good. Something felt wrong. Everything felt wrong. Being here, with Karro. Alive. Sitting in this room, acting as though nothing had happened.

"Yeah." I kept my eyes down.

The entire night, my heart had raced, and a pit had grown heavier in my belly. The hairs on the back of my neck had been erect all morning. Something was wrong. I could feel it.

I ran the tip of my tongue across my chapped lips, tasting the remnants of toothpaste balls from earlier. My face was still damp from when I'd splashed it with water.

It was useless. Nothing was shaking the uneasy feeling in my core.

"Come here," Karro said.

A muscle in my jaw ticked. I looked back up at him, sucking in a breath. My entire body felt heavy as I watched him. My feet felt as though they were stuck to the ground, keeping me in place.

I couldn't do it. Not when the memory of him was the reason I couldn't sleep. How could he comfort me when he was the reason I felt so raw to begin with?

I slowly shook my head.

A few moments passed, Karro staring and waiting for me. The silence ran through the room, almost as loud as my breathing. I didn't understand why I was so nervous, especially with him.

Karro pushed himself off the bed, standing with a swift swing of his legs. My muscles tightened as he approached my side of the room. I kept my eyes on his feet.

When had I become such a fucking coward?

He reached for the side of my face, cupping my cheek in his calloused hand. With his thumb, he grazed the area under my swollen eyelids. It felt like I'd let out a lifetime's worth of tears the night before, silently. Could he tell? I hoped not.

I closed my eyes as Karro leaned down toward me. He planted a soft kiss on my left eyelid, and then my right. They were sore.

My stomach fluttered when he pulled away from me. He was so gentle and delicate—I'd never felt him in such a way. It was abnormal. Everything about him was abnormal.

I opened my eyes, meeting his close face. His lips were parted, as if he was going to say something, but no noise came out. Instead, a loud clicking echoed through the room.

Karro and I both turned our heads toward the door. The open door.

"Ready?" Karro asked, his eyes locked it.

I slowly looked at the tallies behind his head. It felt like it'd been a few weeks since last time, as the nurse had said. He'd done it. He'd actually done it. She was going to help us.

I straightened my spine and looked back at the door. I wanted not to care, but I couldn't help but feel my belly burn at the thought of what Karro had done to gain her trust. He'd seduced her.

"Naga?"

I sucked in a breath and nodded. I wasn't ready. It couldn't possibly be this easy. Karro had been here for so long; if it had been, he would already have gotten out.

I grabbed the scalpel, nonetheless, and tucked it into the back of my pants.

Soldiers. Nurse. Spaghetti. Margarita. Death.

I followed behind Karro as he exited the room. The hallway was as it had been last time, and the time before that. Soldiers lined the walls as we made our way toward the lone room. I stared at them, noticing their lack of breath and their eerily still posture. I felt if I were to lean over to them, and rip their masks free, I would see lifeless eyes bulging from dead bloated faces.

I shifted my attention to the back of Karro's dark hair. The entire walk to the office, I focused on his head and how his strands felt between my fingers. It'd felt the same as it once had, but nothing else did. When we'd fucked, it had felt like I was fucking a stranger; would it be the same if I held him like I used to?

He slowed, pulling me from my spiral down my mind, and my stomach twisted when we reached the office.

I took a step toward Karro. There were only a few inches of space between my front and his back. His large figure concealed me as we entered the room. He had seduced the nurse. It had fucking worked. We were here, weeks later, as she had promised.

My body tightened as we stepped inside. I watched Karro's head dip toward the nurse; I looked away when he began to look up at her through his lashes. I remembered that look. I myself had knelt to it once.

I scanned the space. As before, soldiers lined the walls. Karro slid onto the table, paying no attention to them. He rolled his sleeve up, and the nurse slowly began to prepare his arm for the injection.

I did not look away from the soldiers.

This time, my hands were trembling. I looked down at them, intertwining them behind my back. *Fucking coward. Poor little Naga turned into a fucking coward.*

I swallowed down the knot rising up my throat.

Karro whispered something under his breath, eyes still trained on what the nurse was doing to his arm. It would make sense if the soldiers were some kind of decoy. Karro and I against a pathetic little girl like her? The soldiers were the only thing stopping me from lunging toward her and plunging the scalpel into her throat. Over and over.

I wanted to. Badly.

"Sweetheart," Karro whispered. The nurse and I both looked toward him. Her cheeks turned a light shade of pink. My face contorted into disgust. "We need help. I know you can do that. For me. Anything will help."

His fingers reached bravely toward her, lingering on the little exposed skin around her wrist. The sleeves of her white dress ended at her wrists and the hem ended just above her ankles.

She hadn't looked up, though her body was responding to him. I focused on the goosebumps following his fingers. Her lips parted as he continued, and her hands trembled against his skin. It was bloody from where she had injected him.

"Anything," he repeated, much quieter. He sounded like he was pleading. At any moment, Karro would drop to his knees and beg her for it. Maybe he would give her everything she'd ever wanted. I'd once believed the same thing. "Please."

I clasped my fingers together. I needed to pull myself together. I didn't want to waste my time on the silly feeling that burned in my stomach as he touched her. He was a man. He was nothing.

The nurse suddenly jerked her head up. I flinched when her eyes landed on me, not Karro. "She wasn't dead," she cried, so loudly that I flinched again. I hadn't heard such a loud noise since I had entered the white room. "She wasn't—"

Her brain matter and blood sprayed across my face before she could finish.

My jaw dropped. Karro and I both stared at the floor as she fell limp to it. A bullet had shot through her eye, blowing clean through her brain.

I reached my fingers to my face. I was covered in the bits and pieces of what she had been.

A soldier stepped forward. Very much real. There was a large gun propped on their right shoulder, barely moving as they took multiple steps toward us. Even with the movement, the room was eerily still. I blinked, wondering if I'd imagined it.

The soldier unmounted the gun from their shoulder. I stared at the barrel. It was pointed directly at me.

All of the soldiers had pointed their guns at me. Not Karro.

CHAPTER

FIFTY

PRESENT

I wondered when I'd become such a pussy. In my prime, violence and outbursts had been my comfort—my first response in a situation like the one with the soldiers.

The nurse twitched and seized at my feet as her muscles reacted to the loss of her brain. Back then, I would have laughed and gloated as I jumped from the table. I would have grabbed a gun and died smiling as I pumped these *things* full of pretty lead.

But it was different now. I was the one looking down the barrels, and I couldn't seem to do a fucking thing about it.

I stared.

And stared.

Even now, the soldiers weren't moving. They weren't supposed to be real.

Karro's hand clamped on top of mine. He, too, continued to stare at them, though I'd expected nothing more of him. His hands were warm and damp against mine. It reminded me that he was here, beside me, though the soldiers hadn't acknowledged him.

I sucked in a breath. I wasn't scared, though I had no intention of joining the pile of meat and brains on the floor. I refused to have my fate sealed in such a way.

"Fuck this." I seethed, pushing myself from the table. Karro's large hand gripped tightly around my bicep, preventing me from attacking as I had planned.

I narrowed my eyes at him. His gaze was focused on the doors that led back into the hall. The soldiers who'd lined the walls out there had relocated to the doorway, guns held high.

I hadn't heard so much as a shift. A breath.

"Don't," Karro warned.

He had more sense than I did. I was prepared to grab a gun and start shooting as many as possible until damnation. I couldn't sit and stare. I had to do something. I was no pussy.

A small soldier stepped forward before I could protest, hooking their slim fingers beneath the bottom of their mask. *It.* They pulled it from their face, throwing it toward the floor.

Her face came into view, very much alive and well.

The soldiers were real.

This soldier was real.

They were made of flesh, meat, skin, and blood, just as Karro and I were. They were going to die like it, too.

How had they been so still? Had The Blood changed this much? How could I have been so stupid?

"Impressive, isn't it?" The woman's voice was soft.

She was wearing the same clothes as the rest of the soldiers: a white uniform resembling a fencing costume. However, she wasn't holding a gun. The soldier directly beside her had been the one to eliminate the nurse. I felt oblivious; how had I not noticed one without a gun?

Stupid. Stupid. Stupid.

The woman took another step forward. She clasped her fingers behind her back and held her shoulders squared with mine. Her chin was high, even as she approached us. Her hair was pulled into a tight low braid. Most of the white strands were tucked beneath the back of the uniform.

Most interestingly, she was thin. Incredibly thin. No soldier, Blood or not, would ever have been able to fight in such a condition. Her cheekbones protruded under her thin skin, as if they would tear it apart if she smiled too hard.

I grabbed the scalpel and launched it toward her deathly face. It spun fast in the air, twisting like a throwing star.

She caught it a few inches from her nose. Her fist tightened around the scalpel, a couple of drops of blood spilling down her forearm. "Tsk." She clicked her tongue. "That wasn't very nice of you, Commander."

I clenched my jaw. I reminded myself I wasn't her anymore. I was more than The Blood—better than that.

I slowly looked at Karro, everything around me a blur. I was going to die. This was it. I was sure of it. I was disgusted by how much of a coward I would end up being in the end, if this was my time for brutality.

Karro's jaw tightened, and his breath was silent. I didn't see him inhale once. He stared at the woman intently, his body tight, as if he were going to leap at her at any moment. She advanced toward us. She must not know us well, or she wouldn't dare get close to either of us.

Her blue eyes jumped from soldier to soldier. She never turned her back to us. In that sense, she may have been smart. "The Blood has improved when it comes to training soldiers. I supposed that's why you thought they weren't real." She giggled. Actually giggled. "A few things have also changed since I last saw you both—you guessed that correctly."

I cleared my thoughts. I didn't want to believe in The Sight, or anything of such a nature. But in case it was real, and she knew what I was thinking because of some *sense*, I thought about nothing but white.

I dipped my chin down and stared up at her from beneath my lids. I thought of white, though a few occasional thoughts of her dead body popped into my mind's eye.

She finally looked over at Karro, her eyes scanning his body for far too long. It was enough reason to gouge her.

Karro's hand tensed around mine.

She smiled hard at it. "Oh! I suppose an introduction is needed." She scrunched her nose and kicked at the nurse's body. The corpse gurgled. In some twisted way, I felt as if I were looking at myself. She spoke so passively, seemed so numb. Only something like The Blood could do that to you.

"My name is Lucreita." She smiled harder.

Lucreita. Pretty name for a walking corpse.

Lucreita reached for a soldier near her. Her fingers lingered on its chest. She continued down the line, caressing every soldier as if they were her pets. Knowing The Blood, they just might be.

"You see, after you two, we realized how much needed to change. Secrecy. Stealth. Fear." She ran the tip of her tongue across her top lip. It was true. It had been far too easy for Karro to escape and for the Murthaa to be killed. The Blood had been falling apart.

She looked up at the ceiling, shifting her eyes around. It looked like she was watching something that was not there. She smiled and responded to something that seemed to be occurring inside her head.

Fucking mental.

It reminded me of my soldiers. When they died, some of them began to mutter things they saw as the spark left their eyes. They would describe the light at the end of the tunnel, but instead of speaking of angels and heaven, they screamed in pure agony. I'd learned a long time ago that death was not going to be pretty.

"The fucking dramatics," Karro growled. "If you're going to kill us, get on with it. You are such a bore." He'd said what I had wanted to.

Lucreita jerked her head in his direction, her eyes narrowing into slits. "Big words for someone with guns being held to their face," she spat, then returned her attention to me. Her face was too pale, her body too thin, and the colors beneath her eyes were far from normal. I could've easily killed her, but I would be dead beside her if I had.

Lucreita nodded her head toward Karro. Seven soldiers made their way over to him, pulling him from the table. He didn't struggle. He couldn't. There were seven barrels pointed into various parts of his body—parts that would kill him if shot.

She hadn't muttered a single word, but the soldiers obeyed her thoughts like dogs.

I didn't turn around to watch where they were taking him. *He is alive,* I reminded myself. That was all that mattered.

I kept my gaze locked with Lucreita. It was me and her. No Karro.

"I am going to kill you," I promised. I mimicked the confidence in her voice. I was scared, but she couldn't know that. I didn't want to admit it.

She smiled. "I know." She took a final step toward me. She was so close. If I just—

She pulled a knife from the back of her uniform. Quicker than a breath, she plunged it deep into my belly. Once. Twice. Thrice.

A strained noise came from Karro as I gave into the black.

CHAPTER

FIFTY-ONE

PRESENT

I dreamt of Karro. Through the many nights I slept, it was him.

CHAPTER

FIFTY-TWO

PRESENT

I'd had my own child cut from my womb by the man I loved; however, *nothing* compared to the pain I was in when I awoke.

I pried my eyes open and squinted toward the bright light above me. My mouth was dry and tasted of a strange metal. For a moment, I believed the room might have been my own hell. I recognized the cold steel table under me all too well.

The doctors.

I turned my head to the side and let it fall limp. My vision was a blur, but I could see that I was alone. No doctors. No Karro. No Lucreita.

I pushed myself up, wincing and grabbing at the sharp throbbing in my stomach. I let out a loud cry, and my breath staggered. It felt like the pain was shooting down every nerve ending in my body, even the small pathways in my brain. I could feel everything so terribly. It felt like when my stomach had been split open and my dead child removed by the hands of my lover.

But worse.

My breath quickened into a panicked state. My fingers trembled as I reached for my belly. I couldn't focus on anything but the pain. I doubled over, noises and cries coming from my mouth as I tried to distract myself from it. I needed to focus, but something was terribly wrong inside of me. I'd been stabbed here before, but never this harshly. This deep.

I pulled up my tank top. The fabric was crusty with blood that had dried over the entire front part of my being. I nearly passed out at the sight.

There were five puncture marks in my stomach. A few of the wounds were much deeper than the others. I could see how far the gaping had been in one wound; even with stitches pulling the skin together, I could see how fat had been split.

But scabs were forming. I was healing.

I gulped. That was not good. I had been asleep for far too long. If a wound like this was healing, I could only imagine how long I'd been unconscious.

"Karro," I called out, turning around and scanning the room. I whimpered. The small movement had caused the pain to intensify. I hadn't believed it possible. My vision blurred from how unbearable it was becoming.

Weak.

The pain twisted, contorted, and then sank to my fucking feet.

I knew the room I was in. Karro was right. It was The Blood. Lucreita had not lied—it was The Blood. It always had been. Not only that, but the room was a part of the War sector.

I'd had many nightmares of this room in my past. Once I'd started my period, this was where I spent most of my days. I'd been broken in until I no longer even thought of lustful acts on my own. I'd never be able to be weak for a man because of the feelings in my belly. I'd learned very young that I was only to fuck to benefit The Blood. This room had taught me that.

It was only missing my doctors.

Nausea rolled over me, and the pain of my wounds became a memory. I was too focused on the memory of how it had felt to be in this room. The first time. The last.

"Shit. Shit. Shit." My heart was thumping hard in my chest. It was the only noise I could hear. I felt unseen hands wrapping around my throat, clamping down hard on my windpipe. I couldn't breathe. I needed to get out of here.

I slowed my breathing and focused on getting out of the room. If I focused too much on the room itself, I would pass out.

I pushed myself from the table with a cry. Cradling my stomach, I clenched my eyes shut tight when the pain shot from my feet to the top of my head. I could have sworn I felt every nerve ending in my body.

The room was exactly as I remembered it. It was too perfect. Too replicated.

This had to be some sort of psychological torture. I couldn't let it get to me. I had to get out. Not for Karro, but for myself.

I stumbled into the wall beside the door. The exit was exactly as I remembered: double-doored with a mirrorlike coat on top of them. It was all too easy. The exit of the room was there, right in front of my face.

I clenched my eyes shut, trying not to focus too much on what I'd once seen in the distorted mirror, when I was tied down with my doctors on top of me. It was like it was happening all over again, though it was only me in the room.

I caught a glimpse of my reflection. My hair had loosened from its braids and hung messy and free around my face. The top of my head was frizzed, and blood dried and crusted the ends of my strands. My skin no longer had a golden undertone. I was pale. I'd never been this pale before in my life. I looked weak.

I pushed all of my weight into the door. It did not bulge.

The hands around my throat tightened. If this was psychological torture, it was working.

"Shit. Fucker. Cunt." I screamed until my throat became raw. I needed to get out.

I slammed my forehead into the door. Hard. My vision blurred, but I did not care. Perhaps it would get the doctors out of my memory. It was all I could think to do.

I began to shake. The temperature of the room and the silence it held were almost too well replicated. Perhaps this was my hell.

The doctors aren't here, I reminded myself.

I pressed my back flush to the door and slid down. Something was damaged. It had to be. In my head and in my belly. I'd been able to move more with my stomach split open.

Licking my lips, I wet my dry mouth. I closed my eyes to avoid the room around me and the false doctors who paced around my memory. Every inch of it was resurfacing. I'd spent twenty-something years repressing these images. I swore I could feel the drops of blood between my legs from when I'd first been torn into. I could feel the eyes of other doctors on the opposite side of the bulletproof mirror. Watching. Analyzing.

But it was a memory. I needed to remember that. *They weren't here.*

I pulled my arms over my face, protecting myself from the people who were in my head. I trembled. I was a child again.

"Karro," I cried, but he did not come for me. I was alone in damnation.

CHAPTER

FIFTY-THREE

PRESENT

"Oh, you have seen better days, *girl.*"

Lucreita stepped entered the room. As she approached me, a large pack of guards followed behind her. My eyes flicked to the door they had come through, but it was shut before I could think of lunging toward it.

My attention moved to the guards. The sound of metal scraping against tiles filled my ears. One soldier was holding a pair of handcuffs. Directly beside them, a few more held on to chain links that kept falling to the ground, rubbing against the tile.

I was too tired to protest. My eyes burned from lack of sleep. My eyelids were heavy, pleading with me to give in to the weighty feeling pinning me to the table. I had fallen asleep for a moment, but the memory of the room kept me up through the rest of the night. I'd been able to do nothing but sort through the memories I had suppressed.

I needed to find a way to prevent the pain from rising out of me and spilling onto the floor in chunks of bile.

A raw groan rattled up my throat as two soldiers stepped between Lucreita and me. One took hold of my wrists and tightly clasped the cuffs over them. The second did the same to my ankles. Lucreita tilted her head and tried to peer around their large figures. She looked fascinated.

I tugged at the cuffs when the guards stepped away. The chain connected my wrists and ankles together in an uncomfortable manner. When I tugged at my wrists, my ankles tugged as well. I was far too tired to try to fight it. I couldn't attack in this condition, the restraints preventing anything of the sort. I could barely walk with the chains.

I missed the white room. Whether it be Karro or the silence, I missed something. Deeply. I would rather have died at his hands in that room over this. These people.

My throat tightened as I looked down. I *hated* being restrained. My chest tightened, and my breath quickened. I was vulnerable to anything. I couldn't protect myself from the devils I knew lurked through the halls.

"Oh, Naga," Lucreita sang. She bit her lip and stared down at me. The corners of her lips were lifted, and her eyes were wide. She looked completely, utterly fucking insane.

She looked the exact opposite of the soldiers around her. They wore white baggy uniforms, as they had in the hallway near Karro's and my isolated room. Lucreita, on the other hand, was wearing a skin-tight black outfit. Her tight bottoms were coated in something resembling leather, and her tight black jacket was zipped to her throat. Her hands, like the soldiers', were covered in gloves; hers were made of black leather.

Even the uniforms had changed since Karro and I had last been in The Blood.

I tilted my head, looking back at her face. She had no armor. No protection. It would be so easy.

Lucreita shifted, muttering something to a soldier beside her. A glint of stitching caught in the light, forcing my eyes to focus on her left arm. Within the Blood, stitching was often done on uniforms to ensure order remained within the ranks. Karro and I had both once worn ones with the letter "C" on our left arms. My Anaka had worn the letter "A" on their small uniforms before their demise.

Lucreita wore an "M."

My breath hitched, but I looked down at my feet. She would not get to see that reaction from me. I focused on a small spot, a crack in the tiled floor. It had been my escape during the last painful day and night. When the room around me became too overwhelming, I'd let my attention disappear into the crack.

My arms tightened around my throbbing belly. I wanted to disappear into the crack now. Crawl inside and never see the light of day again.

Lucreita crossed her arms over her chest and stared down at me with a wide smile. For a moment, I thought she might have been gloating. I slowly blinked and cleared my mind. I wished I had believed in The Sight earlier. I would have known how to protect my mind from this thing I didn't understand.

"Where is Karro?" I asked, keeping my voice as slow and controlled as possible. I wanted to scream. Cry. I wanted to grab everything around me and yell to an unlistening god. But I didn't.

Karro would help. If he were here, everything would be fine. We could figure it out.

She let out an exaggerated gasp, clasping her hand over her chest as a dramatic teenager would. Her eyebrows pulled tight together, and her jaw hung low. "I stand before you as a stranger, and the first thing you ask about is your lover? Oh, Naga, how soft you have become."

I had, but she didn't need to know that. Nor did she need to tell me that.

I sat up straight, rolling any cracks from my neck. "Shut the fuck up, you stupid bitch," I replied, my voice calm.

Lucreita tilted her head and pouted her bottom lip. It was all too exaggerated. Fake. It felt as if I was looking at myself back when I'd been cocky enough to believe I had the entire Blood in my hands.

"You aren't curious how I know you? Your questions? You only care about your lover?" Her fingers flexed under her leather gloves.

"No."

I was curious. Karro and I had once been spoken about like celebrities at The Blood. More Karro. No one had ever escaped the way he had, and no one had ever been tasked with retrieving someone as brutal. Anyone might know who we were. I did not care who she was. She was the Murthaa—the "M" on her arm told me that.

But us still being alive? The terrain-like area I had been trapped in was no exception either; I hadn't aged once. Something was not normal, and I was beyond curious to understand it all. I wanted Karro and me to be free from this place.

"Hm," Lucreita hummed. She looked down at her feet, white strands falling in her face. Why did she seem so disappointed?

"Wh—"

"So this is where it happened?" She looked up. I was slightly taken aback by the sudden emotional change in her face. She looked happy again. Gloating. "The reason your thoughts are so fucking loud. Is this where poor Naga was broken in?"

I tensed, pulling at my chains. No one had known about this. Only the people who had orchestrated my raising.

Shame crept up my neck. Every person in this room had to die. I did not want anyone to live with the knowledge of what had happened to me in here. I was weak for it. I wanted to peel off my own skin so I wouldn't feel how horrible I felt. Even though it had been years, and my doctors were long dead, I could still feel it in my skin.

I cleared my mind and reminded myself of the ability this woman had. I didn't want to believe it, but a young Anaka had proved it to be true once. Lucreita was proving it just as much.

My stomach twisted. My mind flashed to the bloody training room after I had found their bodies.

She was not going to receive a reaction from me. Not over something like that. I kept my face and mind blank.

"You don't talk as much as I thought," Lucreita said with a sigh. She huffed and leaned her back against the wall. She was inches from the door. "You used to be so fun." Her gaze was lazy as she looked at me. Her lids hung low, and she seemed bored.

I did not respond.

Lucreita gestured for the soldiers after a few moments of silence had passed. She was not patient with my lack of speaking. I could tell she wanted a reaction from me. Words. Anything.

Everything she said was followed by analysis, like she was trying to figure out my reactions.

The soldiers complied with her gesture. Two of them grabbed ahold of my biceps tightly, pulling me from the table. I groaned and folded over from the movement. The pain in my stomach felt like it had erupted.

Lucreita didn't notice. She'd already walked out the door. The soldiers were rough, pulling me behind them. I was folded over, trying to cope with the pain she had caused.

"You know," she began, walking a few feet in front of me. There were ten soldiers behind me, two on either side of me, and a very unprotected Lucreita ahead. "You always were such a selfish cunt."

I scoffed quietly, looking around the hallway. It was exactly as I remembered. It was not the hall Karro and I had walked down to go to the nurse's office. It was The Blood. The air and the smell were exactly as I remembered them. I wanted to throw up. On her. I'd never thought I would smell that iron and decay again.

"Not the slightest bit curious who I am?" she continued. I'd forgotten she was speaking. She was rambling about selfishness and my lack of interest in her. I zoned it out. I wanted to find Karro. We would figure it out and be free; I knew we would.

"I don't care," I repeated.

Lucreita sighed, though it was obviously exaggerated. She stopped after a few more feet. My stomach was in pain, but I was able to focus more on the things around me. I could see officers moving fast in the distance, though they scattered at the sight of us. For a moment, it appeared as though it was Lucreita they were running from.

"Come," Lucreita said, turning to face a random area of wall. It was as the rest of the hall: white. There had been nothing special about this area until she turned to face it.

The wall reacted to her presence.

The Blood was mostly accessed using biometric data. In most big cities, there was an entrance to The Blood. There were elevators you could use for transport at advanced speeds toward the sector you wished. War, Order, and Intelligence. This appeared to be the same thing.

A red hue shot from the wall, scanning down Lucreita's face. I flinched. It reminded me of the nights I'd snuck into The Blood, despite whatever city I was in. We were everywhere. The War sector alone took up the entire city of Chicago.

Lucreita smiled and turned to me. She looked familiar. I couldn't deny that. I pushed the curiosity aside before it could ruin whatever chance of freedom Karro and I had.

The wall had recognized her cells and biological code. It split into two, revealing a new hallway beyond it. My lips parted, and I took a step forward, peering down the large corridor.

"What is this?" I asked.

The hallway was the same as those in the rest of the sectors, but I had never seen it before. In the Intelligence sector, there were small designs traced along the floor made by those who were too creative. The artists usually lived in the Intelligence sector. In Order, there was much more glass, offering a view into the water, as it resided under the lakes. But this? I had never seen this before.

I took another step toward it. Karro was no longer in my mind, nor was the pain in my stomach.

"Let me show you what they hid from you."

CHAPTER

FIFTY-FOUR

PRESENT

I stared at Lucreita. Her back was to me as she walked through the open wall. She stopped once as she stepped over the threshold, waiting for me to follow.

The soldiers didn't push me toward her; they were letting me decide. I wondered if any of the ones I had seen were ones I'd worked with. When I was commander, there were some very young soldiers among my charges. If any of them were here, they would be very old by now.

Or dead.

I didn't know how long I had been in that room. Or in that place before, where Karro had sent me.

"Are you coming, Commander?"

I chewed at the inside of my lip and looked behind Lucreita. In the past, when I wanted to be The Blood and everything it considered perfect, this would have been my dream. I wanted to know everything. It was power. I wanted to become the Murthaa and live for an eternity. Once, that had been who I wanted to be.

"What is this?" I repeated.

"Aren't you curious why you haven't aged? The place Karro sent you? He couldn't explain what he didn't understand. You can't understand something you never believed to exist." Lucreita looked around the room. The glint in her eyes returned. It looked like she was watching something that was not there.

I cleared my mind. She knew everything I wanted an answer to. I wanted to rip out my hair. She was in my fucking head.

She thrust her open hand in my direction. To take. I stared down at it. There were small stitches on the seams of her leather gloves—the word "Murthaa" spelled out in embroidery over and over.

I took a step forward into the new hallway, but I did not reach for her hand. Her smile deepened. I'd made the wrong decision; I knew it.

"God, I missed you!" She sounded batshit.

I didn't ask how she knew me. I was curious, but I knew it would eventually come to light. Karro, on the other hand, was my concern. It felt wrong to be without him. The room had made me too dependent on the man I'd once considered an enemy and a lover. I couldn't sleep without him. I couldn't eat. I needed him here, or it all felt wrong.

I wondered if he was being escorted the same way I was. Did he have more soldiers with him? He was much larger than me. I bet he had more soldiers.

Taking another step forward, I focused my thoughts on nothing but light. I turned to peer back over my shoulder as I continued to move closer to Lucreita. It was difficult to walk with the chains, let alone attack her. I could barely move my arms from their restrained position in front of my belly.

The soldiers remained in place, despite how close I was getting to Lucreita. It was only she and I in the new hall. They stayed where they were. Unmoving.

"You put a lot of trust in these shackles," I said. The chains around my ankles dragged against the floor with a screeching noise.

Lucreita clicked her tongue and continued forward. She was walking fast, unlike me. I limped and struggled to keep up as a result of my restraints. I had to focus on where my hands were in order to move my feet.

"I'd be impressed if you could free yourself from those," she replied. If I'd had more strength, I would have tested it.

I kept my attention on the "M" on her uniform. She was the new Murthaa. It made sense. She was young, and at the time of her promotion, she would have stopped aging. The Murthaa had died before Karro's and my imprisonment, and a new one would have been promoted during our time away.

"Do you ever wonder why we stop aging?" Lucreita asked as she walked.

I was beginning to sweat, and my stomach hurt terribly. I made my mind go blank. I didn't know how to stop it. To protect myself from it. It wasn't even supposed to be real.

"No," I said shortly. They stopped aging—that was a fact. But how? That had never been my place to ask. To even think about it would have risked my relationship with the Murthaa.

I supposed she was dead now. It didn't matter. This new one had no problem speaking about it.

I noticed a few doors on the walls ahead. They ran along either side and went on as far as my field of vision went. I had *never* seen this place before.

"We have control of it all. The Murthaa. We control The Blood. All of it. Karro had found this sector. I am not sure how, but he did. It's time." Lucreita stopped in front of the first door we came across. She turned around and faced me with a wide smile. "What makes a body age?"

"Time," I replied, responding only for myself.

My eyes rounded, and I looked from door to door. It felt like I was being sucked back into the part of myself I had destroyed. The curious part of me. This had once been all I ever wanted. I'd wanted to be powerful. To know everything. Be everything.

This sector was something I had never imagined existing. And now I was standing in it. The part of myself that was creeping up from the darkest shadows of my brain considered this power. The Blood was power.

"Yes, time." She traced her fingers along one of the large metal doors. There was around a foot of space between them.

This was where it happened. I scrunched my eyebrows together, remembering the night I'd clung to Karro after our child had been removed from my stomach. I held on to the man I believed to be my salvation as he threw me into one of the rooms.

My mouth went dry. This was hell. Perhaps being among Man—what I'd once believed to be atrocious—was heaven.

I took a step back, and Lucreita jerked her head around to face me. "Oh, don't worry, I'm not Karro." She smiled widely, as if this was some inside joke that had happened between him and me. Did everyone know what had occurred that night? Were there cameras? Had my mind somehow shown her?

She reached for the door and pushed it open with a groan. There was no knob. There was no lock. It simply opened.

I took a slow step toward it. I could feel myself slipping back into my mind, letting the dark parts flood back. Karro and freedom were no longer in my thoughts. The pain in my belly and the familiarity of the girl before me were the least of my concerns.

Power. I could have had it all.

"These are pockets in time," Lucreita continued. "When people of this sector mess up, a pocket is made. It's a moment stuck in time. A day repeating itself. Something horrible occurs when you meddle with time. It stops it completely."

I looked through the door. Inside was a beach, though the water was all dried up. The sand stretched for miles, with a slightly darker area where ocean had once been. The sky was the color of raw meat. My hair blew slightly it the breeze coming through the door. It smelled like salt despite the lack of water.

"It can be used as a prison. The most powerful prison in this life is time. If you are stuck repeating the same time over and over, well . . ." She stopped, looking at me.

That was what had happened to Karro and me. The prison of nothing but white was stuck in time. It was why we hadn't aged. The forestlike area he had thrust me into. It was time.

"It's a prison for eternity."

Lucreita smiled hard and clapped her hands. "Usually not a prison. We don't imprison people for being traitors."

No. They hanged them. The Blood allowed all three sectors to congregate and stone the traitors before they were hanged. My spine straightened. Karro and I had both known this before betraying The Blood, but that made it no less brutal.

"Or just a moment of time tucked in the corner of The Blood."

"How do I know you aren't lying?" I asked.

Lucreita gestured to the door. I stared at it, but did not enter it as she was telling me to. I slowly shook my head. I'd been in one of the rooms before. I'd spent the nights waiting for something to happen. Anything different. And when the time came for my freedom, I was thrust into a new prison. With Karro. Awaiting anything, yet again.

I had no doubt this dried-out beach was no different.

"There's more."

We continued down the hall. I no longer doubted her. Everything she had said was lining up with the unexplained experiences I'd had prior.

I occasionally tugged at my wrists to see if there was any way to contort my body into strangling her to death, but based on her lack of care or protection, I assumed there wasn't one.

I stayed silent and counted my steps as we continued down the long hall. If somehow I managed to escape, I needed to memorize how to get here. Anywhere. Anything besides following Lucreita around like a limping dog.

Sweat formed at my brow line. I wondered where we were in relation to the city above.

"War, Order, and Intelligence came to create The Blood. You know the creation story. But did you believe that was all that was needed to control man? To become a creator? You never struck me as someone who subscribed to the traditional beliefs."

I looked at her feet. There were some who believed it was all that was needed. Others believed in change and reform. I did not.

I should have believed in it. I would have questioned The Blood more.

"There is so much more to us. Things that your previous Murthaa didn't believe you would ever be fit for. She believed you to be for Order, War, and Intelligence. How pathetic."

My blood heated. If she was trying to crawl into my skin and into my head, it was working. She knew it was all I wanted. I needed to stop fucking thinking.

"You don't know me."

Lucreita turned around to face me. Her eyes lit up. I couldn't wait for her face to be as blue as her eyes.

"Oh no!" She forced her lips into a pout and scrunched her eyebrows together like she was going to cry. "I'm so scared. Little Naga, who only knew about three sectors. Naga, who would never live up to her potential. You were born to capture Karro. It's pathetic. That's all you were. You didn't know anything because you were never going to become anything. Fuck, you couldn't even do what you were fucking raised to do."

Her entire body was tight, as was mine. I wanted to hurt her very badly.

"But, I'm so fucking scared," she hissed.

I tilted my head and watched her. She had spoken like she was spewing venom at me. I *must* have known her. That kind of hate did not come from nowhere. It was pure poison. In the past twenty-four hours, it felt like she'd picked at every wound I'd healed. No stranger would do that.

I didn't react to her words. She was reacting on her own. Her face was red, and her hands were clenched. For a split second, I'd seen something in her expression. When she had forced herself to appear scared, I'd seen the young girl I'd once shot bullets at as she cried for it to stop. I'd seen her round baby-blue eyes staring up at me, brimming with tears as she cried from the loud pangs. The one who had never been able to make it across the course with the other children.

She'd been so fucking scared. I'd thought of her for nights after finding my Anaka. I thought of how scared 7437 must have been in her final hours.

Except she was staring at me. And she was not scared.

My tongue was on the verge of bleeding from how hard I was biting it.

"Bingo." She seethed, popping the word. I couldn't tell if she was excited or livid. She seemed to want to hurt me as badly as I wanted to hurt her. But here she was, answering the questions I'd always believed would remain mysteries.

"Holy shit," I began. I kept my words slow and controlled. "7437 finally fucking grew a pair." I looked her up and down with a scrunched nose.

She tensed, and her frown deepened. It wasn't fake. I knew how horrible it felt to be called by your number. I grew nauseous thinking of my own.

She took a moment before taking a deep breath. She smiled and forced herself back into the manic state she'd been in. "And I am so much more than you'll ever be, Naga. Closer than you ever could have been."

She continued forward like nothing had happened. I closed my eyes and focused on nothingness. She had The Sight. She'd had it before, and she had it now. I had to keep my mind clear. I had to figure out how to get out of this, to find Karro.

I followed behind her. Her pace and words sped up. "You were a fucking commander, Naga. You knew nothing. You were not as powerful as you thought. How could someone like you believe you were powerful when you knew nothing about what was above you?"

She was *not* happy.

I kept quiet, staring at the back of her head. I could feel the heat radiating from her. I hoped my silence was angering her.

When the hallway of time pockets ended, we approached a much larger room. It was large enough to fit at least ten hallways in it. My lips parted as we entered the massive space.

The ceiling was so high it disappeared into a blur; even when I squinted, it was out of my field of vision. It was just as wide, though I could see a few soldiers very, very far in the distance. They lined the walls but were not close enough to hear anything being discussed.

These soldiers weren't wearing masks, unlike the ones in the previous sector. They were all women, but I could not see far enough to make out any details.

There was a massive old tree in the center of the large white room. It gave the illusion of an atrium of sorts, though there was no glass covering it. The roots were thicker than my legs.

The floor was the most peculiar part. I looked at my feet to examine the multicolored lines I was standing on. There were hundreds of them, crossing together or isolated from the rest. Each system of lines was a different color, similar to how a subway map might be constructed.

I noticed there were small squares spaced out along the lines. Some of the lines ran into much larger shapes, like a giant square.

One system looked nearly identical to the one I'd been raised in. I recognized the small rooms on either side of the tunnel, leading to much larger rooms where others had slept in the War sector. I frowned at the sight of them. It was where the Anaka were trained.

"Exactly," Lucreita said.

I cleared my thoughts and looked up at her.

"It's a map," she continued, crouching down toward the floor.

I leaned closer, though my restraints only allowed me to bend over slightly. Not as close to the map as she was.

"This is War." She traced her finger along the tunnel I recognized. "Order. Intelligence."

I watched her trace the systems of tunnels. There were hundreds of them, and I only knew of three.

"The rest are—" I looked around. I recognized the system beside War. It was identical to the hall we'd just walked down. Time was directly beside War. But hundreds of systems covered the giant floor. It would be impossible to explore it all in a single lifetime.

"So much more than you will ever be," she replied.

I jerked my head, causing her to smile. "Why show me this? Do you want to rub it in before you execute me? Euthanize me? Why do all this? Why take me from one prison to put me in another? Why keep Karro alive? Why keep me alive? You know what the protocol is for traitors."

Lucreita sat down on one of the large roots. She gestured for me to take a seat a few feet away. I didn't move. 7437 had every right to seek revenge. I had been cruel to her. I didn't want to be cruel, but I had been. But I was still here. Breathing.

"I'm curious, that's why. Why leave in the first place? Why did you want to leave this? You could have had it all. You were on the path for your destiny, but you threw it all away." She looked down at my stomach. "For a boy that is no better to your womb than I am? Why?"

I kept my mind free of any thought.

"I think you made the wrong decision. You became weak, and you know that." She bit her lip and looked up at me. "I want you to come back and work for The Blood. All of it. You were born and raised through brutality. This place is where you are meant to be. I want you to see that."

CHAPTER
FIFTY-FIVE

PRESENT

I laughed harder than I had in a while.

Lucreita laughed harder, though I'm not sure what she found so amusing. I assumed it was something going on in her head.

"No," I bit out. "Was that your plan? To try to get Karro and me to return?"

Lucreita stopped laughing, and she scrunched her nose. "Karro? No. He's back in the room you two were in. I have no intention of him leaving it. He was put there to stay."

I went quiet. I thought of Karro alone in there. Was he struggling as much as I was? We had once been very independent from one another; I wondered if he was channeling that. I tried to.

"What did you say?"

Lucreita shrugged. "You were never meant to be imprisoned. He did that. We put you in the room to see how you would . . ." Lucreita seemed to be searching for something in her mind. "To see how you would *be*. If you would be weak and fall for him again. If you would resent him."

"Stop speaking like you know me. It wasn't weak loving him." It had been. That was why I had been broken in by my doctors—so that I would never look at a man and think of love or sex. I looked at men the way I looked at my doctors.

"But you didn't decide," she said, ignoring my previous comment. "You tried to convince the nurse and escape with him, but you're not like you were before. Something is different, and you know it. He is different. So, I'm giving you the choice: return as loyal as before or die with him."

Lucreita leaned her head against the old tree. She closed her eyes. "It's different with Karro. He never had potential. You had potential, and they didn't see that. I see that now. You will have everything you ever wanted. You will be a part of God."

The room slowed. The words she spoke slid through my ears, but when my cognition grabbed hold of them, everything turned into a scattered mess. 7437 had become everything I'd once wanted to be.

Karro had been my opportunity to become it, to be what I was made to become. He'd ruined it all. Everything. But was that for the better? It didn't feel like it was for the better. Not when Lucreita spoke of what I'd once fantasized about.

The brutality. The murders. My officer, whom I had beheaded. The Murthaa. I was out of touch from The Blood. They'd wanted me to become something. And I became nothing.

I thought of my Anaka. I hadn't been trained like they were. I was trained for the purpose of becoming something. I could have been everything.

Something flashed in Lucreita's eyes. I didn't recognize the emotion. For a moment, I'd been too distracted by her words to remember she was supposed to be a part of the dead.

"They cried for you."

My mouth went dry. I cleared my thoughts and locked eyes with her. "What?" I had to have heard it wrong.

She smiled and looked down at her lap. Her smile was weak. Her dimples were not as deep as usual. "I said they cried for you," she repeated, much slower this time. She looked up at me. I could see *her* staring up at me—the girl who'd been too afraid to run. She was far from it. She might have been far from it for a while now. "Pity."

Her eyes were locked with mine, but a part of her was not there. Dissociated.

"You—" I couldn't think of the words. I contorted my body until I was able to fall on my ass. My arms and legs strained against the chain and shackles. I couldn't stand much longer, however. I would faint.

Lucreita slowly shook her head. "Not me." The part of her soul that had left her eyes when mentioning the Anaka led me to assume she had either done it or seen it. Her reaction was not normal. I could have sworn I'd seen something split in her gaze when she'd gone back to the memory of the room. A part of her she had hidden.

Coward.

She cleared her throat, and the most manic parts of her returned. She began to tap her fingers against her leg and smile wildly. "Take it out on me." Her grin was so broad I could see every tooth. "Kill me. Figure out a plan to torture us all. Be angry. Brutal. Fucking do something about it. You can't do anything if you are rotting in that cell for eternity. *Coward.*"

I couldn't breathe. Everything was spinning. Every wound that I'd healed felt raw and violated.

I slowly shook my head and closed my eyes. She was right. Every word.

"You will know everything that happened. Why it happened. You can avenge them. Hurt us. Kill us. Kill everyone you see fit. *If you can.*" She was challenging me with what I wanted most. It was working too well. "You can't do that dead."

The air between Lucreita and me had shifted after the mention of the Anaka. It was thick. However, we shared the same expression at the thought of them.

You can't do that dead.

I would end up back in the room with Karro, forever mourning my Anaka. I would mourn what could have been between Karro and me; I would shame who I had become. In the prison with Karro, and the prison before, it had been all I thought of.

Lucreita's face softened. Her smile dropped as she watched me. Many minutes of silence had passed. She wasn't challenging me anymore, or trying to convince me what to do. She knew what I would decide.

"Karro," I started. Lucreita rolled her eyes in disgust, but I continued. "If I did, what would happen to him?"

I hoped she would say something different. She did not.

"He would remain in the room to die."

"How would he die? If it is a prison of time, he would be immortal. That's how the Murthaa's are."

Lucreita smiled. "You catch on quick."

I stared blankly at her, waiting for an answer.

She sighed before continuing. "He has become symptomatic. He won't have much longer. You would join him, and this time, you'd receive the same substance as him. Yours was a fake when you were injected. His was not."

My throat tightened. I felt like all of their little hands were wrapped around my throat at the simple thought of returning to The Blood. I could feel Karro in the back of my mind. His fucking mother was dead because of me.

But if I cowered away from The Blood, they would be nothing but a casualty of War. I could only tear it apart from the inside.

I cleared my thoughts. Lucreita was still in her slightly dissociated state. She was zoned out, peering behind my head. She had no reaction to my thoughts.

"Symptomatic?" I asked.

She nodded, pulling herself from the trance of the Anaka memory. "Weren't you curious what the black liquid was?" She smiled hard. "It's cancer. We created it to control the population. Don't you think we used it against our own people, too?"

My breath picked up. I searched between her eyes, desperate for some sort of punchline. None came. I wanted to crawl into the corner and hold my head in my arms until I disappeared.

Just as she had in the training rooms.

"If we can create it, we can cure it." My voice came out as heat. My body had begun to shake. I hadn't even known of our involvement with the disease. I'd believed it to be something of Man. Not The Blood.

Karro had been injected with *a lot* of it. Much more than I had, even if mine was fake.

Lucreita clapped. "Exactly! So when we inject your weakness with it, we plan to come to you and offer you a cure for your loyalty. But your stupidity and attempts with the nurse sped things up."

I frowned and lost myself to a small crack in the floor. Karro would die. I would not.

It was just as it was meant to be.

Lucreita pushed herself from the root of the tree and tapped her foot against a small system of tunnels. They were a dark forest green, unlike the rest of them. "This is the disease sector. You come back, loyal as ever, and he will be sent here for the cure."

Everything I'd betrayed to prevent Karro's death was irrelevant. He was going to die. Whether I found a way now, like I had before, eventually death would come to claim him. It was how God had intended things to be—how The Blood had.

It felt like everything I had known was gone. My perception of The Blood, my Anaka, Karro, power, and Lucreita. It was a distorted mess. I didn't even know how I felt anymore. I couldn't think for myself without her finding her way in.

"You would cure him if I worked for you? I would spend my entire life trying to kill you. To destroy this place. To free him and myself."

Lucreita clapped wildly. "So fun, isn't it? Just like how you were before."

I remained quiet, staring at her.

She did too.

I kept my mind blank in case that was what she was waiting for. I knew what I was going to do. I could figure it out. I couldn't figure it out imprisoned.

"You go back to Karro, you die as the dust Man believes in. You stay . . ." She looked away for a moment. "Well, I can't wait to see what you try to do to us. It's always fascinating to see you try."

I recognized the challenge as bluff. I lapped up every drop of it. With Karro, I could find a way to kill a world. Karro and I were no cowards. She was.

Unless that, too, had all been a distorted perception.

"Karro stays with me. Whatever I am to do, Karro is to do with me. He is cured immediately, and I'm given the footage of the night with the Anaka. Whoever was there will be executed by my hand."

I kept my face blank and my words steady. I couldn't allow Lucreita to hear why I wanted it to be this way. She couldn't hear the plans I was hiding over the thought of nothingness.

Lucreita ran her tongue across her top teeth. She stared up at the ceiling, lost in thought. "Everyone knew what Karro did. The murder of the Murthaa before me was done at the hands of Karro, and it will remain that way."

My lips parted. They had pinned it on Karro. Everything I had done, he would take the stones for. Would have.

"No one knows of your betrayal, and no one ever will. Karro, though, everyone knows of. If he were to be allowed to walk down the halls, what would stop a janitor from killing an officer? If Karro is simply given a slap on the wrist, so would everyone."

"I'm sure you can figure something out."

I understood what she was saying. She wanted to make an example of him. To prove that if someone betrayed The Blood, they would be punished. It was about fear and control. Even in traditional beliefs—of nothing but War, Order, and Intelligence—fear and control had to be instilled in The Blood. Without it, we were a faulty god.

"By the time he's done with his treatment, figure it out." I was stern.

For some reason, Lucreita listened. "Okay," she said slowly. "Soon."

"How soon?"

She groaned and closed her eyes. "You have become such a bore. So concerned with Karro." A few moments of silence passed. "After his treatments, I'll figure something out—*if* you agree to the terms I laid out. Work as loyally as before. You won't leave The Blood, ever. You will be monitored by senior soldiers and will report to multiple senior officers, as well as to me. Just as it was before." She waited for me to say something, but I remained as quiet as my thoughts. "So, are you returning to your chambers, or Karro?"

I looked down at the chains. My wrists were raw from the metal rubbing against my skin. I couldn't do anything in these or in that God-fearing room. "I agree."

Lucreita let out an excited noise and began to clap. Something horrifyingly unfamiliar flashed in her eyes. "Come," she called to the soldiers along the walls. I'd forgotten about them; they were too far away to see.

I watched her quietly, wondering if she had been the one who'd killed the Anaka. She'd been far too tiny at the time. I didn't think she could have done something as brutal as that.

I would find out, and whoever had been there was going to die.

The soldiers worked on my shackles, and Lucreita took many steps backward. There were too many of them around for me to try to hurt her—or them. However, she still was cautious. The restraints required multiple keys to unfasten. The handcuffs alone required five separate ones.

OF BLOOD AND LIES

I needed to make sure Karro was healthy. Alive. I needed to find out what happened to my Anaka. When that was done, I was going to burn this place to the fucking ground.

Lucreita's lips twitched. She looked away from the cuffs and locked eyes with me. "I can't wait to see you try."

ALSO BY LAYLA GRIM

Sacred Ties

CONNECT WITH ME

Make sure to follow for more updates on the remainder of this series and anything else to come!

TikTok: thelaylagrim
YouTube: authorlaylagrim
Instagram: laylagrim
Goodreads: Layla Grim